"We've got company! Weird company!"

> ➤ ➤

Between her and the wall half a dozen creatures were anchored by their feet (or whatever they stood on) so it appeared she looked down on them from above. The little rural Texas girl inside her squirmed. They looked, more than anything else, like giant golden-brown cockroaches. Cockroaches her own size. Cockroaches with gunbelts and guns pointed at her.

Another being caught her astonished eye. It was smaller, of more slender build, apparently unclothed, but covered from head to foot either with soft scales fringed at the edges, or stubby feathers. Like the insect-things, it wore a weapons belt....

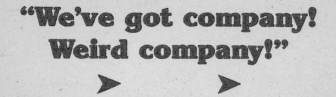

CONTACT AND COMMUNE

CONTACT AND COMMUNE

L. NEIL SMITH

POPULAR LIBRARY

An Imprint of Warner Books, Inc.

A Warner Communications Company

POPULAR LIBRARY EDITION

Copyright © 1990 by L. Neil Smith
All rights reserved.

Cover illustration by Wayne Barlowe

Popular Library books are published by
Warner Books, Inc.
666 Fifth Avenue
New York, N.Y. 10103

W A Warner Communications Company

Printed in the United States of America

First Printing: January, 1990

10 9 8 7 6 5 4 3 2 1

This Book Is Dedicated, with affection and admiration, to Karl Hess, who wields the Hammer of Volund at the Forge of Liberty.

Table of Contents

Prologue
The House of Eneri Relda

A fountain sparkled in the broad, tiled courtyard of the hillside villa, cooling the afternoon breeze, sprinkling the sandaled feet of a lean-muscled young man seated before it. His sleeveless tunic, its decorative metallic border just reaching his knees, was the lightest in his wardrobe. As always, Eichra Oren wondered in an absent way how the air could remain so warm after passing across the Inland Sea from the ocean of sand where it had been born.

At his master's feet, also enjoying the cool spray, Oasam, a heavily-furred white dog, grinned into the slanting sunlight, sniffing with contented curiosity at the hot, scent-laden air from the countryside beyond the villa. A colored bird chirped in a wicker cage hung from a mimosa tree nearby.

As on countless previous occasions, Eichra Oren listened (as absently as he wondered about the wind) to his mother regaling guests in the Original Language with oft-told tales of life before the Continent was Lost. From an unobtrusive corner, a lyrist, hired for the day, counterpointed the burbling of the fountain, weaving notes between the woman's words. More dignified than beautiful in the flowing drapery of her girlhood, she was much respected by those who considered themselves honored to hear the old stories once again from the lips of Eneri Relda, one of the remaining few who had lived them.

Although he still felt bone-weary as he sipped his bowl of wine, the young man centered his thoughts, couched in a Successor Tongue he had only yesterday been asked to learn, less upon the perilous task he had just performed than upon whatever he might be required to do next. Eichra Oren was skilled and enjoyed most aspects of his trade. A short, broad-bladed sword, the badge of his profession—representing all those things about it he enjoyed least—leaned in its unembellished sheath against the graceful stuccoed archway leading through the villa's atrium to the cobbled street beyond.

Of a sudden, he heard insistent shrilling behind his eyes. Others heard, as well. The lyre-playing creature paused to brush its bristly mandibles with claws enameled in the latest fashion. A guest ruffled feathers, stretched flightless wings, scratched powdered beak with scaled foot. Another splayed glistening tentacles over the courtyard tile, turning its awkward, encasing shell to peer at the tunic-clad figure with a giant, placid eye. Eichra Oren's mother gave him a brief, irritated scowl, then resumed her story. Glancing at his wristwatch, he swore a soft oath in the Original Language.

His dog looked up, remarking, "Boss, there goes the doorbell—what'll you bet it's a snake on a bicycle?"

I
The Golden Apple

The answer, once they had it, only generated more questions. As usual. Regrettably, they were a people for whom it had become difficult—because they'd been taught the hard way—to ask and answer questions.

"*Front and center, EVA team, you're about to earn your pay.*"

The familiar voice crackling over the intraship comsystem was that of Brigadier General Horatio Z. Gutierrez, commonly referred to as "the Captain" by virtue of his appointment as expedition commander.

"Aye, aye, Commodore!"

The source of the facetious reply was the team's geologist, Dr. Piotr Kamanov, one of a few token Russians participating in what, in due course, would be advertised at home—provided they could stake a claim to anything resembling success—as an international undertaking. It was accompanied by a characteristic grin, a wicked twinkle contrasting with the icy and penetrating blue of the eyes that had produced it, which the remark's intended recipient wasn't present to appreciate, separated, as the men were, by two hundred fifty centimeters of hard vacuum and a pair of aluminum-epoxy-graphite bulkheads.

From several others, who were present, a ripple of nervous laughter followed. Despite the technical fact that he rated it, Gutierrez, a career AeroSpace Force officer, had admonished them all, with an identical grin, just after the voyage had begun, that any crewperson addressing him by that irredeemably naval title would be immediately ejected from the airlock.

Since this was precisely the fate now awaiting the EVA team, it had perhaps seemed worth the risk.

"Major?" Technical Sergeant Toya Pulaski whispered. "The EVA team's about buttoned up—everyone but Dr. Kamanov, of course—would you like some help with your suit-seals?"

The gloves, with their knurled lock-rings, were the hardest part to finish by yourself. Pulaski was one member of the EVA team who wouldn't be venturing outside with the others. To anyone who'd given it a thought (no one ever had), it wouldn't have seemed in character for the hesitant-voiced young woman who offered every appearance, deceptive though it must be, of frail timidity. It was her job to see that those suiting-up got through their checklists without skipping items which might cost them their lives.

"What?"

In many ways a perfect contrast to Pulaski, Marine Corps Major Estrellita Reille y Sanchez, the EVA team's nominal leader, blinked and shook her head at her subordinate, a bit chagrined to be caught wool-gathering at a crucial moment. The multilayered bulk of vacuum-armor enveloping and disguising her full, feminine form (one of several differences between the major and the less endowed sergeant) failed as yet to conceal her thick, wavy red hair, trimmed just short of shoulder length. Giving the fabric an overly positive tug, she pulled the suit's upper torso flap over the waist ring and reached for the soft helmet which the yellowed NASA manuals labeled "communications carrier," but which everyone else called a Snoopy cap.

"No, thank you, Sergeant, I believe I can manage."

Reille y Sanchez faced the forward bulkhead, every meter of which was bedecked with storage lockers, shelf grating, and gear attachment points. The bulkhead stood between her and, across a narrow gap of empty space, the flight deck of the refitted and rechristened shuttle *Daniel P. Moynihan*. Once the property of NASA, it now served as flagship to the little fleet it was a part of. The major's small, space-booted feet were tucked into nylon stirrups projecting from the curved wall of the cargo-bay passenger insert, a twelve-faceted cylinder, four meters by fifteen, which had been home to more people, for a longer time, than she liked to think about even now, when at last they'd reached their destination. Her sense of smell alone, she felt, would never be the same for having made this journey.

Others, flight crews, scientists, engineers, mining and ag specialists, refinery technicians, the Vietnamese-American physician whose name she always had to struggle to remember— Rosalind Nguyen—forty-two individuals, had been just as cramped, dirty, and uncomfortable. This and the other two eighty-year-old vessels, the *Howard M. Metzenbaum* and the *James C. Wright*, had never been intended for flights of this duration, let alone interplanetary travel. Fourteen souls per shuttle, seven forward in crew quarters, seven aft in Hell. Three hundred forty-nine days, eleven hours, seven minutes. She was grateful consumables were stored in an emptied auxiliary fuel tank, fastened in Earth orbit under the flattened belly of each ship.

Tucking an intransigent auburn strand into her cap, the major settled the phones over her ears, plugging their leads into a receptacle just under the gasketed neck-rim of her suit. Peering over the rim, she adjusted her oxygen flow and reached for her gloves, detaching them from the bulkhead with a ripping noise. The nylon thumb loops fastened to her cooling undergarment had already begun irritating the soft webbing of her thumb, but the gloves went on without a hitch. She snapped the lock rings together and turned them from the ⟨OPEN to the CLOSED⟩ position without Pulaski's help, smoothing the cuffs back over her wrists.

She reached for the bulky helmet which invariably reminded her of a gumball machine she'd been fascinated with as a child. It still stood, she imagined, in a dusty corner of the grimy Trailways station in the central Texas town where she'd been born. One of her earliest memories was of wondering what it had looked like, full of the multicolored spheres it had been placed there to dispense by the McQueenie Kiwanis or some other long-gone local pillar of a now-defunct establishment.

Reille y Sanchez had never seen a gumball, let alone tasted one. This had failed to strike her, even then, as any great personal tragedy. In a global civilization reeling into the second quarter of an already ragged twenty-first century, small children everywhere had at least been as equal as possible in their deprivation. At that age (twenty years ago, she mused; she must have been all of eight or nine last time she'd been home) she couldn't appreciate the desperate situation in detail, but even then she'd understood, to some small degree, how a nation locked into a collapsing international economy couldn't spare resources on trivialities.

She wondered why she was thinking about it now. Perhaps it had something to do with that same nation's eleventh-hour gamble (things hadn't improved since she'd grown up), employing obsolete machinery, mothballed for decades, which had never been that good to begin with, to explore and exploit the swirling belt of flying mountains circling between Jupiter and Mars. . . .

"Major?"

Before she was entirely aware of it, the airlock ready-light had turned green and the lid swung aside. She squeezed into a compartment beyond the bulkhead, allowing herself to be sealed in. Across from the hatch she'd come through, another led to the crew compartment mid-deck. Her helmet brushed a third hatch, pierced with a tiny porthole like the others, leading outside. She had room to draw her CZ99A1, a twelve-shot .41x22m/m, from an insulated pocket on her right thigh and gave it a final check, an awkward task with the gloves, despite the special oversized trigger guard, yet one she'd been reluctant to perform in front of the others. When she'd satisfied herself that the chamber was loaded, the magazine full and locked in the grip, and that the three spares were in their places in her left thigh pocket, she reholstered the weapon, smoothing the velcroed flap. Clanking and hissing noises faded as the machinery which made them reclaimed precious oxygen from the compartment, replacing it with nothingness.

Instead of looking up, as might be expected, into the starry depths of space (Gutierrez was preparing a hasty getaway, and a view of the major's real destination, a kilometer aft, was blocked by the bulk of the passenger insert, the cowled OMS pods, and the tail assembly of the shuttle), Reille y Sanchez peered back through the thick transparency at her companions, soon to follow, she hoped, despite a mixture of less-than-enthusiastic expressions—nervousness, anxiety, uneuphemized terror—on their lens-distorted features. She wondered how her features looked to them.

Again before she knew it, this being a calculated result of countless Earthside simulations and endless drilling afterward in space, which had taught her body what to do while rendering it independent (in these matters, at least) of her mind, she'd observed the second ready-light, opened the overhead hatch, and was outside the free-falling craft with the lock dogged shut behind her. Nylon tether clipped in place, space-gloved fingers laced into one of the several handholds at the rear of the flight deck, she waited for the rest of her team to emerge. Through paired windows high in the after bulkhead, she could discern human-shaped silhouettes. Too much yellow glare interfered to make out whose they were.

The airlock hatch swung open. First came Kamanov, his tanned, handsome face framed in his helmet, his grin belying not only the birth date in his dossier (the geologist would turn seventy before his feet touched the Earth again), but the silver of his beard, mustache, and thick, unruly hair. Nor was the major ever altogether unaware of the Russian's broad shoulders and flat stomach, even concealed beneath the unflattering bulk of his suit. Clipping his tether to a ringbolt, he pivoted in "midair" and dogged the hatch. With a gentle kick at the stubby cylinder of the lock, he floated up beside her, giving her a friendly pat on the arm before turning his attention back where he'd come from.

This expedition, the major thought, represented a triumph of some kind for senior citizenry. After Kamanov came Colonel Vivian Richardson, the seams in her black face softened by reflections in her visor, just as the salt-and-pepper of her close-cropped hair was hidden by her cap. Expedition second in command and captain of the *Wright*, she was also Gutierrez's emotional surrogate, since he wouldn't be obeying his strong personal inclination to accompany them on the initial EVA. Displaying none of Kamanov's athletic grace, Richardson closed the hatch and joined them aft of the flight deck, well out of the way of the airlock.

As they waited, the major squinted against what seemed to

her a blinding glare. It was less actual light, she'd been informed, than a moonlit night back on Earth. At the *Moynihan*'s stern, the inexplicably featureless surface of a miniature planet shone like a golden apple in the sun. Training for this expedition, no one had been able to tell her why the astronomers had taken so long discovering 5023 Eris, bright as it was compared to most bodies like it, nor why it displayed this particular shade of yellow. The odd color had drawn them, that and a spectrographic signature rich in hydrocarbons, lifestuff which promised to make establishing themselves here possible. Observations made closer at hand every day told them the hue was that of the same residual minerals which lent color to the fallen leaves of autumn. Yet the answer, once they had it, only generated more questions, and they were a people for whom it had become difficult—because they'd been taught the hard way—to ask and answer questions.

The expedition's political officer, Arthur Empleado, was the last to squeeze out through the lock, his sweat-beaded scalp glistening through his thinning hair. To the major, he looked incomplete, somehow, insecure without the complement of "associates" who normally followed him everywhere, an oddly assorted lot of, well, "thugs" wasn't quite the right word. He looked uncomfortable without them, even through the vacuum suit he was bundled up in. Like Kamanov he was a civilian, rare among the crew. Short-winded, overweight like most of his professional brethren, he had nothing else in common with the perpetually youthful geologist.

Clever of Gutierrez, Reille y Sanchez thought, and daring, to place all of his rotten eggs in one dangerous basket. Expendables (including the major herself as chief of security) would take first risk. For many reasons (not the least of which was an undeniable yearning for every personal advantage footnotes in their records like "heroic" and "historic" might earn them), none of them could do a damned thing about it.

Empleado joined them at the bulkhead. Now it was time to make their mark on history, whether for the greater glory of their individual dossiers, their nation's honor, or perhaps a hungry world. Even if the bay doors hadn't been spread wide—superconducting solar panels sucking up the feeble sunlight—the major's team were at the wrong spot to look back along the foreshortened hull and read the blue block letters stenciled there, a meter high. Each of them already knew what they spelled out. Once the team had tethered themselves together and—propelled by the reaction pistol their leader accepted from Kamanov, who helped her plug the rabbit-eared device into her backpack—begun drifting aft of the shuttle's stubby, swept-back wings, the letters would be legible.

First they'd see the flag decaled on the fuselage to the left of the lettering, the same familiar banner a dozen generations of Americans had known, with thirteen horizontal stripes of red and white. The blue field in the upper left hand quarter contained a stylized yellow hammer and sickle.

And the lettering would say:

AMERICAN SOVIET SOCIALIST REPUBLIC

The United World Soviet, what Madison Avenue, on the air and in the pages of *American Truth*, would be calling—as their Russian predecessors had three quarters of a century earlier—the "Cosmic Collective" (or at least its latest, and, in whispered opinion, most important dominion), had come to the asteroids.

II
The Catwalk

"Holy Mother of God!"

The words slipped unbidden from Richardson's lips into the open mike of her carrier. It occurred to the major that, whatever nominal allegiance they all owed Marxist doctrine, by some coincidence each of her team, even the black American colonel and the Russian geologist (whose grandparents, in an earlier ambience of *glasnost*, had partaken of a sanctioned Orthodox revival) had been brought up Catholic.

"5023 Eris does appear rather impressive, does she not, for all that she is a very small asteroid," Kamanov responded with a grin, *"and a somewhat minor deity."*

"Belay that chatter!" Gutierrez interrupted from the flagship, unable to avoid nautical jargon even at a time like this. *"Keep the frequency clear!"* More than cost, security precluded television. The only eyes following this expedition for mankind as a whole were those of the KGB.

"Quite so." Empleado sounded no nearer to the major than the general. *"How unfortunate were a religious oath the first words relayed to the United Peoples of the World Soviet."*

"Not to mention," Kamanov suggested, *"your many and varied superiors, Comrade Political Officer?"*

In the privacy of her helmet, the major smiled. The Russian had raised a sore and complex point. Marxism's first century had been notable for its undisguised hostility toward religion which, despite an official easing of positions, still colored Eastern attitudes. You were free to believe what you liked without sanction, even manifest your belief openly, but never expect to rise in the bureaucracy if you exercised that freedom. In the West, with the Savior reborn to lead the revolution, the situation differed. Representing an organization ostensibly subordinate to Moscow, Empleado must reflect that hierarchy's policy. A member of KGB America, he must act on principles diametrically opposed. It was what came of serving too many masters at once, she thought, and no more than he deserved.

Bereft of moral support from his "corporals four," Empleado refused Kamanov the dignity of an answer, which was how he usually played it anyway. At less than a meter, the peculiar surface of 5023 Eris loomed before them like a wall, curvature unnoticed, the evidence of their senses in dire conflict. Eyes told them they were about to take an endless plunge down its flat, featureless face. Bodies, long since adjusted to the sensations of free-fall, told them no such thing. Even worse, the wall appeared (and perhaps was) every bit as slick as their polished visors, affording not the slightest hand- or foothold.

"Doctor"—the major's part was to pretend to ignore the byplay between Kamanov and Empleado, civilian loyalty and discipline being the concern of the KGB, not the Marines—"if you'd assist?"

They'd anticipated difficulty and were prepared. Swimming closer to what appeared a boundless palisade of yellow-green plastic, Reille y Sanchez drew a five-centimeter steel ring from a kevlar bag. Made from half-centimeter stock welded to a seven-centimeter steel disk, a dozen of these makeshifts had been fabricated in a sparse facility inboard the *Metzenbaum* by a grumbling old machinist, another of the senior-citizen contingent, when instruments during the flight had begun giving foreboding hints about the real nature of the expedition's destination. The major let the reaction pistol drift on the long plastic tube which fed gas from her backpack. Peeling a thin, circular polyethylene cover from the underside of the disk, she exposed a surface coated with a descendant of cyanoacrylic "crazy" glue. Extending her arm, she placed the disk in contact with the asteroid's glossy surface. Within heartbeats, nothing short of explosives might have removed it.

Kamanov, floating beside her, spring-latched a plastic hook into the ring and shook out paired nylon lines attached to it. Reille y Sanchez reclaimed the reaction pistol, pressed the trigger, let it pull her a few meters left. Kamanov remained where he was. The slender lines slipped through her gloved fingers until she reached the spot, indicated by the tautness of the lines, where she intended anchoring a second adhesive piton.

That task accomplished, the free ends of the lines snapped in place, the major hung parallel to the surface as Richardson pulled closer on the single line to which they were all attached, seized an anchored line in each hand, brought knees to chin and performed an awkward somersault, pressing booted feet against the asteroid and standing "up," held "down" by the lines. The vice-commander was followed by Empleado, who required assistance from both women, and afterward by the major. For a moment, Reille y Sanchez stood where she'd alighted, struggling against warnings from her kinaesthetic sense to reorient herself, to see herself standing on the surface of a planet, looking up at a trio of winged spaceships hanging a kilometer overhead. As she knew it would, something readjusted itself inside her head with a mental *pop*. She was aware of watching Kamanov, a hand wrapped around each line, shuffling toward them from the other end of the odd catwalk they'd just built.

With Empleado's more-or-less useless help—they could all hear the man's labored breathing, and his helmet visor had begun to opaque with condensation—the colonel attached a scrap of colored fabric to one line, red, white, blue, and yellow. "I claim this world," she announced to her comrades and the universe, "for humankind, on behalf of American Soviet Socialism and the United World Soviet!"

"We copy that, EVA team, and are relaying it back to Earth," Gutierrez informed them. *"America, and, uh, the United World Soviet, have landed on 5023 Eris!"*

During this ragtag bit of ceremony, the major searched within herself for a feeling of achievement, finding only weary awareness of how much still had to be accomplished during this EVA. It was more than possible, should they fail to produce results, should some disaster, foreseen or unforeseen, befall them, that "humankind" would never hear those words. The expedition was being conducted in secrecy rivaling that enshrouding pre-Soviet American development of the atom bomb. It wouldn't be reported until some spectacular discovery or success could be reported with it. Earth was poor and hungry, much of its populace homeless and hopeless. While its present rulers were less responsive to public pressure than the state which had constructed the shuttles, it would nevertheless be prudent to justify the enormous expenditure this undertaking represented before announcing the expenditure had been made.

The major's companions relaxed a bit, marking a conclusion. The next item on their agenda was a secure mooring for the three space vehicles themselves, each the size of an airliner. Detailed radar survey, as the expedition approached 5023 Eris, had informed them that the asteroid's composition, whatever unknown circumstances had created it, was more or less uniform. Under a polymerized surface only centimeters deep lay a radio-opaque core, presumably of accreted metal and hydrocarbons. It made slight difference where they attached their docking equipment.

A dozen words from Gutierrez, an orange flash from the airlock of the *Wright*—atmosphere would have conveyed the dull boom of gunfire—warned the major that those inboard were ready for the next stage. In a long moment, during which she observed several space-suited forms around the *Wright*'s engine-mounted tail, another nylon line drifted into view, its many kinks elongating until they disappeared, propelled by a huge-bored Webley line-throwing gun at a tangent to the asteroid's surface.

"Got it!" Richardson, who happened to be nearest, caught the line as it snaked between the pitons they'd secured. She handed it to the major, who tucked an end through the ring behind her. Reille y Sanchez pulled, a clumsy Empleado winding slack around a hand and elbow, until a heavier line jerked into view.

"Easy," Reille y Sanchez shouted to no one in particular, "keep it taut! That thing out there weighs enough to break bones!"

The latter line, like those of the makeshift catwalk, was also paired, consisting of a doubled-over single length of nylon passing through a steel and plastic pulley which could be clipped to a ring. Seemingly of its own accord, the wheel began turning. Soon, attached to one side of the line like someone's washing, a bulky cargo hove into view. Shouting instructions into her mike, the major guided the object to a safe landing. Except for its size—the base of the device was a meter in diameter—it was identical in every respect to the pitons they'd just glued to the asteroid's surface, fabricated by the same man, by the same means.

Not trusting Empleado, the major summoned Kamanov to hold it while she peeled off the protective sheeting. Together they placed it two meters from the second of the smaller rings, at right angles to the nylon catwalk, waiting for the cyanoacrylate to set.

"One down, my dear major," the geologist sighed wearily, *"and too many more to go!"*

Unclipping the pulley and retracing Kamanov's steps, they squeezed past the colonel and the sweating KGB officer, approached the first piton, snapped the pulley on, and took delivery of a second giant attachment. In minutes, they'd glued it on a line paralleling the smaller devices. A third parcel was the concern of Richardson and her dubious assistant, a trestle-base like a miniature, truncated Eiffel Tower, to be set between the two giant rings. The major and the geologist had their own task, but kept an eye on the operation as they lifted their feet, reversed positions relative to the asteroid, and, not without trepidation, let the reaction pistol pull them up the face of 5023 Eris toward a new location. There they anchored a small ring, received the pulley via the line attaching them to the other explorers, and hauled in a third large ring from the *Wright*. This and the initial large ring would anchor a second shuttle. The first and second rings would hold the first spacecraft that landed.

It was when they'd floated over the catwalk, to a point on the opposite side where they intended to prepare a berth for the third shuttle, that they ran into trouble. As Reille y Sanchez placed the last small ring, it sank into the solid-looking surface, taking her thumb and fingers with it. Without a sound, without thinking, she tried to withdraw her fingers, which were caught fast, dragging herself down until her helmet bobbed within a centimeter of the surface.

She let the reaction pistol float and extended her other hand to stop herself. It, too, sank in, and her helmet made contact. The spherical transparency before her face met the surface over a sharp-edged circular area the color and consistency of butter-scotch pudding.

Now, she screamed. At the slightest motion, she sank deeper and deeper, drawn by what force, she didn't know. She could no longer turn her head, could see nothing but the uniform, grainy color of the surface material. Short of breath despite an ample oxygen supply, she felt Kamanov's hand on her, tugging at her life-support backpack. She presumed he'd snatched her reaction pistol, their one hope, and was firing it away from the asteroid. If so, it was without effect. Whatever energy acted on her, it was many times stronger than that minuscule thrust.

"I fear it is too late, Estrellita," exclaimed the Russian, using her first name for the first time in the three years they'd known each other. *"I have become stuck, as well, at the elbow. Try to relax. Breathe evenly. I can see the shuttles. I have the pulley in my hand. I believe they intend to pull us up with the Wright's reaction motors."*

By now, her helmet was half-imbedded in the treacherous wall. Light around her face grew dimmer. Whatever the shuttle was doing, it made no difference. She felt strain where Kamanov gripped her suit. Breathe evenly, he'd advised. In her phones, she heard the geologist's breath coming in shorter, more painful-sounding gasps. The pull between shuttle and asteroid must be terrific, his merely human body part of the linkage. At the moment, however, she was more concerned about an ominous hiss from the vicinity of her helmet collar and a drop in her own suit pressure.

"No good, Doc!" It was the *Wright*. *"We're slacking off! Looks like the ship was being pulled in with you!"*

Kamanov remained silent, releasing a lungful of air. *"Thank you, Wright. I confess your slacking off is something of a relief."*

"Roger that. Your suits'll keep you going awhile. We'll get you out!"

"Estrellita," Kamanov squeezed her shoulder, *"did you hear?"*

It was now dark. She took a breath. "Yes, Piotr, I heard. I can't see a thing, and I think my suit's leaking."

A long pause was followed by a sigh. *"It is an ill wind which blows no good to anyone. You need not worry about your suit, you are now covered with the surface material. As for myself, I shan't be able to see much longer. I have kept my face clear until now, but I believe I dislocated my shoulder when the Wright attempted to pull us out. Looking back is a strain. The Wright has performed an OMS burn, and resumed its original station."*

"Running out on us, the rats!"

The geologist chuckled. *"Precisely."*

The major shook her head inside her helmet, drops of perspiration burning in her eyes. Not being able to see the muck she was imbedded in was much better. She began calming down. "And to think we left Earth and came two hundred million klicks to die in quicksand."

"*Hush,*" Kamanov's answer was gentle. "*Do not say it, even—especially if it is true. The Commodore will dig us out, somehow.*"

"Richardson and Empleado." She struggled to remain conversational. "Did they—" She stiffened. "Piotr, I can see light! It's brightening up in here! I don't know what it means, but . . ."

"*Yes,*" the scientist asked her, "*what is happening?*"

"My helmet's broken through, like coming up through muddy water! The radar was wrong, Piotr! Underneath this epoxy or whatever, it's—"

"*What is it?*"

"It's hollow, and we've got company! Weird company!"

The major didn't exaggerate, as she knew he'd soon see for himself. The asteroid coating must be radio-opaque, for it was no more than centimeters thick. Two or three meters before her—below her, thinking of the asteroid's center as "down" —was another wall, or floor, of a plastic-covered mesh like lawn furniture used to be made of, the open spaces between the wires not quite large enough for an ungloved fist.

This wasn't what seized and held her attention. Between her and the wall, half-a-dozen creatures were anchored by their feet (or whatever they stood on) so that it appeared she looked down on them from above. The little rural Texas girl inside her squirmed. They looked, more than anything else, like giant golden-brown cockroaches. Cockroaches her own size. Cockroaches with gun belts and guns pointed at her.

Another being caught her astonished eye, smaller, of more slender build, apparently unclothed, but covered from head to foot either with soft scales fringed at the edges, or stubby feathers. Like the insect-things, it wore a weapons belt, although whatever device it carried there remained holstered. The creature lay supine on the mesh as a courtesy, she somehow knew, so she might examine it full length. It raised a "hand," fingers spread wide to display translucent webbing, and spoke to her in Spanish.

"A good afternoon to you, Major Reille y Sanchez. Or perhaps I may be privileged to address you as 'Estrellita,' a most charming and beautiful name. Welcome to what you call '5023 Eris.' I'm Aelbraugh Pritsch, administrative assistant to the Proprietor. As you no doubt surmised by now, you and your party were expected."

III
The Proprietor's Assistant

"I, uh . . ."

Even had her state of mind permitted it, Reille y Sanchez hadn't, in fact, had time to surmise anything. Before she could order her thoughts to speak, the feather-scaled thing preempted her.

"And here, unless I'm mistaken, is the distinguished Dr. Piotr Kamanov." Without perceptible effort, the creature had switched to a language the humans shared, standard English, but with a fussy, pedantic accent. Reille y Sanchez realized in a corner of her mind that it sounded like an actor in one of those old gorilla movies which, despite their marginal legality, she, like most of her generation, had somehow managed to see while growing up. Or the gold-plated robot, what was its name? "Good afternoon to you, sir."

She glanced at the spot the bird or lizard thing had indicated. It seemed, for once, that the geologist was as speechless with amazement as she was. His helmet bubble, a gloved hand, and the toes of his boot thrust from the ceiling like one of his fossils, embedded in a matrix of yellow silt. That, too, reminded her of an old movie, although she couldn't remember at the moment what it was. The major shook her head in disbelief: Kamanov was winking at her!

With a grunt, the entity climbed to its feet, which were built, Reille y Sanchez noticed through a lucid tunnel in her bewilderment, like those of a parrot, with two long toes in front and another pair jutting backward where the heel should be. It was hard deciding if its appearance was more birdlike or reptilian. Its overall color lay between silver-gray and lavender. Veins in the scales (or were they feathers?) were bright red. Body color shaded from human-looking shoulders, along broad, odd-jointed arms, to hands with delicate, powdery-white fingers. The creature's chest was stooped (scholarly, she thought), tapering to a paunch. Its hips, for all they supported an ordinary holster belt, reminded her of the allosaurs or tryannosaurs in the San Antonio museum and in children's books. The legs supporting them, heavily muscled under the feathers (or were they scales?) appeared mammalian, but bent in the wrong places. The feet, as she'd observed, were birdlike, except that they ended in round toes with flat black nails like those of the fingers.

Aelbraugh Pritsch's scarlet-crested head was unquestionably that of a sentient being, with shrewd amber eyes under the same domed shape which afforded volume for her own capable brain. The face was as flat as any human face, with a pair of small nostril-holes beneath the eyes. A flattened beak, no more than a triangle of black horn scalloped twice along its bottom edge, met a mammalian-looking lower lip. As the thing spoke, the major watched for teeth, but wasn't surprised to see none. The tongue, too, was black, and looked as if it would be dry to the touch.

"My associates"—the alien indicated the insect beings —"whose names, I regret to confess, are impossible even for me to pronounce, will assist you. Please don't be alarmed at their formidable appearance." A couple of the living nightmares raised pairs of many-jointed arms to lift the major down. Despite herself, she shrank away. "I assure you, Major, they're quite as civilized as you or I. Their drawn weapons were merely a precaution, occasioned by the rather fearsome reputation of your own species. But don't underestimate them, whatever you do. Their reflexes are a bit slower than yours or mine, but they're a remarkably hardy folk, singularly difficult to dispatch, in particular with firearms such as you wear.

They'd wreak havoc before they expired, and my employer would be most distressed with me if you should happen to be damaged.''

Shoving revulsion aside, Reille y Sanchez cooperated, only half hearing what the entity said. She could see now that its companions were more like marine crustaceans, giant lobsters, than giant roaches. What made accepting them most difficult was that they lacked anything like a face. The carapace covering the—the word was "thorax," she recalled—was ridged, made up of plates like samurai armor, showing hints of green on the high spots. The pattern seemed to vary with the individual. Golden-brown shaded to black at the edges of each segment. Below the thorax a lobsterlike tail seemed disproportionately small.

She never made an accurate count of the limbs. An upper pair of arms ended in mutually opposed chitin-covered fingers. Several middle sets boasted serrated claws. The weapons swinging at their sides were stubby cylinders, fifteen centimeters long, half that in diameter, attached to stirrup-shaped handles. Despite her resolve, she felt grateful when they released their hold on her. Looking into their compound eyes, their only identifiable facial feature, she managed a ragged "Th-thank you."

Together, using claws, the creatures snapped out a faultless "shave-and-a-haircut," conveying several messages at once. She was welcome, they appreciated her courtesy under trying circumstances. They were intelligent creatures, not trained monsters, and they'd done their homework when it came to twenty-first century humanity. Their impossibly long, slender antennae (each creature seemed to have several pairs) waved in what even she could tell was meant to be a comical manner. Aelbraugh Pritsch chuckled.

Standing upright (whatever that meant where gravity was an ill-remembered ghost), she reoriented herself for the second time that day. The meshed platform was a huge shallow basket suspended on cables seemingly too light for their impressive length, from a half dozen massive green columns, each a klick apart, three or four meters in diameter, blending without embellishment into the ceiling. The surface of the mesh was tacky enough that her boot soles stayed where she put them (accustomed to velcro inboard the shuttles, she knew to keep one foot on the floor at all times), without inhibiting movement. Reille y Sanchez watched another pair of crustaceans assist Kamanov from what now appeared to be the ceiling. He grimaced as his shoulder moved, tears in the corners of his eyes, but was silent until they set him on his feet.

The geologist addressed Aelbraugh Pritsch: *"Tell me, sir—or perhaps 'madam'—can our people hear us?"* Kamanov's voice came by radio and air-conduction. By the way their suits hung, the place had plenty of atmosphere. What particular gases, the major thought, was another matter.

Aelbraugh Pritsch raised feathery brows, bent its arms at misplaced elbows, and turned up webbed palms in a shrug. "It would be 'sir,' Dr. Kamanov, were my species given to honorifics in our own languages, which we are not. I'm a reproductive male. And to answer your question, I regret to inform you that you aren't being heard. The canopy's designed, among other functions, to filter harmful and unwanted energies. This precludes communication in the radio wavelengths, which haven't been employed by our civilization for . . . well, for rather a long time."

The chief of military security had an imaginative flash of condensers, tubes, and other early components petrified in the geological strata of some far-off planet. "We're to be held," she stated, "incommunicado?"

Aelbraugh Pritsch blinked, looked at its—his—hands, turned one over and placed it in the other. "Great Egg, no! On the contrary, you're free to do anything you wish, within the bounds of my employer's propriety. I'll order an antenna (is that correct, or is it aerial?) exserted through the canopy, if you insist. I suggest patience, since your colleagues, Colonel Richardson and Mr. Empleado, will join us in a moment, along with Corporals Wise, Roo, Hake, and Betal, who've been sent to 'dig you out.' In due course, a matter of mere hours, your entire group will be invited in, spacecraft and all, if it should be their desire."

The major opened her mouth to reply, but the being snapped his digits. "That reminds me: feel free to remove your helmets!

I'm a bureaucrat by inclination, an execrable host. Your suits are stuffy. Our atmosphere's the same as you're accustomed to, twenty percent oxygen, most of the rest nitrogen. It contains less trace lead and carbon monoxide than you must feel comfortable with, having poured so much into the air of your homeworld.''

The humans glanced at one another, shrugging at the same time, Kamanov with a grimace of pain. Reille y Sanchez pushed fabric out of the way to unlock her helmet ring, only to discover it had been damaged and wouldn't detach from her suit. For his part, Kamanov made a half-hearted attempt to remove his helmet with one hand, and gave it up. His left arm floated useless.

"Dear me, I'm remiss again!" their host exclaimed. "Allow me. I'm rather good with primitive mechanics. The major first, as I believe that is the custom."

With the assistance of the nimble-fingered being and two crustaceans standing nearby at parade rest, Reille y Sanchez's helmet was soon free, its sealing ring warped, accounting for the leak she'd experienced. She set it on the mesh and strode to Kamanov, her boots making tearing noises like velcro. With the help of the aliens, she removed the geologist's helmet, revealing a pale, sweaty countenance. His eyes still twinkled.

"Are you okay, Doctor?" she asked, admiring and alarmed. If she'd felt the way he looked, she'd be lying down by now, or throwing up.

Kamanov bit his lips, then let it go. "You were calling me 'Piotr,' when we thought we were going to die."

She frowned. "Okay, Piotr-when-we-thought-we-were-going-to-die, you don't look well. I think your arm's dislocated."

He began to nod and stopped himself. "I am afraid so." With this, the geologist's body slackened, his knees bent, his arms began floating to a half-horizontal position. His eyes were still alert, but his companion knew he was in shock and not far from unconsciousness.

"First Nest!" Aelbraugh Pritsch exclaimed, failing to suppress a canarylike trill of alarm, "I didn't realize he'd been injured! He must be seen to immediately! Section chief, a vehicle!" One of the crustaceans clacked claws and reached to its belt with armored fingers. Making more noises, somewhere between those of a dozen sets of castanets and a pan full of frying bacon, it communicated with someone or something somewhere else, received an answer composed of the same noises, switched off, and made noises at the bird being. Aelbraugh Pritsch turned to the major. "A vehicle will be here any moment, to take your friend to the surface below to be looked after."

"We have a medical doctor," Reille y Sanchez protested, "aboard the—"

"It will require an hour, I believe the interval's called, to get her here. If my information's correct, Major, Dr. Kamanov isn't a young being. He could die of shock, however superficial his injury."

The woman shrugged. "What do we do when the vehicle gets here?"

Aelbraugh Pritsch thought, then examined Kamanov without touching him, peering into the collar of his suit. "The important thing is what we do beforehand. Like me, you're endothermic creatures. Dr. Kamanov is warmed by his suit. His isn't an open wound, no fluid loss must be staunched. In absence of gravity, his circulatory system—"

"Kamanov? Reille y Sanchez? Is that you?"

The interrupting voice was Empleado's. True to Aelbraugh Pritsch's word, the hands and helmets of what turned out to be the expedition's political officer and second-in-command weren't long emerging from the substance of the ceiling. Beyond those first few, fearful words, Empleado was as speechless and shaken when finally freed from the matrix as the geologist and the major had been, content to be led aside by gentle claws and armored fingers as all turned their attention to the colonel.

Richards was in much worse condition, paralyzed and pale despite her complexion, unconscious despite wide-open eyes— until the bird being's assistants began reaching for her arms and legs.

"Get back all of you! Don't touch me! Don't touch me!"

With a screech, Richardson burst into a blurred flurry of furious motion, slapping hysterically at the creatures' manipulators, kicking at them with her heavy boots. The startled and dismayed crustaceans exploded from around her like pins in a bowling alley, adding their sizzling expostulations to the woman's shouts of terror and warning. No one, human or otherwise, dared approach her without risk of serious injury.

"Blessed Hatching," declared Aelbraugh Pritsch, almost unheard above the stream of noise and abuse, "can't you do something about her, Major?"

Reille y Sanchez shook her head without speaking, keeping wary eyes on the colonel while trying to watch the injured Kamanov as well. Windmilling her limbs, the black woman slipped, unassisted, from the ceiling. Any one of those wild kicks might have sent her spinning in any direction, transforming her into a deadly, bone-breaking human missile. Instead, still flailing, she began settling toward the mesh below amidst screams and curses which filled the air about her and reverberated painfully in the major's suit communicator. Kamanov seemed inert, oblivious to it all.

By the time Richardson reached the mesh, she had a glove off, a tiny gun in her hand, and was swinging the black eye of its outsized suppressor back and forth at a variety of targets, failing to exclude her shipmates. The major thought she glimpsed the dull gleam of a hollowpoint deep in the chamber at the rear of the suppressor and short barrel, which she recognized as that of a double-action SD9 9m/m, a favorite of covert agencies.

The bird being and his party knew what the weapon was. They scattered, ducked, and flinched, no less enthusiastic in their effort to avoid being shot than the humans, including Empleado, who found themselves on the wrong end of Richardson's little automatic. Briefly, from behind a pair of hunched-over crustaceans, Reille y Sanchez considered drawing her own CZ99A1 and putting an end to this insane display. Before she could act, however, despite his own physical difficulties, Kamanov had come to sudden life and somehow managed to slip behind the colonel and seize the SD9 before it went off.

Exhaling a deep-throated moan into her suit mike, Richardson slumped into the relaxed posture which, in the absence of gravity, meant she was truly unconscious. As everyone else relaxed as well, Reille y Sanchez noticed that, this time, the woman's eyes were closed.

"Major?" Reille y Sanchez almost jumped, despite Aelbraugh Pritsch's mild tone. With Empleado's help, the crustaceans were attending the colonel and the geologist. "I'll order that aerial run out, now. The vehicle's on its way. You can let your people know what's happened."

She nodded, watching the orders being carried out. Despite her experience of darkness when she was within the ceiling, it now seemed to transmit abundant sunlight of an eerie yellow-green character. No wonder she and Kamanov had been expected! She could make out, she realized with astonishment, fuzzy-edged silhouettes of her would-be rescuers, Empleado's four musclemen, who'd be the next to come through unless they exercised extraordinary care.

She glanced down, wondering about the vehicle. Beneath her feet, through the supporting mesh, she noticed a sight which severely tested her recent reorientation. The thick green columns seemed to reach into a nether region an infinite distance away, lost in shadows and obscuring haze. Gravity or not, a fall of a kilometer awaited before one encountered, at whatever velocity, the genuine surface of the asteroid. Nor, she became aware, was the bottom of the basket entirely flat and floorlike. Where she'd emerged, she'd just missed dropping into a long central depression worked into its shape, as if made to nest a piece of enormous, oddly shaped equipment. This provoked a laugh: it was just right to cradle one of the shuttles!

A crustacean handed her a stiff copper lead terminating in an ordinary alligator clamp. It took a moment to find the right place to clip it. Following the wire with her eyes, she observed that it had been thrust through the substance of the ceiling. She should have watched how that was done, she admonished herself. On the other hand, there was too much to be watched all at once.

Meantime, a soft humming from below announced the arrival of the vehicle. She'd have to hurry not to be left behind. She recited the names of three honored statesmen who, according to her books in school, had made America what it was today:

"Moynihan, Metzenbaum, Wright? General Gutierrez, this is Major Reille y Sanchez. Do you copy?"

IV
White Gloves, Trousers Optional

"Have you seen the ones," hissed a voice which had been born to gossip, "that look like giant spiders?"

AeroSpace Force Brigadier General Horatio Z. Gutierrez looked up from the tiled floor he had been staring at, into the small, porcine eyes of Arthur Empleado, KGB (ASSR). Having been brought up properly, he promptly glanced away again. Pacing this brightly lit area for what seemed hours, worried about his friend, preoccupied with a dozen other trains of thought, he was vaguely aware he'd been wondering, all along, why a corridor should be forty meters wider than the suburban streets of Walton Beach, the Florida panhandle bedroom community for nearby Humphrey Field (also known as Engels Auxiliary #9) where he and his family had lived the last six years. His concerns of the moment didn't include a zoological catalog of the inhabitants of 5023 Eris.

The general opened his mouth. "Art, don't—"

"Spiders have eight legs, comrades," another voice interrupted before he could finish. "These have six, although appendage-counting's the last item one thinks of in their presence. I take it you don't mean the major's friends, Arthur. Toya says they're marine crustaceans."

The portal Gutierrez paced in front of (no human architect would have designed a door two meters high and five wide) had evaporated without a sound. Rosalind Nguyen stood before him, incongruous and unmedical in these hospital-like surroundings wearing her frayed and faded ship-suit. Like his own, it had served during the months they'd traveled to this place, only to discover that someone, *something*, had gotten here first. Already it seemed days, rather than six short hours, since two of his people had dissolved into the surface. Two more had been lost before rescue could be mobilized and one victim had relayed an alien invitation to come in from the cold of interplanetary space. He'd refused to consider it without the return of the major and Empleado, their unfettered presence serving as assurance—frail, since the aliens intended keeping Kamanov and Richardson, ostensibly to treat their injuries—that they weren't walking ("sinking" might be a better term, or "being sucked") into a trap.

Handing him the first of many new riddles, the major had been compelled to return under her own power, Empleado and a catatonic Richardson in tow. In the view of nonhuman therapists, the latter wouldn't regain sanity in their company. Rising from the muck she'd vanished into, the major had used a reaction pistol to pull her party to the waiting shuttle. The bird being who called himself "Proprietor's assistant" had apologized for the inconvenience, explaining that his group on 5023 Eris possessed no spacecraft. But if that were true, how the flaming hell had they gotten here? Asked the question (in more diplomatic tones), Aelbraugh Pritsch had begged Gutierrez to hold his inquiries for the Proprietor. One of many items on the general's crowded mental agenda was an appointment with that individual an hour hence.

"Sir"—Dr. Nguyen didn't wait for an answer from Empleado, whose four oddly assorted henchmen stood nearby as usual, trying unsuccessfully to look like casual loungers—"you can see Dr. Kamanov, now. I assured myself that they did a good job with him."

Gutierrez blinked down into her exotic features. Neither he nor Empleado was a big man, but both loomed over the little Vietnamese. This silly mission, he thought, remembering it was a good thought to keep to himself, consisted of every obsolete loser and disposable misfit the ASSR could find room for (an iconoclastic brigadier, for example, who never kept his mouth shut at inopportune times), but it also included, by accident he was sure, some of the most beautiful women he'd ever known. It was a toss-up, he'd long since decided, whether the doctor, with her delicate face and flawless skin, or the major, with her striking combination of Irish and Mexican attractions, was easier on the eyes.

As always on such occasions, he reminded himself of the darkly beautiful woman he'd wed thirty-two years ago, more Indian than Spanish in appearance, whom he loved with whatever heart and soul the service left him, and with whom he'd raised eight splendid children. His second eldest, Danny, happened to be a junior officer aboard the *Metzenbaum*. As always on such occasions, he tried not to think of his eldest, blown to radioactive vapor in a recent, less-than-successful attempt to bestow the benefits of American Marxism upon the benighted denizens of southern Africa.

"Thanks, Doctor," he answered, "I'll see him now." Followed by Empleado, who left his sinister cohort behind, he headed for the wall where the door had been, too conscious of his dignity in KGB presence to approach it with caution. He hoped the damn thing would remember to go away before he broke his nose on it.

"Horatio!" At the sight of his friend, Kamanov propped himself on an elbow. He lay on a platform extruded, as far as the general could see, from the floor, the surface of which grew more resilient the closer it came to the man's skin. He was covered, in homely contrast, by a worn blanket from one of the shuttles.

"Pete." The general glanced around the chamber, failing to discover a flat surface (except the floor and the bed) or straight edge. The room's plan was kidney-shaped. Soft light glowed from every centimeter of the low, domed ceiling. A meter away, in a sort of corner where a sort of chair had been created the same way as the bed, Pulaski, whom Dr. Nguyen often drafted as an assistant, sat at rigid attention. To the general's surprise, Kamanov smoked one on the Cuban cigars which had seemed almost an appendage back in the pre-mission planning days in Florida. Near one wall lay the twisted cellophane of its wrapper. Gutierrez stooped to pick it up. "I'm surprised," he observed, "they let you smoke that thing in here."

"Leave it, my friend, it is an experiment—they seem content to let me go to hell in my own way; notice that no trace of smoke or even of the odor remains—the sergeant and I have been watching that wrapper creep toward the wall at a rate of about fifty centimeters per hour.''

''What?''

''In an otherwise seamless surface, a fine line runs about the room centimeters up the curve where floor turns into wall. This is what caught my eye: subduction, as on Earth, one tectonic plate flowing under another. The surfaces are self-sweeping—dust and litter are carried by the 'current' to disappear into the crack. The same mechanism provides a certain tackiness, allowing firm footing in almost nonexistent gravity. You, too, would drift across the room if you stood motionless. Unless, like this nightstand, you wore small spikes which penetrate the surface, placing you in contact with the substrate. The surface then flows around you. Fascinating.''

The general shrugged. ''Ven Kamanov draws final breath,'' he intoned in a theatrical accent, ''he vill dictate notes about it.'' He turned to the little sergeant, bestowing an imperative glance on Empleado as well. ''Take ten, Pulaski.'' She jittered out into the relative sanctuary of the corridor, perhaps unaware of the four awaiting her outside. There had been some kind of trouble between her and one of Empleado's men earlier in the voyage, although Major Reille y Sanchez had taken care of it, and Gutierrez didn't know the details. The KGB man gave his head a microscopic shake, intending to stay through Gutierrez's conversation with the Russian. The American let out an exasperated breath, and, despite the fact it had never been raised, changed the subject. ''Glad to see you looking well. Rosalind said you'd pulled your arm out of the socket trying to rescue the major.''

Kamanov grinned. ''What man with testosterone in his blood would not?'' His eyebrows suggested he excluded Empleado from that category—and that, if no one else did, he'd hold the man responsible for the behavior of his underlings. Assuming a frozen expression, Empleado sat in the seat vacated by Pulaski, feet flat on the floor, arms folded in front of him. The general remained standing.

''Trying to rescue myself, as well,'' Kamanov continued. ''It was the *Wright* which did the pulling. You know, the *sound* of a shoulder separating is worse than any pain." He shivered, shaking his head. "It's like the idea of sliding down a fifty-meter razorblade into a barrel of vodka." Across the room, Empleado squirmed at the words. "Thanks to the dexterous manipulators of our esteemed hosts, I now feel fit and hale. I wish they would find it in whatever they use to encourage circulation to let me out of this place." He brushed the blanket from his shoulder. No scar or inflammation could be seen. "We have arrived, Horatio. I have work to do. And many, many questions to ask."

"Like everybody else aboard Earth's three best, and only, spaceships!"

"Except"—Kamanov glanced at Empleado to observe whether he'd caught the general's unpatriotic complaint—"that everybody else, tovarich, has had the advantage of seeing all that has happened so far with his own eyes. While I have been occupied thus far—what is the expression? Making zees?"

Grinning, Gutierrez told Kamanov about the major's return. "The landing went pretty much as planned. Instead of mooring to the rings Corporal Owen manufactured, we used RCS thrusters, sinking into the surface as you did. Our hosts had suspended docking cradles to support the shuttles—made up in advance! That's something I want to know more about, Pete. We were *expected*, even though we left Earth under strict secrecy and radio silence. Like everything about this place, it gives me a creepy feeling."

"And the colonel?" Kamanov asked. "I am told she is not here, in the infirmary, where they might help her."

"You're told correctly. Your multilegged doctors are afraid they'll drive her down even deeper, and I think they may be right. She's limp as a dishrag now, has been since you took her gun away—with one exception. She threw another fit when the shuttles were settling through the roof. Bloodied several noses, including mine, broke one wrist, not her own, and damned near ruined a couple of the crewmen for life."

"This reminds me, Comrade Doctor Kamanov." It was Empleado, speaking up for the first time. "Whatever became of Colonel Richardson's weapon after you took it away? And the silencer? I haven't seen it since."

"An excellent question, Comrade Political Officer, but you ask it of the wrong individual. You tell me where they took my trousers, which I would like very much to have, and I will tell you where Colonel Richardson's gun has gone." The Russian dismissed the KGB man and let his head swing from side to side. "I have seen this sort of thing before, Horatio. After a great fire or an earthquake. So have you, I suspect, in combat."

"It's like she's asleep," Gutierrez nodded, "only we can't wake her up. Rosalind says it's a simple retreat from reality, because she can't stand talking to a big bird, or the sight of giant bugs with guns, or something."

"Possibly the worst case of culture shock on record, my friend. Our first contact with a nonterrestrial intelligence. Some will be affected worse than others. Some, like you and I, may even be immune. How is the rest of our little party standing up to it?"

The general shrugged. "Certainly no more reactions as bad as Vivian's, but there's something like a flu bug, ugliness at both ends, going around. I suspect it's partly relief after being cooped up for so long, and partly tension on account of what we've found here. Or what's found us. We've already had to break up a couple of fistfights."

"You may eventually have to restrain me, if they will not let me out of here," Kamanov nodded. "You have seen everything I missed by passing out like a schoolgirl. What is it like outside?"

"You've seen sequoia forests in California." Gutierrez shrugged. "It's like that, moist without feeling humid. Somber, but not depressing like you'd expect. The asteroid's covered with huge plants, Pete. I'm not sure they're trees. Thousands of them, a kilometer tall and the same distance apart, not arranged in any regular pattern. Remember the redwoods tunneled out for Model Ts? Some of these could accommodate a freight train. They spread at the top, fusing into an airtight, self-repairing canopy that forms the artificial upper surface of this place. It fills the area below with a diffuse yellowy-green light, and retains, probably even manufactures, oxygen and water vapor for a worldwide shirtsleeve environment."

Kamanov nodded again. "This much I managed to learn

from Rosalind and Toya. As I understand it, even yet we are not on the surface?''

''Within a dozen meters. They use more than the surface of this world, Pete. The hanging baskets—they're down with us now, by the way—weren't invented for our benefit. This area of the asteroid's full of platforms, catwalks, what you might call 'treehouses,' all the way to the canopy. A dozen living and working environments for use by at least as many species.''

Again Kamanov glanced at Empleado, but for what reason, besides polite acknowledgment of his existence or an unconscious effort to include him in the conversation, Gutierrez couldn't guess. ''Tell me about them.''

''You saw Aelbraugh Pritsch, a kind of bird or reptile. And the lobsters, soldiers of some kind. The place reminds me of a cross between a paleontology exhibit and a cartoon where the animals wear trousers.''

''Three-fingered gloves.'' Kamanov chuckled. ''In cartoons, trousers are optional. I have seen the insect folk, the ones who fixed my shoulder.''

''Okay, so far I've seen a walking quilt made of gray plastic and a big rubber flower, yellow and red, covered with a half-invisible film that's silvery at an angle. I wouldn't have known it was intelligent, except that it was pushing a cart with wheels roweled like a vaquero's spurs. Now I know why. It offered me a cup of coffee in unaccented Spanish.''

''Coffee?'' Kamanov's expression was almost greedy.

''Something that smelled like coffee, and a doughnut! I turned it down, politely as I could, until Dr. Nguyen tests a sample. It wasn't easy. I could use a cup of real coffee. Have you eaten?''

Kamanov made a sour face. ''Rations, from the ships.''

''Probably all to the good. I asked this creature—call it 'she'—why, with all the mechanized wonders surrounding us, she was stuck pushing a cart. She replied that in convalescent circumstances, the 'human' touch was more to be desired than efficiency. That's what she was providing.''

''Hmmm.''

''Hmm, indeed.'' Gutierrez was reluctant, but needed his friend's advice. ''There's more. While I had her attention, I asked after the Proprietor, what he's like, what species he belongs to. A long pause, during which I'm sure she stared at me with an expression of profound pity and amazement, although I don't know how I know it. I certainly didn't know what part of her to watch in order to see it. She said, in words approaching religious awe, that the Proprietor's one of the '*Elders*.' Pete, I've got a bad feeling—''

"One bad feeling at a time, Horatio. What happened after you docked?''

"The *Moynihan* was last. We were met at the platform by a squadron of wingless aircraft like the one that brought you here.''

The icy blue eyes twinkled. "Tell me what that was like. I missed it.''

Gutierrez sighed. "Like an amusement-park ride, flattened spheres four meters in diameter, each a different color. Open tops, padded floors and walls. No controls, no seats, either. I suppose because they accommodate a variety of species with equal discomfort. I thought they had antigravity, but it turned out to be fanless hovercraft, operating, so Aelbraugh Pritsch said, by ion exchange. I didn't tell him I don't know what that means, but I asked him other questions. He gave up and told me I should see his boss, which I'm planning to do in about twenty minutes.''

"I see.'' The Russian scratched his chin thoughtfully. "We could always send Arthur in your place.'' He grinned at Empleado, who ignored him.

Gutierrez shoved his hands in his pockets, looked first at Empleado, then at Kamanov. "Aelbraugh Pritsch told me an odd thing before he shut his beak and referred further inquiries to the Proprietor. I thought I'd figured it out. Despite how well they're established here, the place has a new feel to it, as if they'd just arrived themselves. Having read some science fiction, I figured it was sort of an advance base for an interstellar expedition. You know, a galactic federation of races from many different worlds?''

"And?'' Kamanov raised bushy white eyebrows.

"I offered my deduction to Aelbraugh Pritsch,'' his friend

told him, "who replied, 'But we're all from the planet you call Earth.' "

V
The Proprietor

"Take my sidearm, sir," the major offered. "I can always draw another from the armorer."

The redheaded Marine officer pulled her CZ99A1 from the synthetic Webb weapons belt slanting across her hips, let the muzzle roll past her extended thumb as the pistol pivoted her trigger finger, and executed a practiced, casual wrist-snap which ended with the automatic's broad backstrap thrust toward her superior.

"Careful, sir, there's one up the spout."

Irritable with preoccupation, and a little short of breath, Gutierrez shook his head. He and Reille y Sanchez hastened down a maze of identical roofless corridors, trying to keep up with Aelbraugh Pritsch, who was faster on those parrotlike feet of his than he looked. Overhead, beyond a screen of overhanging foliage, for the first time since they'd arrived on 5023 Eris, they could have seen the yellow "sky" darken as the asteroid rotated into night—corridor walls glowed to make up the deficit—but neither of them looked up to see the change.

"Thank you, Estrellita," he puffed. "I understand that you're paid to be paranoid. I'll even grant you that paranoids live longer. But I don't think going armed to this meeting would be a very auspicious way to start official relations with the Proprietor. Do you?"

Life was difficult enough, he thought. Nothing about this expedition was going according to plan. Their shuttlecraft were parked inside the asteroid, more or less, instead of out, which saved on valuable consumables, but involved them with an advanced technology they didn't understand, meaning that they required local cooperation to get back outside, which placed them at the mercy of their hosts.

Vivian Richardson, his vice-commander and captain of one of the three shuttles, had become, well, not a vegetable, exactly, since she appeared to be subject to unpredictable outbursts of violence. The fact that, over the many months the voyage had lasted, he'd come to believe the colonel was a covert KGB observer—in a manner of speaking Empleado's second-in-command, as well as his own—made things nice and complicated. Hell, maybe Empleado was *her* second-in-command.

Worst of all, any claim they made here would now be disputed. One item of news he hadn't discussed with his friend Kamanov, and not just because Empleado had insisted on hanging around, was the detailed report he'd radioed Earthward soon after his three spacecraft had been bedded down, via the antenna provided by their hosts, the resulting orders he'd received from Washington, and certain conspicuous differences between them and the equivalent orders Moscow might have issued.

"I guess not, sir." With reluctance she didn't bother disguising, she flipped the grip of the pistol back into her palm in a maneuver which, in her part of the country, had been known for two centuries as the "road agent's spin," shucking the .41x22m/m into its kevlar holster, refastening the flap. As Gutierrez struggled to remember what it was he'd asked her, he realized the holster was balanced neatly by the big wire-cutting Bowie she wore at the off-side of her waist in a matching scabbard. "But it might be a good deal safer, sir," she added, earning her pay. "Isn't anyone going with you, sir, not even our political officer or one of his four—"

"Hoods? I had that out with Art not five minutes ago." The general dropped his heels, out of breath and suddenly heedless of how the dinosaurlike bird being outdistanced them. "I won't repeat the same argument with you. Thanks, Estrellita, for caring, but I was invited to this party by myself. I'll go by myself and fill Arthur in later, for the edification of his bosses.

He needn't worry about my leaving anything out. The crime that got me sent here was saying too much, not too little.''

He resumed his forward motion, but not the previous pace. Beside him, Reille y Sanchez nodded, but offered no immediate reply, first of all, he suspected, because he was correct in his assessment of the political realities, and she knew it. Second, because she probably didn't wish to contemplate whatever crime had gotten her volunteered for this expedition. Third, he thought, there was always the possibility that even Estrellita had bosses outside the normal chain of command to report to. Instead, she seemed to wait for what felt to him like the regulation decent interval for changing the subject in conversations with a superior officer.

"As you will, sir. I'll be back at the *Moynihan*." She tossed him a salute and turned to go.''

"You do that, Major. On your way, look in on Dr. Kamanov. He's restive in durance vile and considers you decorative.''

For that matter—he watched the rakish slant of her pistol belt as she retreated down the corridor, fighting knife slapping at her thigh—*so do I.* Enjoying a reflexive moment of guilty feelings about his wife, he began taking longer strides, pivoting to follow the Proprietor's assistant around a corner. That obviously impatient individual now awaited him at the end of the passage where it T-junctioned with yet another.

"You mustn't be late, General,'' the avian fussed when twenty such strides had brought Gutierrez even. The man resisted an urge to rub his eyes, seeing motion, or thinking he saw it, near the base of the birdlike being's neck, a flash of turquoise and perhaps the slender whip of a reptilian tail. "At the end of this passage a pressure door and a flight of stairs lead to the Proprietor's quarters. Don't be alarmed to find them awash with a colorless, odorless liquid.''

Gutierrez stopped again. "What?''

"Oxygenated fluorocarbon. Some of our staff here substitute it for the marine environment they're naturally adapted to. My security party, for example, the individuals you call 'lobster people'?'' The bird entity gave the flapped holster an unconscious pat where it hung at his belt. Gutierrez experienced a momentary doubt about having rejected Reille y Sanchez's sidearm. Hadn't officers and diplomats once worn ceremonial swords on occasions like this?

"Yes?" the man asked, struggling to gather up loose ends of thought and recapture the subject at hand. Maybe Vivian wasn't the only victim suffering from culture shock. "What about them?"

"You may have noticed the protective membrane they all wear," replied Aelbraugh Pritsch. "In some respects, it's like your own spacesuits, I'd venture to guess, devised to retain the moisture, temperature, and pressure necessary for their survival. Off duty, they inhabit quarters similar to those of the Proprietor."

Gutierrez hadn't noticed, now that the avian mentioned it, and couldn't blame Pete or the major for failing to take in this minor detail earlier. There was just too much here, all at once, to see and wonder about. What did Aelbraugh Pritsch do, for instance, about the way his gunbelt seemed to crush the feathers at which should have been his waist? Pressure, too? That hinted at an even more advanced technology than he'd imagined. It did explain the silvery appearance of the quilt-thing he'd seen himself. "I take it your boss isn't one of these lobster people?"

"Dear me, no!" The creature actually clucked like the barnyard fowl he resembled. "Great Egg, the Proprietor's no crustacean! Like them, he simply happens to have evolved in a saline medium. The artificial liquid I referred to permits him to remain comfortable, while others, land-evolved organisms such as you and I, may confer with him under more convenient circumstances than water would afford."

More confused than ever, Gutierrez shook his head. "I don't get you."

"You will, General. Here we are."

This passageway terminated in a dead end. The oval panel before them was the first real door Gutierrez had seen in this place, and fifteen centimeters thick. At Aelbraugh Pritsch's touch it swung aside on heavy hinges, allowing a faint scent of iodine to waft outward. Within a well-lit, roofed-over chamber, a steep flight of plastic coated stairs disappeared into a clear, mirror-surfaced liquid.

"Down there?" Recognizing a pressure lock when he saw one, Gutierrez laid a reluctant hand on the door frame, turning to confront his strange guide with an expression, more than skeptical, which he wondered if the nonhuman could read. "What the hell do I wear, scuba gear?"

There it was again, that blue-green flash amidst the powdery gray-white of scaly feathers. Aelbraugh Pritsch blinked at him. "If you refer to mechanical breathing apparatus, not at all, sir. The liquid's fully charged with oxygen, every bit as breathable as air, and rather pleasant to the tactile senses. Nor will it damage anything you wear or carry with you, even the most primitive electronics. In that sense, it's quite inert. However, I do advise you to exhale completely before you take your first breath, as an uncomfortable cramping, owing to bubbles trapped in the respiratory system, may otherwise result."

Now the general braced both hands against the door frame, like the family dog, he realized, reluctant to be bathed. His ostensible purpose was to lean in for a better look. "Let me get this straight: I'm supposed to walk down those stairs, duck my head, take a breath—"

The Proprietor's assistant raised a long, slender, admonitory finger. "Remembering to exhale thoroughly first."

This time Gutierrez blinked: "Remembering to—remind me to take you skydiving some time. You're not coming along?"

The dinosauroid's scaly plumage fluffed out around his body, as if in alarm. In vain, Gutierrez watched for another glimpse of the turquoise-colored symbiote or parasite, wondering why it seemed so important. "Oh, no, sir! Not at all. This interview is to be private. Besides, I've other business to attend."

"I'll bet you do." Feeling a good deal less jocular than he hoped he sounded, he trod down the steps. "Well, my GI insurance is paid up. Here goes nothing!" He entered the liquid, which surprised him with its warmth where it lapped his ankles, his knees, his thighs up to the crotch, the waist, and at last his chest. It wasn't entirely odorless, but the odor wasn't entirely unpleasant. With all the trepidation in the world, he exhaled hard and ducked his head.

A moment passed.

A small string of bubbles rose to the surface.

Unable to overcome a lifetime of reflex, Gutierrez crashed back up through the wave-chopped liquid without having taken a breath of the stuff, coughing, his lungs aching for no reason he knew.

"Do keep trying, General, please!" Aelbraugh Pritsch stood, a single amber eye peeking around the door at the top of the stairs. Another pair of eyes, black and tiny in their turquoise settings, glittered down at Gutierrez from the feathered creature's shoulder. The avian's voice echoed in the bare-walled chamber as he raised it over the man's spluttering. "The first breath's the hardest!"

Gutierrez wiped the liquid from his eyes. It wasn't entirely tasteless either. "That's what they told the guy in the gas chamber!" Nevertheless, he set his jaw, exhaled, and took two steps in a single, inexorable bound, and was surprised to find himself breathing. As with water, he discovered he was quite nearsighted. It gave him a shut-in, claustrophobic feeling. Hand on the rail beside him, he approached another door, placed his free hand as he'd seen his guide do upstairs, let the oval panel swing before him, and stepped through.

It closed behind him, plunging him into darkness.

For more than a moment, this time, he regretted having turned down Estrellita's offer of her pistol. No expression he could think of was adequate to describe the utter blackness that enveloped him, after the cheerful glare of the pressure chamber upstairs. He was blinded, cloaked in silence as absolute as the darkness. Adjusted now to the surrounding liquid, its smell, its taste, its temperature, his sensory deprivation was complete. Nameless fear of the unknown rode his spine in waves which threatened to paralyze his mind altogether.

Concentrate! he ordered himself. What was there left to feel? The floor still retained its tackiness. The liquid medium in which he stood was less dense than water. The faint currents he could feel running through it didn't prevent him from maintaining an upright posture. When thirty seconds had crawled by, he began to make out blue-gray outlines. This wasn't an empty room, *something was moving around him!* Panic almost overtook him before he realized that the moving objects were marine plants, undulating with the gentle motion of the liquid.

Despite his fear, Gutierrez stepped forward, slowed by the fluorocarbon which made it all seem even more like the nightmare it was beginning to remind him of. Another slow-motion step. In the distance, blurred and exaggerated by refraction, he could make out the faint sparkle of colored lights. They twinkled at the far end of the chamber like pilots on a console, winking on and off apparently at random, appearing, disappearing, replaced by others which winked on and off in turn. They formed a pattern, he thought, like faraway Chinese lanterns strung on a line, bobbing in a breeze.

A few more steps brought him closer, but not to any better understanding of what they were. Darkness seemed to lift by stages as his eyes adjusted. The room, more and more visible in shades of gray-on-gray, began to assume dimensions, a ceiling low and oppressive overhead, enclosing walls more palpable than seen. Humped amorphous shadow-forms lurked about him. The blackest, most shapeless lay ahead. The chill he felt wash through his body had nothing to do with temperature.

Without warning, the darkest of the shadows pivoted before him with a low moan, a grating noise. Moved by a reflex he hadn't known he possessed, he slapped at his thigh, feeling liquid stream between his outstretched fingers, clawing for the weapon he wasn't carrying. A tangled mass of thick, writhing, fleshy ribbons squirmed toward his unprotected face, each illuminated along its undulating length by row after row of the bioluminescent spots he'd first seen a moment before.

A deep voice boomed. *"You are the human leader, General Horatio Z. Gutierrez?"*

The general gulped the sour taste of panic, prevented from taking mindless flight by nothing more than the density of the liquid around his body. He opened his mouth, only to discover that whatever knack speech required in this medium, he didn't have it. In front of him, the thrashing horror grated closer, the obscene mobility of that portion nearest him somehow limited by a grotesque, massive object at the rear.

Unbidden, the surrealistic image came to him of landed eels, horrible, slimy, maddened by barbed hooks in their tongues, squirming to regain the water, yet cruelly fastened by their tails to a granite tombstone grinding across the bank behind them.

Above the unthinkable junction where the tentacles found root, a pair of cold, golden, luminescent eyes regarded him, englobed in glassy corneal spheres and slitted, like those of a jungle cat. Behind them, the meter-thick tube of the monster's gigantic body disappeared into a vaster spiral-wound shell which might have garaged an automobile.

Somehow, Gutierrez found his voice, deepened by the liquid medium he forced it into.

"You're . . . the Proprietor?"

VI
Beer and Sympathy

A tentacle-tip stabbed toward a wall.

Illumination sprang up in a sudden flood, making Gutierrez blink. Before him, across the diameters of eyes the proverbial size of dinner plates, vast pupils shrank to fine, black vertical lines.

"Forgive me for not having done that sooner. You're rather earlier than expected, General Gutierrez, doubtless at the urging of my over-punctilious assistant, and I'm afraid you startled me. I'm descended from abyssal species, you know, and in any event, like you, would enjoy my dark, quiet hour of contemplation."

"I startled you," Gutierrez gulped, "the Proprietor?"

"'If you prick us, do we not bleed? If you tickle us, do we not laugh?'" A respiratory organ two hundred centimeters long and forty in diameter seemed to generate a colossal, godlike chuckle, rattling the man's teeth. "I'm a simple tradesman, my boy, no distinguished military hero like yourself, with nerves of steel. The only individual who refers to me as 'the Proprietor' possesses an unfortunate predilection for the melodramatic.

Also, I suspect he thinks it looks good on his résumé. Everybody else calls me Mr. Thoggosh, for the excellent reason that it happens to be my name.''

Nerves of steel. Now that the danger was past, another humiliating wave of panic swept through the man's body, this one worst of all. This, he thought, must be what Vivian's been feeling, maybe even what Art feels all the time. "I'm pleased," he lied, attempting to control his bodily functions, "to meet you."

"Do try to relax," the giant told him. "I realize I'm something of a spectacle for anyone who's never seen the like, but I assure you I'm quite an ethical being. I wouldn't dream of eating you."

Gutierrez found himself muttering an inane, "That's nice . . ."

"And before we start, my boy, the next time you come to see me, by all means wear your sidearm. Everybody here carries personal weapons. You appear quite unclothed without yours."

Gutierrez suddenly wished for a chair, although most of his weight was supported by the liquid filling the room. Growing calmer, he glanced around. In one corner, suspended on light, decorative cords between floor and ceiling, hung a cage about the right size for a small parrot. Through the bars, he could see, "perched" in "midair," a brightly striped, spiny fish, trilling an undistracting, if not exactly musical, song.

"I'll, er, try to remember."

If there is a next time, he thought. His recent, peremptory orders from Earth intruded themselves into the forefront of his mind, although it wasn't as if he'd forgotten them. He tried to breathe deeply. The floor directly in front of Mr. Thoggosh, an area perhaps three meters wide by two across, was set aside as a sort of desk, handy to the giant being's sinuous manipulators. Behind the house-sized horror lay an unnaturally broad door (now he understood the infirmary's architecture) flanked by a pair of large, upright boxes resembling stereo speakers. Gutierrez realized he hadn't been listening to Mr. Thoggosh, but to their output, balanced so the sound seemed to emanate from the great mollusc.

Mr. Thoggosh noticed him noticing. "Your surmise is correct, my boy. My species is quite mute, incapable of uttering a sound. Although our hearing's rather keen. For reasons peculiar to our evolutionary history, we communicate by what would no doubt strike you as telepathy, although, in point of plain fact, it's rather less romantic than that. You'd understand better if I told you that, had you worn your space suit to this meeting, I might be able to speak with you directly."

Gutierrez peered at the monster. "Natural radio?"

"I assure you, sir, your vocal ability to compress and rarify the medium about you at will is no less marvelous to me. We're all beings, are we not, of infinite wonderment?"

Mr. Thoggosh chuckled, his many tentacles twining a complex pattern. Gutierrez couldn't estimate the number of those writhing limbs, but he remembered that a squid (which his host resembled) had ten, while a nautilus (which he also resembled) had more. One of them lashed across the "desk" and touched a colored light. A wave of pressure passed through the fluid. Gutierrez glanced toward the ceiling, from which an object—a plastic-coated wire chair—sank to the floor beside him.

"Will you be seated, General?" Mr. Thoggosh asked him. "I prefer eyes at a level. And, as I suspect this conversation will continue rather a long while, I'd be more comfortable if I felt you were."

"Thanks." Gutierrez sat.

"And so, my boy," Mr. Thoggosh began, "contact has at long last occurred between humanity and another sapience, just as your species dreamed of for so many centuries. And on your first real deep-space voyage, at that. Yet none of you seems much prepared to celebrate it."

The general grunted. "Mr. Thoggosh, before this goes any further, I have an important—an official—message to relay to you from my superiors. I haven't been looking forward to it."

"A moment, sir." two of the mollusc's tentacles were longer than the others. Instead of tapering to slender ends, they possessed splayed tips. Mr. Thoggosh laid one across his "desk," crossing the other over it. "Do you care for refreshment? I'm having beer. This liquid we steep ourselves in has its uses, but it will dehydrate the tissues."

"Beer?" Gutierrez felt his eyebrows rise. At the rate they were getting exercised here, he thought, they'd eventually take up residence at the back of his neck. Suddenly, to his even greater astonishment, one of his host's tentacles separated from his body with a plop, swimming like a snake toward a wall on the right.

"Surely, General, you can't imagine yours the only culture, in a universe far wider than you know, to have discovered fermentation."

Open-mouthed, the human watched the mollusc's disembodied limb wriggle through the handle of a round-cornered door (inside, a light came on), remove a pair of containers, and place them on a tray.

"Not," Mr. Thoggosh told him, "by at least two hundred million years."

At the desk, the tentacle wound itself about a small gold-colored metal accessory, piercing the top of a container and bringing it, with a slender plastic tube trailing behind, to the general. Mr. Thoggosh reached for his own beer and reclaimed his wandering limb.

"This, for example, and at the risk of sounding like your legendary Captain Nemo, is brewed from a variety of kelp native to the waters off the landmass you call New Mexico. Or is it Old Mexico?"

With another tentacle, Mr. Thoggosh inserted the tube where Gutierrez knew his mouth must be.

"Or perhaps it was California. In any event," the mollusc sighed (no other word could describe it), "I find it very satisfactory. My only regret is that I can't invite you to smoke, a fascinating habit which does seem to be unique with your kind. This liquid carries heat away too quickly and won't support combustion."

The songfish warbled in its cage. Gutierrez sampled the exotic beverage, surprised to discover he agreed with his host's evaluation of it. He admitted as much.

"I'm highly gratified to hear it," Mr. Thoggosh replied. "And now, my boy, if I may help you: you've been instructed to inform me—that is, whoever's 'in charge' among my party—that this asteroid, indeed every celestial body and the entire volume of space within the 'Solar System,' is the property of

Earth, under the authority of your United World Soviet, as 'the common heritage of all mankind.' "

Gutierrez's jaw dropped. The beer-tube floated free. "How—?"

Tentacles lifted and spread in a shrug. "It must certainly have occurred to you by now that our command of English, Spanish, Russian, and quite a number of other human languages results from the fact that your planet, in certain frequencies, is quite the brightest—or, rather, the loudest—object in the Solar System."

"Yes, but—"

"Further reflection would make it clear that the computative sophistication requisite to sort this tangle of signals out from one another—and, in a word, 'decode' those languages—empowers us, by necessary implication, to comprehend them whatever enciphering may have been imposed upon them. It isn't so much that we set out to break your rather childish codes, General—our apparatus simply removes interference, be it from solar radiation or our own machinery."

Gutierrez reached for his siphon. "Which is how you knew we were coming, the names of some of the people onboard the shuttles—and the rest of my message."

It was as if the mollusc sighed again: "Sir, you've my profoundest sympathies. The spectrographic signature of this little world signifies to any observer a concentration of minerals highly desirable to the prospective colonist expected to support himself as soon as possible. Moreover, the planetoid describes an orbit which carried it near quite a variety of other such bodies. To your American Soviet Socialist Republic, as it is to us, 5023 Eris is perfectly conceived as a base for science and exploitation. Thus you're ordered to evict us, no allowance being made by those with the power to command you, for the priority of our claim, or the fact that you possess no means whatever of carrying out that order."

Now that it had been mentioned, Gutierrez found himself wishing for a cigarette, although he'd given up the habit a quarter of a century earlier. "Well," he told the mollusc, "at least all my cards are on the table. I ought to thank you. I was dreading it."

Mr. Thoggosh emitted a chuckle. "As I would in your place,

my boy. Permit me to put my cards on the table, as well. Let us discuss what alternatives present themselves, before you try to carry out that preposterous command. First, we'll dispose of this 'common heritage' nonsense: that a body lies within the same stellar system as your United World Soviet scarcely means that you own it. I gather that this pernicious doctrine was first promulgated to prevent the assertion of private property claims in space, in effect assuring a Marxist revolution there before your species even arrived on a permanent basis.''

The chuckle became Olympian before the great mollusc managed to get it back under control.

"Do forgive me, sir, I beg you. Where was I? Oh yes: those penalized most by this doctrine nevertheless felt compelled, for some reason, to accept it, to their eventual fatal disadvantage. Now it's being used to *assert* a property claim—a collective one, your own—in the face of our having arrived here first. In short, those you call your superiors wish to retain their pie and consume it at the same time.''

It was probable, the general realized, given government control of education and the media, that the Proprietor was better informed regarding Earth's recent history than any member of the expedition, with the possible exception of Piotr Kamanov. In his profession, Gutierrez couldn't help understanding how eventual American acceptance of United Nations treaties governing such unclaimed territories as Antarctica, the ocean floor, and outer space (after earlier periods of rejection) had deprived it of resources and defenses appropriate to the late twentieth century, and disproportionately influenced subsequent political events. It was one of the things that made him a dangerous liability to the ASSR.

"Cake,'' he corrected, "although I wouldn't want to go on record agreeing with you about that.''

The mollusc waved a negligent limb. "For reasons that will become more and more obvious as you get to know us better, my boy, this isn't going onto any sort of record. However, I do sympathize with your dilemma. One grows accustomed to free speech, and the casual opinions I've just expressed would get you sentenced to Siberia, would they not?''

"Labrador." Gutierrez grinned. "We Americans take care of our own."

Great pupils widened in what the human believed was a smile. The mouth, probably a great three-jawed beak, wasn't visible, even if it were capable of expressing Mr. Thoggosh's feelings.

"Labrador," that being said and shuddered. "I'm not overly fond of the cold, being a creature of tropical waters. In fact, General, I come equipped with a full complement of prejudices. I confess that I'm disposed to regard this Marxism of yours, indeed collectivism of any sort, as a manifestation of primitivity, a pitiable, aberrational phase in the otherwise progressive development of any culture which it nevertheless appears all intelligent species must go through. They do grow out of it eventually, provided they survive its immediate economic and ethical consequences."

Mr. Thoggosh stirred. "Which brings us to the nub of the situation, and to words I don't mind telling you I've dreaded saying quite as fully as you dreaded conveying your superiors' message to me. I, too, have principals, General, investors I must answer to. Not to mention employees who traveled here with me in good faith. I'm not a free agent. My policy will be to remain amiable as long as your superiors permit me, but we'll not be dispossessed, whatever consequences we're forced to bear. We pursue important business here, touching deeply upon our civilization's most ancient and fundamental values and beliefs."

"I wanted to ask—" Gutierrez began.

"I trust you'll not regard me as persisting with perverse mysteriousness if, for the nonce, our business here remains unspecified."

Believing he was being dismissed, the general rose.

"You've your imperatives, as well," his host conceded, "and we may soon confront each other in mortal conflict. Yet I'm reminded, in all courtesy, that, whereas I know exactly who and what you are—to the extent those things can be known about anyone—you've still many unanswered questions about me and my associates."

Gutierrez sat down again.

"Will you have another beer, while I anticipate some of

those questions? Has anyone informed you, for example, that we aren't the extraterrestrials of your folklore?''

"Yes, thanks. Aelbraugh Pritsch told me you were from Earth—"

"But he didn't bother to elaborate upon what must seem to you a remarkable assertion." A snorting noise came from the speakers behind Mr. Thoggosh. "How very like him. There are times I . . . but I suppose it's best to start at the beginning."

Gutierrez took a sip of his second beer, nodding agreement.

"We are, indeed, from Earth, sir," the mollusc told him, sampling his own beverage, "not from the Earth you know, but from what you'd no doubt regard as another dimension."

"I'm familiar with the phrase," the human replied, "although I never understood what it means."

"You're refreshingly forthright, sir. Indeed, it's been truly said that 'To know what you know, and to know what you don't know, is to know.' In this instance, it means an alternative branching of historical probability. I haven't the time or temperament, nor, I suspect, have you the patience at the moment, for a lecture on metaphysics. Let it stand, then, that my people discovered long ago that each choice which reality offers us, in a wider reality, is resolved in every possible way it can be."

Gutierrez resisted the urge to wrinkle his brown and scratch his head. "Would you like to try that again?"

"To be certain," Mr. Thoggosh replied. "In this continuum, you accept my offer of kelp beer. In another, altogether separate from our particular consciousness yet somehow nearby, your counterpart refuses. In a third, my counterpart was niggardly and never made the offer."

He took a draw on his own beer.

"Farther out upon the bell curve of ultimate reality, you and I never had this meeting. Human beings never came to 5023 Eris. At the farthest extreme known or conceivable, the 'Big Bang' never happened and a universe was stillborn. In this context, in addition to its other manifold attractions, 5023 Eris presents us with something of a conundrum. Its counterpart fails to appear in our version of reality."

"I—" Gutierrez tried to interrupt.

"But I digress." Mr. Thoggosh ignored him. "You see,

General, in my version of prehistory, exactly as in your own, during what your scientists term the 'Ordovician Period,' the dominant life-form on Earth was a small and unprepossessing ancestor of mine called a 'nautiloid.' This, you must understand, was five hundred million years before anything even remotely resembling human beings evolved.''

Gutierrez nodded. "I think I follow you."

"I should hardly have expected otherwise, my boy. In your prehistory, with perhaps a cetacean exception or two, none of the ocean animals developed high intelligence. In due course, they were supplanted by other forms, culminating in your own."

He raised a tentacle-tip, "Ah, but in mine..."

In its cage, the striped fish trilled a mindless melody.

VII
Rumors of War

They reminded him of embattled prairie Conestogas.

Only in this case, they were surrounded by jungle, and were merely three well-worn orbiters—spaceships only by the most generous courtesy—lowered to the crumbling gray-brown surface where they lay now, cradled in plastic-coated wire-mesh baskets, and a triangular configuration was as close as they could get to a circle.

Nestled within, what was beginning to be the human camp-site on 5023 Eris occupied the space left by the shuttles' backswept, stubby wings, which served as tents of a sort. They might be needed, thought Piotr Kamanov. The asteroid's organic canopy enclosed more than enough volume to support rain, and the humidity had been increasing since sundown.

In the jungle, beyond the geologist's night-shortened vision, something rustled leaves, some kind of animal life, he guessed, brought along to balance the great plants. Approaching the camp, he took his time, squeezing between the blunt nose of the *Metzenbaum* and the scorched tail of the *Wright*, not overly anxious to rejoin his fellow voyagers. He'd bidden his nonhuman well-wishers what he hoped was a temporary farewell as one of their electrostatic craft, apparently the only mechanized transport on the asteroid, had left him on the ground to return "upstairs," walking the remaining distance, a matter of five hundred meters, to the human enclave. Rosalind and Toya had descended with him, but he'd urged them to hurry ahead on the strong, swift legs of youth, so that he could be alone to think.

Kamanov's arm hung in the sling he'd be wearing, if he obeyed doctor's orders, another couple of days. It no longer pained him, and hadn't from the moment he'd been placed in the care of the insect-surgeons a level up in the series of complex structures built under the canopy. It wasn't his injury which filled him now with a feeling of weary sickness.

It was news from home.

"Pete!" Kamanov watched his friend Horatio rise on stiff knees, a malady of middle age he identified with. The general was hunkered by a tiny fire of branches and huge fallen leaves. As new as the alien colony appeared, the ground between here and where they'd dropped him already had a scattering of debris he associated with forests. Among their other uses, the growths were already creating soil for a miniature planet.

His geologist's eye noted that the fire was built on an upcropping of iron-bearing rock, an obvious accretion feature on a world mostly composed of carbonaceous chondrites. He was also aware that there was no objective need for such a fire. No one was cold, no one was cooking, but he understood the primeval necessity. Toya huddled near, despite the mild temperature, as did others from the three shuttle complements.

"Horatio." Not quite recovered from his ordeal, Kamanov leaned, a bit short of energy, against the mesh basket under a shuttle wingtip. He waited for Gutierrez, but didn't wait to speak, nor bother keeping his voice down, despite the presence, beneath the wing, of a dozen figures curled in makeshift sleeping bags. "What is this nonsense they speak of at the infirmary, that we are about to declare war on our hosts?"

Two or three recumbent figures stirred. A faint, general muttering passed through the camp. Gutierrez shrugged as he met his friend and took his arm. "I guess I shouldn't be surprised that their grapevine's as good as ours. It's orders, Pete, straight out of an old B-movie: Earth versus slave-warriors of the Elder race."

"Orders?" Kamanov halted halfway from the center of the little compound, only pretending to catch his breath. Having become an old man, he'd long since discovered, offered one excuse after another for stealing time to think. He turned to look at his American friend, this time lowering his voice. "Washington's or Moscow's?"

Gutierrez blinked, deadpan. "Orders are orders. Should it make a difference?"

Meaning, Kamanov knew, *should you admit in front of this many witnesses that it does?* Beyond the firelit circle he heard noise again, squirrels rummaging for acorns among dried leaves. He took another breath, dropping to a whisper. "When they are such exceptionally stupid orders, commanding me to murder—or be murdered by—sapient beings I have grown to like and respect."

Gutierrez looked him in the eye, but refrained from contradicting him. For an American in this part of the twenty-first century, that alone represented fervent agreement with a politically dangerous opinion. They resumed walking. Within a few steps, they stood beside the fire, which threw grotesque, wavering shadows on the flanks of the surrounding orbiters. The general thrust both hands into his pants pockets.

"If I'd known earlier they were going to release you so soon, I'd have stopped for you on the way back from my talk with Mr. Thoggosh."

Kamanov surveyed the scene about the fire. Despite the relaxed postures and exotic setting, it had the look of a meeting, Empleado taking part, along with Estrellita, who was sitting at attention. He often had to think twice before recalling that the redheaded beauty was *Spetznaz*, a military security officer, although at the moment she looked every centimeter of it. Several others added their silhouettes to the eerie shadows: Lieutenant Colonel Juan Sebastiano, captain of the *Metzenbaum*, and young Danny Gutierrez, a mere second lieutenant but the general's son. Rosalind was absent—catching up on much-needed sleep or checking on her charges, among them Vivian Richardson, Gutierrez's missing-but-accounted-for second-in-command—while Toya Pulaski, her occasional assistant, sat with her forearms on her knees, staring into the fire, stirring it with the meter-long skeleton of a gigantic leaf.

Watching everything and everybody from scattered points somewhere in the nearby darkness were Empleado's crew of KGB enforcers, blocky Demene Wise, Broward Hake, the oily one, the deceptively charming Roger Betal, and sinister Delbert Roo.

"The Proprietor?" Kamanov asked.

"None other. Pull up a rock. I'd just started filling everybody in, so I won't have to do much backtracking on your account."

Kamanov found space, as usual—although he didn't notice it, himself—between a pair of handsome young women, the major and Lieutenant Marna, a husky blond life-support tech from the *Metzenbaum*. Stretching at full length on the ground, he cradled his head in his good hand. Campfire and flickering shadows sent his memories back a lifetime, to red-neckerchiefed childhood outings with the Young Soviet Pioneers.

Horatio must be right about the speed of informal communication among their hosts; this would be an attribute of all intelligent life. But most of what he thought of as "grapejuice" he'd squeezed a drop at a time from his own doctor and her aide, not their new acquaintances. As Gutierrez spoke, Kamanov understood that it had been hours since he'd returned from conferring with the alien leader, soaked in rapidly evaporating fluid but otherwise intact. Naturally, Gutierrez had been required to report Earthside, via a kilometer-long antenna lead, before talking to anyone, even the local KGB. This surely would have rankled Arthur.

But the geologist was most startled to learn that, following this initial report, each and every one of the expedition's half-dozen department heads had been privately summoned to the mike as individuals, apparently to receive specific, highly classified orders direct from Washington.

"I was telling Pete," Gutierrez continued, "this Mr. Thoggosh is the one Aelbraugh Pritsch called the Proprietor. And before you ask, we didn't go into it: beyond informing me that he had stockholders to consider, I've no idea what authority he exercises. You have to see him to believe him. He calls himself a nautiloid, sort of a big squid in a giant snail shell. He's preoccupied with some kind of search on this asteroid, but from what little he said, it looks to me more like a religious exercise than anything else."

He described the great mollusc as best he could, the medium in which he lived, something of his dissertation on alternative probability. It took several tries, with Kamanov's help, before everyone understood that, in their own version of reality, nonsapient creatures similar to Mr. Thoggosh had been supreme on Earth far longer than humans—even mammals, Kamanov told them—had so far existed. Conveying the length of time involved, hundreds of millions of years, almost required starting over.

"Such organisms dominate Upper Paleozoic strata," the geologist added, "but may be found, in one morphology or another, from the Cambrian through the Jurassic. Unless, of course, one includes the famous chambered and paper nautiluses, in which case they survive even today. They are a hardy form, vulnerable only to whatever mysterious force exterminated the dinosaurs." He shrugged, not an easy gesture with his stiff shoulder. "But why listen to me—it is not my specialty—when we enjoy the fortuitous presence of an amateur, but competent, paleobiologist?"

Gutierrez frowned a question. No such specialty appeared on the roster. The major and several others looked to the general. His son glanced from the major to the blond lieutenant and back again, there being little about Toya to hold his interest. Like his henchmen, Empleado glared suspiciously at everyone, frustrated, it seemed to the Russian, that he couldn't glare suspiciously at himself as well. In the silence, Kamanov heard that rustling again, from outside the encampment. He could tell from their expressions that the others heard it, too.

"Toya is perhaps too modest to inform you of the fine conversation we enjoyed on this very topic in the infirmary. An intrepid fossil hunter and collector in her girlhood, she remains a part-time delver into the past even now. She identified those beings—whom most of you Americans, through ideologically colored glasses, seem anxious to view as soldier-slaves—as descendants of sea scorpions."

Empleado gave the Russian a sharp glance which he may have believed no one else noticed. KGB or not, however, he'd learned that there was little he could do to restrain the geologist.

"How about it, Pulaksi?" Sebastiano stroked his goatee. "A zinky for your thoughts." Faces turned to look at the girl. The expression, originally meaning debased American coins of the lowest denomination, was now applied to kopecks, as well, just as dollars and rubles were often and interchangeably called "ferns," in reference to unsecured banknotes once issued by the Federal Reserve system. Toya kept her eyes on the fire and cleared her throat as her thin, nervous hands wrung the end of the fire-stirring stick she held.

"On Earth—our Earth, sir—sea scorpions were crustaceans which, in normal history, followed nautiloids as the dominant life-form. The soldiers evolved from them, as we did from primates." This evoked muttered comments, nothing intelligible enough to reply to. She stopped, her small supply of courage consumed by what had been, for her, a terrible effort.

"You see," Kamanov smiled, "not so difficult." To Gutierrez: "What did I tell you?" Gutierrez looked down at the fire with a hand over his mouth. The geologist had no way of knowing that the general was torn, as he'd been for his entire acquaintance with Kamanov, between exasperation and amusement at his friend's instinct for treating women of all shapes and ages in a manner which attracted them like a magnet. That the attraction was quite mutual had no doubt made his life very interesting. Kamanov turned to Pulaski, "Explain the rest of your remarkable theory, if you will, Toya."

"*Doctor Kamanov!*" she protested in a hoarse whisper, blushing and pleased by his encouragement, if not by his having made her the center of attention. "*I'm so embarrassed!*"

"Not as much as I have embarrassed *me*"—the reclining

Kamanov lifted his good hand, palm up, in a half-shrug—"by not thinking of it myself." The casual motion assumed more ominous proportions, exaggerated in a huge serpentine shadow on the fuselage behind him.

Grinning into the flames, Sebastiano peered at Kamanov where he lay between the two good-looking women. "We can all see how embarrassed you are, Pete." He looked around the fire. "Poor guy must've had something else on his mind at the time."

In the laughter that followed, Pulaski reddened further. "I, that is, Captain, they..." Her voice trailed off in bashful paralysis.

"What the hell's wrong with you, Pulaski?" snapped the major. "Spit it out!" Estrellita must be as nervous as everyone else, Kamanov observed; she was usually a good deal more patient with the shy little sergeant.

A fist-sized flying something swooped through the dark overhead, under-lit by the fire, and disappeared again into the jungle.

"What Toya is trying to say, Major"—Kamanov ran fingers through his shaggy white hair, as if even he found her idea staggering—"and I remind you it is her idea, is that we see here creatures, not from one alternative world, but from several, perhaps dozens."

"What?" Marna, the life-support specialist let her jaw drop. Danny whistled, then cut it off.

"Hundreds," the embarrassed girl stammered into the ground. "I've seen beings descended—like we are from simians, the way Mr. Thoggosh is from nautiloids—from cartilage vertebrates like sharks." Her eyes jerked away, toward the shadows beneath the nose of the *Wright*. The night-flapper had confirmed Kamanov's theory about animal life on the asteroid. As the evening cooled, he surmised whatever he'd heard earlier was being attracted to the warmth of the fire. Pulaski shivered, huddling closer to the coals.

"Do not forget," he added, trying to distract Toya from her fear, "those who patched me up. All who see them believe they might be insects."

Gutierrez agreed with what he heard. "How about the

ever-popular Aelbraugh Pritsch? Nobody seems to know what
he's descended from. I'd be surprised if he does himself.''

''Some flightless avian, I'd guess, or dinosaur, sir. I'm not
certain which, or that it even matters, given the warm-blooded
hypothesis.'' Toya had surprised everyone but Kamanov by
speaking up again. As she warmed to her subject, some of her
shyness seemed to slough away. ''I'd be surprised if there
weren't at least one true fish species living in the same
environment as Mr. Thoggosh. Of course, I've seen two or
three creatures I couldn't recognize at all. Sir.''

''What gets me''—Reille y Sanchez sounded calmer, yet still
edgier than Kamanov was used to seeing her—''is that every
individual, all these other species, refer to the nautiloids,
molluscs, cephalopods, whatever they are, as 'Elders.' With a
deference I'm beginning to find—''

''The nautiloids,'' Gutierrez interrupted, ''do give the impression of being wise and ancient. Mr. Thoggosh certainly
did.''

''Wise and ancient,'' Empleado snorted, ''when their notion
of terraforming consists of planting this runaway kudzu and
letting it do all the work?''

Kamanov sat up. ''Arthur, even someone with your obliga-
tions appreciates the absurdity of the labor theory of value. The
point is—how did you call it, super kudzu? You Americans
have such a flair for phrases. Whatever you call the stuff, it
works. The plant is gene-designed to germinate in the airless
cold of space, grow to a predetermined—''

''Enough biology, Comrade Scientist,'' put in Empleado.
''The point is, what do we do about these *molluscs*? Goddamn
it, they're individualists!''

''Goodness.'' Kamanov widened his eyes in mock horror.
''How shocking!''

''And worse,'' the KGB man added, ''they're *capitalists!*''

Kamanov laughed out loud. Empleado's men glowered.
Gutierrez exhaled. ''Down, Pete. Funny thing about that, Art.
Mr. Thoggosh described himself to me as a merchant-explorer.
Yet when I tried to follow up on that, to make some accommo-
dation between us, he regretted, on behalf of his fellow Elders,

that in all conscience he couldn't trade with us. Not as representatives of the United World Soviet."

"We have become," Kamanov grinned, "the kind of kids our mothers warned us not to play with."

Gutierrez glared at Kamanov. "Lay off, Pete. 5023 Eris is rich in resources. I thought we might work them, sell the results in exchange for a claim. But the Elders didn't travel to this dreary place, Mr. Thoggosh informed me, at great peril and expense—underline expense—with trade in mind. Whatever they find here for themselves will, they anticipate, just pay a fraction of their costs."

"They came," nodded Kamanov, "for a more important purpose—"

"Which they won't—" continued Gutierrez.

"Perhaps cannot—" Kamanov interrupted.

"Reveal," Gutierrez finished with annoyance in his voice. "In any case, he explained—or he thought he was explaining—in the matter of trade, their ethics forbid them to receive stolen property."

"Meaning what?" Reille y Sanchez raised her eyebrows, then: "Did anybody else hear that? Some kind of scrabbling under the ship?"

"A peculiar attitude," agreed Sebastiano, "for a self-admitted capitalist. I heard it, too, Major, and I don't like it."

The general shook his head. "I've been hearing it all night, myself. Little animals, I guess. You'll find this even more peculiar, Juan." Gutierrez glanced at Empleado. "Or something. And try to remember Mr. Thoggosh said it, not me. That's all—stolen property—he says any collectivist society, founded on 'theft, brutality, coercive central planning, and murder,' has to trade."

The resulting silence lasted several heartbeats.

"Then there will indeed be war." The Russian geologist was sober at last. "Although, as with many another war in human history, no one on either side seems to want it."

VIII
Texas Marxism

"Comrade Doctor Kamanov." Empleado folded his arms. "The Earth is hungry. We must have what we came for, whatever the cost."

Kamanov shook his head. "This must be a very popular view, indeed, Comrade Thought Policeman, back on Earth, among your colleagues who are at no personal risk of any kind."

"He's right," Marna muttered, almost to herself. "What chance do we have? They're millions of years ahead of us."

Reille y Sanchez snorted. "It'll be more even than that, Lieutenant. Sure they've got a head start. If you believe this Thoggosh, a couple of *hundred* million years." She slapped the scabbard on her left hip. "But a man with a rifle can be killed with a knife, so I figure a thing with a deathray can be killed with a rifle. We aren't savages to be cowed by technology, no matter how much it looks like magic. From what the general says, I've got an idea they take a long view and their progress is slow. Soviet humanity's way behind, but we're capable of catching up!"

"Spoken as a true daughter of the Lone Star People's Republic." Kamanov grinned. "And valid, provided we can steal enough of their magical technology, soon enough. For what it is worth, however, both sides always believe a fight will be more even than first appears to be the case."

"There's something in what she says." Gutierrez wrinkled his brow, suspended between a tactical need for truth and a political necessity to weigh his words. "I gathered that most of the Elders, including Mr. Thoggosh, and, no doubt, his fastidious assistant, have little stomach for war. In fact, they seem to abhor the prospect.''

''War is bad for nautiloids,'' Kamanov misquoted a saying from the previous century, ''and other living things.''

''That seems to be the attitude. Also, it's bad for business.''

''One expects such a craven attitude,'' Empleado sneered, ''from a—''

''Warmongering capitalist?'' Kamanov supplied with his sweetest smile. Empleado glared back and clenched his fists. In the shadows, his men tensed.

Gutierrez ignored them both. ''Worst of all, from their point of view, it may interfere with the all-important—''

Kamanov interrupted once again. ''—albeit unstated—''

By now, Gutierrez was used to interruptions. ''—necessity which brought Mr. Thoggosh and his people here in the first place.''

''I shall be in the minority, so let me be first,'' offered Kamanov, ''to echo the opinion of Mr. Thoggosh. Do you not realize that, in its current pitiable condition, the World Soviet must learn to *tolerate* the Elders, if only for the sake of regaining what is lost by conquering the world?''

Around the fire there were actual gasps. ''I warn you,'' Empleado snarled as his corporals took a step forward, ''I tire of your sarcastic revisionism. You Russians are all alike, making a world united under scientific socialism sound like the worst thing that could have happened—what's that?''

They all heard it that time, dry leaves blown in a breeze. Yet there wasn't any breeze. The principal result, quite acceptable to Kamanov, was that the women on either side of him moved closer.

He went on. ''It is certainly the worst thing that ever happened to scientific socialism. Deny, Arthur, that no Marxist nation ever managed to survive without—let us be kind and say 'inputs'—from non-Marxists. Always they import innovations they cannot generate for themselves. Endless supplies of food-stuffs. Most important, price information essential to planning. Was this not why the Union of Soviet Socialist Republics was compelled so long to suffer—with a smile—the independent existence of the United non-Soviet States of America?''

"*I'm KGB, you fool!*" All four corporals were a step closer to the fire. Empleado was furious. "*Stop this slanderous sedition, now!*"

"On the contrary, Comrade Inquisitor, if it be sedition, let me make the most of it. We Russians are all alike? Yes: horrified at the way Americans became what they are with scarcely a shot fired! 'Scientific socialism,' like Negro slavery before the cotton gin, was used up by expansionism, discredited by universal failure, convicted of a hundred million murders! Even Europe, with its tradition of preserving and parading every mistake ever made by the human race, had finally given up on this one! Those suffering its tender ministrations looked forward eagerly to its imminent demise!"

Dark-faced, Empleado opened his mouth, thought better of it, and closed it again. His hands appeared restless, as if he didn't know what to do with them. Suddenly, he exploded, leaping atop Kamanov, fingers around the older man's throat. With an arm restrained, the geologist seemed helpless. Before Gutierrez or any of the other men could move, the women acted, prying Empleado off and throwing him half across the fire, half into it. Amidst a shower of sparks he scrambled backward, clothes smoldering, and lay red-faced and panting, eyes filled with murderous hatred.

Demene Wise rushed forward to help his superior to his feet, brushing nervously at Empleado's jacket. A large, square-headed, broad-shouldered figure, cursed with jowls twenty years before his time, Wise's effeminate movements seemed even more grotesque in contrast to his solid stature. Growling, Empleado pushed him away. A more determined movement toward the geologist on the part of Broward Hake, a short, compact man with a round, slick head, was stopped cold by Major Reille y Sanchez, with a shake of her head and a subtle gesture of her hand toward her holster.

"Go ahead, Arthur," Kamanov levered himself up, "take your notebook from your pocket. Get it all down. I promise not to go too fast for you. America is a tail wagging the dog. It is regarded by onlookers everywhere as typical of your character that, once you adopted Communism, you strove to become the biggest and best Communists of all. This, you may be interested to know, is referred to, everywhere but in America, as 'Texas Marxism.' "

"Pete—" Gutierrez began, then let it go.

Kamanov wheeled on him. "What has perhaps not occurred to Washington, Horatio, what they will not admit, will be uppermost in the minds of those in Moscow who have lived for generations with the shortcomings of unworkable theory. Will they countenance throwing away this contact with a superior technology? And another likelihood which no one appears to have considered: people being what they are, wise and ancient to the contrary, it is certain there are factions on the other side who will welcome conflict."

"They'll see us as interlopers," Reille y Sanchez agreed, "or vermin, better off exterminated before we cause real trouble."

"More to the point," added Kamanov, "I suspect yet another motive behind Washington's sudden enthusiasm for the shedding of our blood."

"What's that?" asked Gutierrez, who'd been examining his own dark suspicions in this regard all day.

"How can your countrymen not fear that the Elder's antisocial, unconventional, but demonstrably practical social and economic ideas may contaminate an Earth just united—and still rather uncomfortably—under a shared hegemony? We all know what we are, do we not, our value to the World Soviet? Would they not perhaps welcome a massacre here, whatever the outcome?"

Several of them shook their heads. Reille y Sanchez put her face in her hands. With a resigned expression, the general pointed to the CZ99A1 at her waist. "How many of those damned things," he asked her, "did we bring with us?" No response. "Major, I asked you a question."

Reille y Sanchez started violently. "Six, sir. 'Forty-one caliber by twenty-two-millimeter, Service, Officers, For the use of'!" Now she looked up with something resembling a game grin. "Sorry, sir. Also an assortment of H&K 11m/m signal flare launchers which might serve as incendiaries. Our main battery's half a dozen semiauto carbines chambered in 7.62x39 Russian, with bayonets. Commercial-issue Rugers, sir. Old. None of that trash from the nationalized plant. Same number of

Remington 12-gauge riot guns, also semiauto, also with bayonets. They might prove more effective in this jungle than the carbines. I still wish they were AKs, or at least selective fire.''

"There it is again!" Empleado had calmed down enough to exchange sheepish expressions with Kamanov, who was prepared to write the whole performance off, his own as well as Empleado's, to whatever tensions had caused earlier fights among the crew as well as Richardson's illness. But now the political officer's eyes widened. The geologist knew from previous conversations that Empleado was city born and bred, unaccustomed to normal noises in the countryside. The KGB man started to get up. "We'll get flashlights and see what the hell that is!"

"Let's finish this first, Art." Relief was audible in the general's voice, that things were returning to as close to normal as they ever were. "Then you can hunt snipe to your heart's content." Gutierrez squinted at the major. "Do we need bayonets in the middle of the twenty-first century?"

"The general," she answered with diplomacy, "perhaps because he's AeroSpace, sir, has less reason to be enthusiastic about bayonets than I do. I like bayonets, sir. They don't run out of ammo."

"Right," Sebastiano agreed, patting a pistol-shaped bulge under his suit which didn't appear on the major's list. "But I wish we had a dozen RPGs."

"I wish . . ." Gutierrez shook his head, not for the first time wondering why the shuttles' meager capacity had been used up sending hundreds of kilos of weapons, ammunition, and accessories to what was supposed to be an uninhabited worldlet. "I wish we'd picked another goddamned asteroid."

Around the fire, not one failed to nod, agreeing with the general. His son reached out to touch him, but was restrained by military discipline. Even Reille y Sanchez rubbed first the inner, then the outer corners of her eyes with thumb and forefinger, a seasoned Marine officer, Kamanov thought, attempting to deny tears many of her comrades also felt like shedding.

He climbed to his feet. "While some prepare for war, Horatio," he asked, "might not others see what can be done to salvage peace?"

The general turned to his friend. "What've you got in mind, Pete?"

"I have no orders," the geologist shook his head, "from Washington or Moscow. I will speak with Mr. Thoggosh." He went to his second selling point before Gutierrez had considered the first. "It could buy us time."

"We don't know these things," Reille y Sanchez asserted, nerves in her voice again. "They might take hostages!" She softened her voice, putting a hand on Kamanov's arm. "I know it sounds crazy, but listen, Piotr, please?"

"Some of us came prepared for contingencies." The Russian fumbled in his ship-suit pocket. "'Peace through superior firepower.' Or, if you prefer, chance favors the ready trigger finger."

The general's eyes widened. "What in the name of God is that?"

Holding a large revolver in one hand, the geologist grinned. "Better to ask in the name of Harry Callahan, Horatio. This is a .44 Magnum, *this* world's most powerful handgun, and it could blow my hand right off, had I not practiced assiduously before we left. A Smith and Wesson Model Six Twenty-Nine, stainless steel, its little barrel not quite eight centimeters—three imperialist inches—long. Highly pocketable, do you not think?"

Gutierrez scowled at what looked to him like a small piece of artillery. The barrel was thick-walled, the weapon's front sight inset with orange plastic, the rear sight outlined in white. The handle was of wraparound neoprene, the overall finish a wirebrushed silver. Hollowpoints, also silvery, and notch-toothed at their front edges, gleamed up at him from six cavernous chamber mouths. Kamanov handed him the revolver. Low gravity or not, the gun's weight seemed immense.

"You'll shoot your eye out." He handed it back. "How in . . . Callahan's . . . name did you get that past security?"

Reille y Sanchez leaned forward, whether to hear Kamanov's explanation, which bore on her efficiency, or to drool over his big Smith & Wesson, the geologist couldn't tell. Her hair smelled nice, so he didn't care.

"Innocent Horatio." Kamanov smiled. "Lovely Estrellita. A geologist's tools are among those items least susceptible to

X-ray or metal detection. Besides, comrades, I am Russian. My people have lived with—and in spite of—'security' a century and a half. There is an old Georgian proverb—Soviet Georgian—'Do not annoy Babushka with instructions on extracting...' Rosalind! Vivian! How good to see you!'' Kamanov spread his arms in delighted invitation. ''Come sit by the fire and join the conversation!''

Heads turned as two figures took substance from the shadows, becoming Rosalind Nguyen and Vivian Richardson. The physician led the taller, heavier woman by the arm, murmuring occasional assurances which were audible, but not intelligible, to the others. The colonel walked in a gingerly manner, half leaning on Dr. Nguyen as if it were her legs which had been injured, rather than her mind. From time to time she stumbled or hesitated over apparent obstructions which wouldn't have been noticed by anybody else.

As she and her doctor drew near the fire, a dazed, exhausted look could be seen on the AeroSpace Force officer's face, as if she'd just been awakened—which, in fact, she had —from a deep, drugged sleep. Looking repeatedly to Dr. Nguyen, her expression was childlike in its reliance on the smaller woman and in its fear of the surrounding night.

Beaten to the social punch again, Gutierrez nodded rather than echo the geologist. Dr. Nguyen smiled at them both. ''We're just taking a little walk. I'm not sure whether we're up to much, yet, in the way of conversation. What was that you started to say about annoying your grandmother?''

'' 'With instructions,' '' the geologist finished, '' 'on extracting yolk from shell.' '' He grinned. ''I did not claim it was a sensible proverb.''

''What a peculiar turn of phrase.'' Something slithered from the shadows beneath the *Metzenbaum*, fleshy and elongated, its surface glistening wetly in the firelight. Toya and Marna yelped rather than screamed. Danny seized a burning branch from the fire, holding it aloft in the hand that wasn't wrapped around a pistol like the major's. In that instant, three other guns snapped level in one motion—Kamanov's revolver, the major's CZ99A1, and the Glock 9m/m Sebastiano had been concealing—muzzles locked on the object like quivering compass needles on a

magnet. The four KGB men assumed similar postures a heart-beat behind them. A voice arose from the apparition, filtered and artificial in tone. *"Good evening, humans. Set your primitive weapons aside. For the moment, at least, I intend you no harm."*

"What is this," Empleado demanded from behind the line of his underlings, "an evolved snake of some kind?"

Kamanov lowered his gun, trying to ignore the way his heart pounded, as if at any moment it would smash through his rib cage. He took several deep breaths. "No, Arthur, it is one of those separable tentacles Horatio told us about. I do not believe this one belongs to Mr. Thoggosh."

"How perceptive, Doctor." The tentacle moved, sidewinderlike, between shuttle and fire. As it drew closer, its filmy covering became discernible. Toward its base, Kamanov also saw a flat three-by-five object between plastic and flesh, guessing it to be a thin-film audio communicator. *"Permit this extension of myself to introduce me. I am Semlohcolresh."*

For once, Kamanov looked to someone else to take the lead. It was his friend Horatio's place, he thought, to receive guests.

"How do you do?" Gutierrez somehow overcame the feeling of absurdity inherent in addressing the disembodied appendage. "I gather you know everyone, Dr. Kamanov, Colonel Richardson, Colonel Sebastiano, Mr. Empleado, Dr. Nguyen, Major Reille y Sanchez, Lieutenant Marna, Lieutenant Gutierrez, Sergeant Pulaski, Corporals Roo, Betal, Hake, and Wise, and myself. What can we do for you?"

The tentacle squirmed and twisted. *"You'll excuse my eavesdropping. You're correct about the existence of a faction among us who hope for an excuse to employ violence against you."*

Gutierrez and Kamanov glanced at one another. Almost forgotten in the midst of the alien intrusion, and unnoticed by everyone but her physician, Richardson had stiffened all over, bone-breaking tension singing through her muscles. Dr. Nguyen's shouted warning preceded the hideous noise Richardson made by only a fraction of a second.

Shaking the little Vietnamese off as if she were an unwanted, flimsy garment, the black woman shoved her aside, bowled through the line of individuals confronting Semlohcolresh, and snatched the weapon from Danny Gutierrez's hand. Sebastiano dived to tackle her at the ankles, but with the speed and agility of determined insanity, Richardson sidestepped. He crashed into Danny, knocking him to the ground.

Richardson raised the CZ99A1 just as Gutierrez and Kamanov shouted at her. She turned for a moment, a betrayed, bewildered look on her face, unconsciously swinging the pistol's muzzle toward them. As they sprang aside, with a different sort of shout she swung the muzzle back toward the disembodied appendage and pulled the trigger twice. The double detonation shocked and deafened the entire camp, dazzling vision with the yellow-orange ball of fire which blossomed at the automatic's muzzle. The weapon bucked with recoil. In that instant, a blue sizzling bolt leaped from the filmy covering of the limb, exploding halfway between the tentacle and the woman, consuming both bullets before they reached their target. Two distinct metallic clinks marked the places on the *Metzenbaum*'s hull where her spent brass struck before falling to the ground.

Screaming with frustrated rage, Richardson leaped between two shuttles, pistol in hand, vanishing into the dark. Gutierrez pointed toward where his son and Sebastiano were occupied untangling themselves. "You two," he shouted, "after her! Arthur, your men, too!" All six followed her between the craft and out into the night.

"*Some among us,*" Semlohcolresh continued, as if nothing had happened, "*believe your species corrupt beyond salvage. I'd say that what we've just witnessed confirms it. I, too, regard your species' eradication as an act of mercy toward you, and a positive benefit to the rest of the universe. Thus it will be me, not my overtolerant colleague Thoggosh, you'll have to convince, if there's to be peace between us.*"

IX
Words of Iron

"Aha!"

Tucking the big revolver into the sling holding his injured arm, Kamanov spoke across the campfire to Gutierrez. "Horatio, this is an opportunity such as I had hoped for when I told you I wished to see about keeping the peace." He glanced about at the "circled" shuttles, grinning at a random thought. "Shall we not have a friendly powwow, Semlohcolresh?"

It seemed to Kamanov that the others around the fire were holding their breath. With the nautiloid's harsh words ringing in his memory, Gutierrez raised his shoulders and dropped them. "Take your best shot, Pete. Just try and keep in mind who the Indians are, here."

" 'We have met the Indians and they is us' "—the geologist winked at the general and laughed—"to paraphrase the philosopher. I shall remember, my friend, never fear." He turned. "Semlohcolresh, I accept you as a being of your word. Let us withdraw to a quiet place where you will allow me to try some of that convincing you mentioned."

In response, the tentacle made a sinister humping motion like an obscene, gigantic inchworm, its remote alien voice crackling through the anxious stillness among the humans. "*As you wish, Dr. Kamanov, although I warn you, I hold little hope that—*"

"Then you will also allow me to do the hoping for both of us, at least for the time being." The geologist sprang to his feet, showing no sign of his earlier injury or weariness. "Where would you feel most comfortable conducting a long conversation?"

Gutierrez and the others couldn't hear whatever reply the entity made as the unlikely pair shuffled off across the leaf-strewn forest floor. They passed between two of the grounded spacecraft and into the mysterious surrounding jungle darkness. *"We can converse as we convey ourselves, if you find that suitable, Dr. Kamanov. My personal quarters aren't far from here, and we'll continue the discussion we've begun, once you and this extension of myself have arrived."*

"Indeed." The Russian followed the serpentine organ over a slight rise and through the trees. "Will I be expected to immerse myself in—"

The tentacle halted on the trail. *"On the contrary, Doctor, you'll not be put to such a thoughtless inconvenience in my house. For reasons of my own, having to do with my position relative to others of my kind, with whom I presently find myself in disagreement, it's my wish to convey, to everyone concerned, every impression of cordiality, hospitality, and a sincere willingness to negotiate with you humans."*

Kamanov grunted understanding and their walk resumed. Dodging a low-hanging branch which tore at his sling, he raised his bushy eyebrows, a gesture lost in the darkness, even had his odd companion been prepared to understand it. "Every *impression*, you say?"

"Every truthful *impression, I assure you, sir. Kindly do me the courtesy not to mistake the firmness of my opinion—regarding a proper and pragmatic course—for a pathological eagerness on my part to initiate or even witness the gratuitous slaughter of other sapients. The position I've taken was arrived at after much thoughtful reflection, and not without a measure of ethical and emotional discomfort."*

"I see. You mean killing us will hurt you," Kamanov chuckled, "more than it hurts me or my cosapients." Having no idea where they were headed, he was careful to keep an eye on the glistening surface of the tentacles's silvery plastic covering as the limb squirmed through the underbrush.

"I mean that—excuse me, Doctor, here we are."

The artificial forest, never very heavy, had opened onto a broad, well-manicured, grassy surface. At the back of this clearing, a long, low half-cylindrical structure lay, yellowish light shining from its small, round windows. Kamanov suspected the building was filled with liquid of some kind. A few pale white globe lamps, hanging from tree branches, shed their own soft light over a dark, ripple-surfaced pool.

"These are the grounds of my quarters," Semlohcolresh continued. *"I'm resting at the moment at the bottom of the decorative body of salt water you see before us. I'm quite an old organism, Dr. Kamanov, older than you can imagine. I'm inclined to pamper myself, and have never much cared, in any event, for the artificial sensation of liquid fluorocarbon. Now I'll summon refreshment. There are chairs beside the water which I believe you'll find comfortable."*

The tentacle gathered itself and plopped over the side, into the water. Kamanov lowered himself into one of the sturdy, yielding chairs at the pool edge. Before he was fully aware of it, a creature of a variety he hadn't seen before—in the dim light he had a fleeting impression of many glittering compound eyes, a hard carapace, thin, coarse hair, and an uncounted number of spindly legs—had appeared at his elbow proffering an engraved metal tray holding a number of colorful bottles and a variety of empty drinking containers. The Russian chose a tall, transparent glass and something that looked and smelled like vodka.

He nodded at the creature. "Thank you, very much."

"Your courtesy's appreciated, Doctor." Semlohcolresh's voice came, still filtered and distant, from a patch fastened to the creature's carapace. *"However, this is a bright and well-trained animal, not an intelligent being. The species is known scientifically as* Leru obilnaj.*"*

Kamanov sipped his drink. It tasted like vodka, too, to the extent vodka tasted like anything. Between where he sat and the forest edge, he made out the pleasant twinkling of ordinary fireflies. "Your people are capable," he asked, "of drawing that line?"

The fireflies winked out and disappeared. A deep, bone-felt rumbling vibrated the chair Kamanov sat in, the ground beneath his feet, agitating the surface of the water. It was joined, first by a mechanical hissing, then by a long series of gurgling splashes as the center of the pool seemed to hump upward two meters, and became a streaming dome of striped and colored calcium at the base of which, facing Kamanov, lay two huge, luminous golden eyes, set over a tangle of wet, thick, fleshy tentacles.

Kamanov felt belated sympathy for his friend Gutierrez, the first human on 5023 Eris to have confronted such a monster. And the general had done it without any warning or preparation. Kamanov's earlier feeling of absurdity at the prospect of addressing one of these creatures now turned to barely controlled horror.

"Yours are not?" Semlohcolresh stretched a sinuous limb across the shimmering surface of the pool to take a strangely shaped glass from the leru's tray. The nautiloid spoke through yet another thin-film communicator, this time fastened somewhere on himself. "Tell me, then, Dr. Kamanov, on what foundation your science of ethics reposes? Take care, lest you confirm my opinion of your kind."

In the distance, one by one, the fireflies seemed to recover their courage and begin twinkling again. Sipping his drink, trying to quiet a yammering subconscious and recover his own courage, the geologist took his time replying. "If you have observed my species with the conscientiousness you claim, Semlohcolresh, then you know perfectly well that we have not as yet developed a science of ethics. This does not mean that we have, as you also claim, corrupted ourselves beyond salvaging, so that our eradication represents an act of mercy. It indicates only that we are a younger species than your own. Surely there must have been a time, sir, however long ago, when your people had developed no ethical science. Would your extermination, at the behest of an elder race, have constituted a positive benefit to the rest of the universe?"

The Russian became aware of a metallic, chipping noise, as if someone were striking a cinderblock with the tines of a steel fork. After a moment, he understood that this was the sound of a nautiloid chuckling to itself. Almost at the same time, another noise distracted him. "Semlohcolresh, is there someone or something in the woods behind us?"

"Yes, Dr. Kamanov, there is. I believe it's your Colonel Richardson, who appears to be peering at us from behind a tree. My instruments tell me that she's in a highly agitated state. And almost as well armed as yourself. Do you think she's dangerous?''

Kamanov shook his head, now free to shift the heavy revolver in his sling to a more comfortable position. He had an odd sensation, as if a pistol were being pointed at the back of his neck. "I do not know. Vivian has not been well. There are searchers looking for her. I trust that they will find her and take her back.''

"So I see. I hope you're right. I'll continue to monitor her location and activity, in any event. Now, where was I? You may be aware," his host informed him, "that we cannot cover our ears to exclude undesirable and distracting noise. That facet of our 'hearing' is electronic in character, and can, at times, be very sensitive. You'd entertain a different opinion of your own race, Dr. Kamanov, were you compelled, as we were, to incorporate dense shielding molecules in our environmental canopy, to shut out the incessant, disgusting, wheedling—''

Kamanov raised a warning hand. "Sir, it would be foolish to judge the unique collection of heroic human beings—your guests on 5023 Eris—by the little whining signals you receive from Earth, which is now embarrassed by its heroes, and has discarded them.''

It was as if the giant mollusc hadn't heard him. "—of the puny territorial agglomerations of collective subsentient incompetence and huddled cowardice which bluster and threaten those they fail to cajole, imagining themselves unanswerable powers in a universe they haven't even begun—''

"And more foolish still," Kamanov insisted, "to underestimate them.''

A surprised-sounding Semlohcolresh choked himself off in the midst of his tirade. "Why do you say that?''

"Take my friend Horatio," the geologist replied, "most heroic of the lot. He appears no more than an aging bureaucrat. Yet, as celebrated leader of the infamous Redhawk Squadron at Kearnysville, Long Beach, and Fort Collins, in refutation of the fashionable view that air power is inefficacious in quelling popular insurrection, he was responsible for crushing the remaining opposition to the ascendency of the ASSR. That he now questions the wisdom of his achievement, as I do, does not diminish its remarkability.''

"If I take your meaning, you warn me that this general of your is a more formidable opponent that you believe we estimate.'' Semlohcolresh paused, resting on the water in thought or at a loss for words, the Russian wasn't certain which. "Dr. Kamanov, I find these inappropriate words for a self-styled man of peace.''

"As a student of history, Semlohcolresh''—the geologist sipped his drink, wondering how marine organisms like the nautiloids had invented distillation—"I am a man of peace who nevertheless understands that a visible willingness and ability to wage war can often preserve the peace. It was a wide lack of this understanding which gave Marxism—an inferior philosophy by every measure of such things—its victory over America, although the latter was superior by all the same measures.''

"Agreed,'' the nautiloid replied, "but willingness and ability at what cost, or rather, what practical limit can there be to such a cost?''

The human shrugged. "The one limit that makes sense, Semlohcolresh, the willingness of individuals—as individuals—to pay the cost. It cannot be by group-decision or coercion. I know, for I am also a social being who nevertheless understands that civilization depends upon the individual for its existence, whereas the individual is quite capable of doing very well without civilization. And it was widespread lack of *this* understanding which doomed those few Americans who, even understanding the relationship between war and peace, misunderstood the relationship between the individual and civilization, coming to believe that defense of the latter required imitating Marxism's disregard for the former.''

"By the Predecessors, a civilized analysis!'' In the center of the pool, tentacles stirred, splashing their owner with water. For the first time, Kamanov noticed that the nautiloid wasn't wearing any sort of protective covering, but was content simply to keep himself moist in the cool evening air. "And the result?''

"What any rational observer would expect. Taxed to a subsistence level, where no real hope for individual advancement was possible, bound hand and foot by ten million laws rendering any difference between their culture and its opposition academic, when the time came, no one was left in America who had anything to gain by defending it."

"This might," the nautiloid offered, "have been foreseen."

Kamanov shook his head, beginning to feel weary again. "I am sure some did foresee it. Perhaps I flatter myself, Semlohcolresh, that, for the rest of us, it represents wisdom won the hard way, never soon to be forgotten. Even so, it is rare wisdom, for my conclusions are not much shared, even today. A species may be young or old. It may have learned little of the universe or much, and, to be certain, its individual members may share in that knowledge and benefit by it, or not. Yet I have an idea that, at some fundamental level, individual beings stay much the same over millions of years. Tell me, if you will, how long did it take your people to discover these things for themselves?"

"Such persistence." In the pool, the creature seemed to heave a sigh. "Despite contrary expectations, you begin to interest me after all, Doctor."

Kamanov sat up, voice sharp. "It was never any part of my intention, Semlohcolresh, to amuse you! Nor to defend my species, like a lawyer, against your blanket accusations, for that would acknowledge a right, which you have merely arrogated for yourself, to judge them!" Startled by Kamanov's tone, the serving animal shrieked and ran off toward the dwelling.

With an abrupt, angry gesture, Kamanov set his half-finished glass on the pool surround and arose, turning on a heel to face the human encampment. As if struck by a final thought, he paused. "I am disappointed, Semlohcolresh! It was my understanding that you nautiloids were rugged individualists! Scheming capitalists! This was the basis for my conviction that we could bargain with one another! Believe me, on such an evening, I would far rather be with a female of my own species."

Semlohcolresh lifted one of his long, spatulate tentacles into the air, his voice as emotional as electronics allowed. "Wait, Doctor! There may be justice in what you say, I confess it, do you hear me? At least insofar as your present understanding of us permits. Do please sit down."

Kamanov heard the same slithery whisper as when Semloh-colresh had reached across the pool for a drink. He felt a feathery tentacle touch on his shoulder. Still facing away from the pool, he allowed himself a small, self-satisfied grin before he turned back, exhibiting great reluctance, and sat again. He had the feeling once more that a gun was being pointed at him. "Tell me, is Colonel Richardson still back there in the trees?"

"Not unless she's well-shielded by minerals or vegetation. It's possible, my instruments are limited in range and penetration. But she appears to have left us. Your searchers are also departing."

"Very well." Kamanov tried to disregard that eerie feeling, with only partial success. "Enlighten me, then, *O Elder*. Answer the question I have asked you three times. Wisdom cannot grow in a vacuum. A species which has learned as much as yours must have a great deal of mayhem and bloodshed somewhere in its background. How long did it take you to arrive at an idea of ethics which would not insult the word *science*?"

Relieved, the nautiloid lowered his long arm, summoned the leru back, and accepted another drink. "And if I were to say that it took us a million years, would that make you feel precocious? It took, in fact, even more time than that before the ideas you've just expressed came to be universally agreed upon, although their origins may be discovered among what remains of our earliest faltering attempts at culture."

"So you, too," the human nodded, "are a student of history."

"Yes. And, as I'm certain you've discovered for yourself, Dr. Kamanov, the great tragedy of sapient history, one of them anyway, is that ethical innovations, unlike technical ones, take rather a long time to make their value apparent to potential recipients."

"Nor," Kamanov agreed, "is progress along those lines ever assured, the way it often seems with technology. People will speak, without thinking, of the swings of a pendulum, but more often it seems like a dance consisting of one step forward and two steps back."

"A great pity, too," Semlohcolresh told him in an absent, musing tone. "I suspect, Dr. Kamanov, that the respective histories of our species might have turned out rather different had it been the other way around.''

Kamanov threw back his shaggy head and laughed, slapping the arm of his chair with his good hand, frightening the leru again, and almost upsetting his half-finished drink. ''So your civilization, too, my friend, has skeletons in its ethical closet! This was my point from the beginning, if you will recall.'' He leaned forward and peered into the luminous golden disks floating in the center of the pool. ''Now, old mollusc, at last I believe we have a basis for understanding one another!''

''Dr. Kamanov, you are indeed a dangerous being.''

X
Sarajevo, *Mon Amour*

Against her better judgment, Reille y Sanchez kept a hand on the multicolored line drawing her toward the pulley attached to a branch overhead. It was that or fall a hundred meters, yet common sense told her that her fingers would be shredded in seconds unless she let go. The only thing that kept them wrapped around the line, braided from strands of a dozen different colors, was her experience that common sense didn't count for much on 5023 Eris.

Bright-winged life fluted and rustled amid the litter of dew-damp leaves into which she rose. No other sapience (she entertained doubts about her own, hanging like a spider on someone else's thread) was in sight. Among its other notable events, last night had brought an invitation—and accompanying map—from Mr. Thoggosh to visit a power plant turning garbage into energy, the appendage sent by the merchant-explorer had explained, on the principle by which quasars burned so fiercely in the extragalactic depths. Representing the humans as a technician, she had no such credentials, but was keeping the appointment as a tactician, with the idea of future seizure or destruction of the plant, which might even the odds should it come, as Washington intended, to open conflict.

She gasped: at the last moment the line writhed in her fingers, half of it unbraiding, passing over the pulley, while the other half remained in her hand below the rim. At the infirmary level where Piotr had spent his brief recuperation, she'd found what resembled ski tows, although she didn't know it, never having engaged in a sport limited to the *nomenklatura*, the upper class of her supposedly classless society, and to special mountain troops. Her instructions had included the color combination to look for. She'd seized a line, been yanked aloft, and carried a kilometer before arriving at the high point of her journey, the pulley she was now passing beneath.

Past the pulley, the line reintegrated and she felt the descent begin. Nearer the surface, it carried her in a new direction and deposited her within walking distance of the plant. For reasons she couldn't explain—she'd never been afraid of heights—she already dreaded the return. Her watch said she would arrive early. Taking her time along a forest path, she kicked through dead leaves like a child on her reluctant way to school, marveling at how quickly this once cold, airless rock circling so far from the sun had come to resemble, in its weird way, the wild reaches of her own planet.

If, she thought—then stopped thinking, certain what the object was the moment it caught her eye. That didn't keep her from stepping closer, kneeling, clearing off the debris that failed to hide it. Under a bush, half-buried in dead vegetation, lay the equally dead body of Piotr Kamanov. She sat on her haunches pondering items she must attend to in correct order. Alone, her first problem was that she mustn't leave the body to the next random idiot who stumbled over it, perhaps without her reasons for leaving it as it was. She needed, however, to inform Gutierrez and summon the doctor, what was her name?

Standing, she saw the building where she was to meet Aelbraugh Pritsch, a quonsetlike structure in a clearing, surrounded by large bins, actually input chutes for raw materials. She wondered what he'd do when she didn't show up.

Glancing about, she also wondered how much damage a bullet would do the canopy keeping the asteroid covered with its blanket of air. She couldn't see all the way to the artificial sky anyway, couldn't risk killing some intelligence up there among the branches. Instead she chose a nearby—super kudzu, Piotr had called it—drew her CZ99A1, aimed at the massive trunk, fired three quick shots, three spaced apart, and three more quick ones. Absently pleased that the slugs all struck within a handspan at sixty meters, she swapped the partial magazine for a full one and bent to retrieve spent cases where they'd arced, glittering, into the brush. It took an effort to stop, thinking that such tidiness hardly mattered, and another to start over when the realization hit her, once again, that this murder would begin the fight which had dominated conversation since yesterday. They'd need to conserve brass.

"Major, what's—*Oh, my!*"

She whirled at a familiar voice. "Mr. Pritsch, you've got to go to the camp! Ask the general and the doctor to come. I can't, somebody's got to stay with—understand?"

"*Aelbraugh* Pritsch, Major, the whole name together. This is beyond belief." The creature looked at her a long while before speaking again, his voice strained and thoughtful. "I believe I do understand. You can't trust me with the body. I expect you're wondering this very minute whether your message will ever arrive at what you call the camp."

Although she shook her head in polite denial, she'd wondered exactly that. Many of her fellow humans would blame his people for this. Suspecting the nonhumans might be inclined to preventive countermeasures, she intended to stay here, holding her weapon. "Just get my boss, please. I'll never ask another favor as long as I live."

The feathered biped nodded and stepped around her, vanishing down the trail the way she'd just come. She rubbed a hand over her face, ran the same hand through her auburn hair, took a breath, and sat. Her watch said it had been half an hour, although it felt much longer, when Gutierrez and Dr. Nguyen arrived, with Pulaski. The sergeant took a look and disappeared into the undergrowth, retching. The major and the general stood by in a silent state of delayed shock. The doctor, kneeling, made the traditional arcane gestures. At last she stood, pronouncing the geologist officially dead.

"A blow on the head, I presume to subdue him, then he was strangled. As you can see, neither the person who did it is immediately apparent, nor whatever weapons he or she used."

"Or *it*," the general muttered between clenched teeth, fighting an urge to imitate Pulaski. Knowing him, the major guessed the only thing keeping him in control was the terrible anger she could read on his face. "Did he have any warning," he asked Dr. Nguyen, "any chance to defend himself?"

She sawed Kamanov's revolver from his jacket pocket, catching its rear sight and the knurling of its hammer in the fabric. She handed it to him. "Six unfired cartridges in the cylinder." From the opposite pocket, she pulled the tiny auto with its long suppressor, taken from Richardson. "That's as far as my forsensic expertise extends, I'm afraid." She looked around to see that they weren't overheard. "Something else: strange marks on the throat."

Looking where the doctor pointed, the major saw a row of indentations resembling the tracks left by a hermit crab in beach sand. Pulaski, having returned, seemed fit enough to volunteer an opinion. "They look like marks," she offered, "from the tentacle of a squid or octopus."

"Let us hope you're mistaken." Aelbraugh Pritsch, having fetched the general and the doctor, had hurried off on another errand. He returned now with four sea scorpions, sounding horrified. Even the expressionless lobster beings were agitated. "It would appear you're not. May forces of randomness aid us, those are markings which the tentacles of an Elder leave behind!"

Gutierrez looked at the avian as he spoke. "I was afraid you'd say that. Rosalind, this is his bailiwick. Back home, we'd have an inquest, but it's up to him to say what happens next. You and Toya go along and represent us, whatever turns out to be customary."

Aelbraugh Pritsch blinked affirmation. "Sir, your cooperation's greatly appreciated. Each of us understands that our situation, already tense, has taken a sudden turn for the worse."

"Thanks to unwanted interference from Washington." Gutierrez ignored Pulaski's scandalized gasp. The doctor's mouth was a grim line. Reille y Sanchez remained silent, curious to see what the general had in mind.

"How very generous of you, sir," the creature replied. "Shall we say, then, that a truce, however momentary and uneasy, still holds between beings who, sadly enough, were formerly just hosts and guests?"

"Gracious hosts and grateful guests," Gutierrez insisted. "Yes, Aelbraugh Pritsch, tell your employer it does, until we find out who did this to my friend. After, well, I suppose that'll depend."

"Yes." The avian gave him a nod which almost amounted to a bow, then, an afterthought, extended a slim hand. "I suppose so." The humans watched him direct his guard in the use of what could only be recording equipment, small antenna-covered devices scanning the area around the body, and the pathways leading away in both directions. Afterward, the aliens helped Nguyen and Pulaski carry the remains back at ground level to the infirmary for examination by both sides. In this gravity, it constituted a burden only in a moral sense.

When the departing company was lost among the trees, Gutierrez turned to the major. "It must seem pretty grotesque to Aelbraugh Pritsch. I tell you, Estrellita, from a military viewpoint, to the poor asshole obeying them in the field, our orders *are* grotesque. Generous, he called me, for acknowledging the truth! The generosity of the helpless, the opposite of noblesse oblige!"

"Sir?" She wasn't sure whether he was talking to her or to himself using her presence as an excuse. It was a difficulty of her trade. She didn't know how to respond, whether to stand at attention or slouched with her hands—which she never knew what to do with anyway—in her pockets.

"You still don't get it, do you? He doesn't want our blood on his hands! He's grateful I'm trying to prevent it! Forty-two lunatics issuing orders to numerical and technological superiors, our only weapons a comic collection of obsolete pistols, rifles, and shotguns. Bayonets. You saw what happened when Vivian shot at Semlohcolresh. What are their professionals like?" Staring at the revolver as if he'd never seen it before, he shoved it in his suit at the waist. He unscrewed the suppressor and tucked the SD9 in his jacket pocket, thrust his hands in his pants pockets, and began shambling up the trail.

The major followed, a light breeze blowing the faint scent of magnolias toward them. In her mind, she reviewed their meager inventory. This, at least, was something she could deal with. "The ammo situation's even worse. We brought no more than a token amount, a few dozen rounds per gun."

"Even that was sent," he told her, "against my better judgment."

The ground became uneven, her reply had to wait until they had threaded their way down a miniature ravine. "We'll just let the enemy supply us, sir."

Eyes on his footing, he shook his head. "We can't afford an enemy. Very few of our personnel, scientists, engineers, have the training or temperament. I'm nothing but a retired pilot myself. Being kicked upstairs isn't the same as a promotion for merit. Against us is an unknown force of unknown size, undetermined capability, and enormous versatility. We might be seeing them at their worst, roughing it with what they consider only the bare necessities."

She agreed with his facts, but this wasn't the attitude she'd expected. The astonished Marine fought a humiliating urge to tears. Stumbling, she began to mutter at the rough going until she realized again that, perhaps not very long ago, this had been a cold, airless crater-scarred waste. "I hadn't considered the possibility, sir. I don't know what to say."

He stopped to smile. "I never know what *not* to say. Between us we might've made one decent officer. One thing I know, we must believe the evidence of our eyes. The Elders possess more numerous and potent weapons than we do, and they're armed to the mandibles all the time."

He resumed walking. She was surprised and hurried to catch up, almost turning her ankle where the ground dropped away. "Another aspect, sir, if you'll permit an observation from one of our professionals."

He didn't look up. "And what might that be, Major?"

"Sir, we're speaking of personal weapons."

"And you think they have something even nastier in reserve?"

"That isn't it, sir. They're like Sikhs or Moros, accustomed to handling weapons on an everyday basis, as familiar with them as we are with—I don't know what. That's worse news than any number or power—''

The general nodded. "We can't all be like you, Major, and with all due respect, maybe it's just as well. Peace is balanced on a knife-edge. Before this is over, you'll see it tilted this way and that, from one instant to the next, by all kinds of conflicting forces and differing—''

"I thought it was just us and the—''

"More deadly, I think, than our dispute with the Elders, are frictions between, let's say ideologues and pragmatists on both sides. I don't imply there's a reason to prefer one or the other; ideology's an ugly word because one in particular gave a bad name to the rest. It's just that it won't be fun to deal with while we're trying to find out what happened to Pete.''

They reached the point where the tow line had dropped her, and went past, still headed toward the camp. The general wanted to walk. It was a pleasant day for it, if they could have avoided thinking about current events. "I meant to ask, sir, how will we find out what happened?''

He stopped to lean against something like a birch tree. "I'd say it was Arthur's job, but he wasn't sent here as a detective, and I doubt he has any talent for it, being no more than a glorified . . .''

She swallowed. "Hall monitor, sir?''

Pushing away from the tree, he grinned. "You said it, Major, not me. 'Of the dead, and the KGB, speak nothing but good.' How brave a quarter of a billion miles makes us.'' He stopped again and turned. "Look, you're in military charge of this mission, I'm in overall command, sheriff and mayor. Whatever they decide back home about who does the investigating—you realize we'll have to ask?—it won't hurt if the two of us talk it over.''

She smiled back. "I'm game, sir.'' This was more like it. Maybe he'd just been shocked with grief, forced to struggle the past half hour to refocus his reasoning power. "How do we begin?''

"By thinking out loud,'' he replied, resuming his former pace. "First we review a list of our shipmates, whom we must now regard as suspects.''

"Yes, sir." This time she was ready and kept up without difficulty. For a man beyond his prime, she thought, his breath short from desk jobs and a little fat from a lifetime of flying, he made good time in the woods. She was a little out of breath, herself. "Also the nautiloids and their allies."

"We'll get to them. Given the effect this is likely to have, our best bet's someone who agrees with Washington and wants to provoke a fight. In no special order, consider Rosalind Nguyen, whose only known alllegiance—known to me, that is—is to her patients. I've studied her dossier, so have you: personal background tragic, but far from unique; granddaughter of Southeast Asian 'boat people' who fled halfway around the world to escape the rising tide, only to discover that their place of refuge . . . well, you know."

Without answering, she pushed a branch aside, ducked under another. The path had all but disappeared.

"Given official attitudes toward such refugees," he continued, "if she has a talent besides medicine, it's for survival. As a doctor, she can be presumed to oppose Washington's policy here, but keeps her opinion to herself, a talent I never had much luck cultivating. Her real position's unknown."

"Probably unknowable, sir."

They stepped over a stream, no more than a trickle centimeters wide, leaving heel marks in the soft ground. "Who next? Well, Toya's the descendant of refugees, too. Her ancestors were escaping Cossacks."

"I like Toya, sir," the major offered, "she's an overgrown Girl Scout. Any loyalties she has are to the ASSR. Deep down, I think she loves learning for its own sake. She'll never love anything more tangible."

"Like a man?" Following the steam, they arrived at a tiny cataract, stood watching the water, then went on. "Pretty rough for somebody you like. Can't say I disagree. From various inarticulate grunts—that's what we're reduced to—I'd guess she'd rather study the Elders than fight them."

"Yes, sir." She sneezed, then sneezed again, violently. They'd wandered into a streamside grove of giant ferns. Spores drifting from the undersides of the broad fronds dusted their uniforms. "Sorry, sir."

They pushed through the plants and took a moment to slap at their clothing. "Bless you, Estrellita, are you all right?"

"Of course I am, sir, what were you saying?"

"I was saying, again, 'Of the dead, and the KGB, speak nothing but good.' But we can't allow that to limit us. It's with friend Arthur that we begin getting to the really interesting suspects. Hell, he might have killed Pete last night in front of all of us, if you and that blond lieutenant hadn't pulled him off."

"Tension, sir," Reille y Sanchez shrugged, "that's what Piotr thought. Art's like anyone who belongs to KGB." She wasn't sure why she dared such honestly with a superior. "Willingly, I mean. Not very deep inside, he's a power junkie, and likes the idea of going head-to-head with the Elders. It represents a good gamble, an obvious path to power."

"Promotions come most quickly in wartime," Gutierrez suggested, "and in the terms you state, power can be seized most easily. Hmmm. I never thought of Arthur as that sincere and open a fellow. I do remember his fingers around Pete's throat, however, and I'm putting him at the top of the list, along with those four flunkies of his. Any one of those mutants might have done it at Art's order while he was somewhere else, providing himself with an alibi. What do you make of Vivian?"

The general didn't know Reille y Sanchez had been forced to pull Hake off Pulaski early in the trip, adding to the difficulty of an already difficult situation, making Toya her friend for life. She wasn't sure she wanted a friend for life. At the time, Empleado had expressed the opinion that she should have let his corporal have the girl. It wouldn't have done her lasting damage, he'd maintained. On the contrary, it might have made a woman out of a wallflower. It certainly would have prevented certain frictions created by the black eye the major had inflicted on Hake and his consequent loss of face. Demene Wise, by contrast, apparently couldn't get it up for anything female, and Delbert Roo, she was certain, couldn't get it up for anything human, whereas Roger Betal simply couldn't get it up. But Gutierrez had asked about Richardson.

The major inhaled. "On the assumption that her illness is fake? I wondered about that, myself. She's a good suspect, sir, loyal to the ASSR and covertly, but not very covertly—well, I just hope it's the American branch of the KGB.''

He laughed. ''You're a cynic, Estrellita! I was proud of myself for spotting her as Art's understudy, but the international wrinkle hadn't occurred to me.''

''It's my job, sir. She'd like to fight for the same reason Arthur would. In addition, she's black, and she's a woman.''

''Too deep for me, Estrellita,'' Gutierrez replied, ''I'm at a loss—''

''Beg pardon, sir, you aren't in a position, if I may speak freely—''

''Major, that's what we're here for. We're not going to figure this out if we hold anything back.''

''It's just that''—she colored from discomfiture—''socialism's been a bit relaxed about the equality it promised for women and minorities. I've heard it said—Piotr said it was originally a Russian saying—that socialist equality means women are perfectly free to do a man's job as long as they hurry home to cook dinner.''

He laughed. ''So, if anything, she'd be more volatile than Art. She could be our killer, even if she's genuinely flipped out.''

''You can bet,'' she nodded, ''it enters into the picture.''

''I'll take your word. Okay, next suspect. How about me?''

XI
Fangs and Claws

''You, sir, a suspect?''

''Or you. How would either of us stack up to anyone who doesn't know our minds from the inside? What would I say is my primary loyalty? The AeroSpace Force? My family? How would they deal with it when I answered that each takes precedence over the other depending on the circumstances? It's illogical, but it's true.''

They were startled by a droning overhead. Three meters above them, on two pairs of half-meter transparent wings, hovered a dragonfly straight out of Reille y Sanchez's childhood dinosaur books.

What would I say, Gutierrez thought, *is my view of the little war I'm about to fight? As a career soldier, I'd say I'm used to obeying orders. By the same indications Pulaski manifests, those around me know I also think deliberately making enemies of the Elders is about the dumbest order I've ever been given. As long as I do my duty, am I responsible for their inferences? Of course I am, this is the ASSR, isn't it?*

Lost in reflection, they walked in silence a few heartbeats, Gutierrez scrambling for what must surely be firmer ground than his own muddy thoughts. "I guess you look forward to a fight, Major, the same way a dog looks forward to dog food. Then again I'd be safe guessing that with any Marine, from the lowliest boot to the commanding general.''

She grinned, yet seemed to remain dedicated to the socialist ideal (one she fell short of less often than he did) of taking orders and keeping her mouth shut.

"Okay, if you don't like that direction, we'll pick someone else. That life-support technician at the fire last night. You realize, somewhere along the line, we're going to have to compile a sort of criminal dossier on every one of the members of this expedition.''

"Yes, sir.'' She was obviously relieved at the change of subject. "We need to supplement the, er, uninformative records we have.''

He nodded. "There are lots of crew members I don't know nearly as well as some we've already considered. Right now, to my professional embarrassment, I can't seem to remember that tech's name. I know I must have examined her records.''

"Otherwise,'' Reille y Sanchez agreed, "she wouldn't have been approved for the mission. Lieutenant Marna, sir. You can't remember everything. From what I know, going by the evidence of last night, she doesn't want to fight, although this could be a pose. Isn't it peculiar, sir, that an unwillingness to fight for the ASSR is reasonable doubt where murder's concerned? All traitors are innocent. But unless we find reason to place her higher on the list, her real thoughts are likely to remain unknown."

What Reille y Sanchez hadn't said, Gutierrez reflected grimly, was that this was true of everyone here. Anyone who'd lived all his life under Marxism. They'd become a civilization of accomplished liars. "That reminds me, Estrellita, your job, as you say: what do you think are the chances the KGB sent us another operative, somebody less conspicuous than Vivian?"

"Triple redundancy, sir?"

"Or quadruple," he told her wearily. "You've made me realize the Russians must have someone here, as well."

"Maybe we should rethink this whole thing, sir. After all, there's an excellent likelihood the killer's someone other than a member of our expedition."

"Yes, God help us, I think that's altogether the best likelihood. It also represents a prolonged nightmare to any human investigator. Set aside the political and military complications which are enough, by themselves, to do us all in. The Elders, if Mr. Thoggosh is to be believed—"

"I think he should, sir, insofar as it's practical."

"So do I—their culture's very ancient and complex. It's lasted half a billion years, a hundred thousand times longer than the Pyramids. At the gut level, I can't get a handle on a number like that, a hundred thousand, let alone half a billion. And we haven't even scratched the surface. Between us, we can't agree about their companion species, whether the lobsters, or Aelbraugh Pritsch, are partners or conscripts, retainers or draft animals, slaves or pets . . ."

"I see what you mean, sir. And there are only three entities we know anything about, Aelbraugh Pritsch, Mr. Thoggosh, now this Semlohcolresh."

He nodded. "You've got the picture. And all we know about them is what they've volunteered. If Mr. Thoggosh can be believed—"

"Excuse me, sir, I hate to contradict myself, but if there's a chance Mr. Thoggosh is the murderer, why should we believe him?"

"A point well taken. His interests lay unabashedly with himself, his investors and employees, and with this mysterious search of his. In general, I'd say that wherever what he tells us doesn't buy him anything, we'll grant him credibility. We have to start somewhere."

"Which logically implies," Reille y Sanchez mused, "that he informed you truthfully. He opposes the whole idea of any destructive—"

"Say, rather, 'unprofitable.' "

"Very well, any *unprofitable* conflict."

"Between you and me," Gutierrez told her, "I always wondered, and mostly kept it to myself, why capitalists get characterized as warmongers." She turned, her expression curious, fearful. "Back home," he answered her unspoken thoughts, "I'd be treading on thin ice, if this were any ordinary situation. It isn't, and we're not back home. We have to understand the Elders if we're to survive here, let alone find out who killed Pete. Between making money and war, the choice is clear. Mutually exclusive. It's more profitable to sell things to people than to kill them, and those occupied with the former are usually too busy to bother with the latter."

"My God, sir, where did you ever hear a thing like that? You've got to be more careful—what if I were Arthur?"

"Oh, I remember reading it somewhere," he grinned, "and instantly agreeing with it. Probably in one of the old comic books I collected as a kid, illegal as hell, but like cockroaches, they were everywhere."

"But think, sir! Capitalism and war go together like—"

"Bicycles and windshield wipers? Oh, doubtless some people make money at the start of every war, selling things to governments on both sides. But there couldn't be any war without governments. And whatever short-term profit you make comes at a risk of seeing your business controlled or seized by one of those governments, with an even chance of winding up on the wrong side and losing everything."

Now the warm breeze carried a homelier odor than magnolia blossoms in their direction, one he recognized as sage and sunshine, mountain wildflowers and cattle. They emerged from the trees into a yellow meadow broken at intervals by the huge trunks of the canopy, and walked around to avoid several large, somehow prehistoric-looking mammals grazing there.

"Major, believe me, I'm not engaging in heresy for its own sake, here. It's just that Semlohcolresh contradicted Mr. Thoggosh, implying that certain unspecified tenets of enlightened nautiloid self-interest make killing humans morally imperative."

She shook her head, frightened, yet fascinated by his reasoning. "If Semlohcolresh is the murderer—"

"About the best guess anybody's made so far."

"I agree, sir. Then why should we believe anything he tells us?"

"There it is in a nutshell. Both Elders say they value profit and self-interest above all else. One claims that this precludes war, while the other claims it demands it. Yet Semlohcolresh has no sensible motive for murder unless he's the one telling the truth! It occurs to me that the easiest approach might be to learn more about this nautiloid philosophy. I've never been sure whether a people's character shapes their beliefs, or their beliefs shape their character—"

"Or both."

"Or neither. At the moment, I can think of arguments for either case—that's the trouble with intellectualism—and until now, I haven't really cared. With the limited goal of exposing a murderer, it might not matter: either might provide us the clue we need to unravel this mess. On the other hand—or would it be the other tentacle?—if the Elders are really after something religious here, all bets are off."

"I'm not sure I follow you, sir."

"Estrellita, religious motivation, even that of my own wife, has always been a mystery to me, more unfathomable and profound than anything we've encountered here. The one thing I like about Marxism was its original attitude toward religion."

"'Was,' sir?"

"Just another politician's pose. I've done more serious reading than illicit comics, and Pete was right. Marxism had run its course at the end of the last century. Organized religion, too. Both twitched with death throes which the West mistook for vitality. An alliance was the only way to prolong their precarious existence, and both pursued it with the ardor of young lovers whose families had been feuding for generations."

Reentering the jungle at the opposite edge of the meadow brought them into territory which Gutierrez thought he was beginning to recognize. They must be nearing the shuttles and the human encampment. It had been a much longer walk than he expected.

"Well, their bastard offspring," he continued, "so-called liberation theology, spelled doom for the West. Or, as Pete suggested, maybe for the whole world. So much for Marx and religion. I understand my own culture, but what'll I do with a totally alien set of religious motivations? My official education left a lot to be desired, Estrellita. I'm afraid my only hope is more illegal literature—murder mysteries I used to read, waiting on alert with my squadron."

"And what do they tell you, sir?"

"Well, sometimes they held that the truth could best be determined from considering the character, not of the murderer, but of the victim. Peter was a charming and urbane gentleman whom everybody liked. Despite his age he was a ladies' man, and, in his last hours, our self-appointed peace negotiator. It struck me the first moment I knew he was dead that he was the last person on this expedition who deserved to die. Still, experience tells me this is the way with murder. Maybe with death in general."

"You're thinking of your son, sir?"

"But I'm not talking about him. First and foremost, Pete was moved by an innocent and limitless curiosity. I don't think he ever wanted anything more sinister or more demanding of anyone than simply to be permitted to learn everything he could about, well, these new beings we've discovered here, for example. Aside from that, he was something of a cynic in his own cheerful way. I was never sure whether he had any loyalty to anything, except the old-fashioned concept of individual autonomy, and his notion, at least, of decency. That's why he opposed the idea of conflict on this asteroid so bitterly and was never afraid to say so."

Hearing an odd noise, Gutierrez turned to Reille y Sanchez,

placing both his hands on her shoulders. "What is this, Estrellita, tears?"

"It's nothing, sir. I'll be all right in a minute."

He shook his head with sympathy and surprise. "Shed some for me while you're at it. I wish I could afford them myself."

Embarrassed, the major searched through all of her pockets, failing to find whatever she was looking for. Gutierrez produced a fold of tissues which she accepted, dabbing at her eyes and finally giving in and blowing her nose. "I'm sorry, sir, I . . . it isn't very—"

"Macho? Look, Estrellita, I loved Pete Kamanov like a brother. I'll miss him more than I ever missed my own brothers. He was the only completely happy individual I ever knew, and a good man to have around, just to remind you happiness like that was possible. If it's the last thing I do, I'm going to find the son of a bitch who killed him, whatever species or gender it turns out to be, and make him pay for it."

Reille y Sanchez nodded agreement. Gutierrez thought he saw the white flank of a shuttlecraft among the trees. Very near home base now, they were beginning to hear familiar, human-sounding noises—although they were still too far away to make out individual voices—and smell the smoldering ghost of last night's campfire.

"And now it occurs to me," the general told her, "that Pete's character might be the key in a different way. I always talked too much about the wrong things, and felt guilty about my lack of caution. Well, maybe we should forget caution altogether. Maybe we should adopt, at least for the duration, the same unflinching scientific attitude he always displayed toward the bitter truth, whatever it turned out to be. Even if it doesn't prove to be of any practical use, it somehow strikes me as the only fitting monument to him. What do you say?"

The major took a deep breath, straightening her shoulders. "The bitter truth, whatever it turns out to be."

He grinned, restraining himself from kissing her or giving her a manly punch on the shoulder. Either would have served.

"Okay, the only sensible motive for Pete's murder was to provoke trouble between us and the nautiloids."

She stuffed the tissues into a jacket pocket. "The problem

with the general's analysis, if you'll pardon me for saying so, sir, is that it fails to narrow the field."

He laughed. "You're right. Probably plenty of folks on both sides would like to start trouble." He paused a moment in thought. "You know, I remember once seeing pictures of a sperm whale covered with battle scars like those on Pete's throat. It looked like the surface of the Moon. On the whale, the craters had been produced by suction organs, tooth-edged, I think, on the undersides of the tentacles of some very large squid. According to Aelbraugh Pritsch, the equivalent nautiloid organs are vestigial, the way fangs and claws are with us, although, as I noticed during my visit with Mr. Thoggosh, they're far from altogether absent."

"Yes, sir?"

"Pete had a good idea about something else." He pulled the revolver from his pocket and gazed at it before continuing. "In nature, animals with plenty of spines and stingers never bother you if you leave them alone. We humans are too evolved for spines and stingers, and much too civilized to carry personal weapons even if the authorities permitted it. Now the same authority wants us to drive the Elders off this asteroid—do or die—and our friend Semlohcolresh thinks he has to wipe us out before we try. I lose my boy when we nuke South Africa to save it, and now someone strangles Pete before he can make peace. It's funny, Estrellita, the more atrophied and ineffectual our natural defenses get, the weaker we become as individuals, the bloodthirstier we all seem to be as a collective."

Before the major could reply, they broke through the trees and were only a few meters away from the *Wright*, *Moynihan*, and *Metzenbaum*, sitting in their wire-mesh cradles. The camp had spread beyond the triangular circle of the shuttles. Several individuals were cutting and stacking wood, an incongruous task to be performing, the general thought, in their silvery-gray ship-suits. A guitar-harmonica duet was being played somewhere out of sight. Sebastiano and several of his crew members sat on the ground with their legs folded like cinematic Indians. Heavyset and naked to the waist, Corporal Owen seemed to be washing his underwear in a large plastic tub.

Closer to where their commander and the Marine major had

emerged from the vegetation, Empleado and his four assorted assistants appeared to be waiting. The general had always privately thought that Delbert Roo was the one to keep a wary eye on. Little and wiry, the half-Chinese, half-Australian leprechaun seemed to have an almost magical talent for hurting things. Dr. Nguyen and Pulaski had returned to the camp and were standing with another figure, not a member of the expedition, not even human, but nevertheless no stranger to any of them.

"General Gutierrez! Major Reille y Sanchez!" Aelbraugh Pritsch had been waiting for them impatiently. "I'm afraid I've the most distressing information to convey to you!"

The music halted without even a crash. Sebastiano and his group stopped talking and arose, almost as one. As they approached, Gutierrez noticed that each and every one had drawn a weapon, probably on their colonel's authorization, from the expedition armory. In addition to his own unauthorized sidearm, which he now wore openly in a holster, Sebastiano carried one of the heavy Remington riot guns.

The general sighed. "You're just in time, Aelbraugh Pritsch. After all, I've been experiencing such a shortage of distressing information lately. What is it now?"

The avian's feathers rustled, and he fluttered nervous hands. The little reptile he seemed to carry with him all the time was nowhere in sight, which Gutierrez interpreted as a bad sign.

"Well, General, you see, as you might expect, the Elders have developed a reasonably advanced science of criminal forensics."

"That makes sense," offered Reille y Sanchez, "considering that they've had half a billion years to do it."

"What?" Aelbraugh Pritsch blinked, his pupils changing size, a sign of fear, Gutierrez knew, in many birds. "Oh, yes, Major, I see what you mean. In any event, as I gather you humans are able do with fingerprints, we've methods of identifying the specific individual who left . . . well, who made the marks on Dr. Kamanov's body."

The general tensed. "And?"

"And on behalf of Mr. Thoggosh, and with considerable trepidation on my own part I don't mind telling you, I've come to report the results of the postmortem examination to you humans. Dr. Nguyen and Sergeant Pulaski were there as witnesses, and—"

"And the apparent murderer," Sebastiano interrupted impatiently, "was Semlohcolresh, that Elder who, more than any of the others, favored war between our species. Now tell General Gutierrez the rest of it, Aelbraugh Pritsch, and get it over with."

"I, er, that is, as the Proprietor's assistant, as spokesbeing for the Elders and their associated species, I confess shamefacedly and deeply regret that I've also to report, and with even more trepidation, I might add, that our colleague—"

"Semlohcolresh," the lieutenant colonel interrupted again, unconsciously fingering the saftey of his semiautomatic shotgun, "seems to be conveniently among the missing!"

XII
Ampersand and Asterisk

"Well, Juan, this is interesting."

Lethal hardware was everywhere. Gutierrez was more than annoyed that weapons had been issued to so many. The major could tell by the set of his lips as Sebastiano, to whom it was also obvious, stepped forward, indicating that what he wanted to say wasn't intended for everybody.

"In the general's absence," the *Wright*'s captain whispered, "I thought it wise to give Big Bird some protection"—his eyebrows indicated the KGB nearby—"considering the traditional fate, sir, of the bearer of bad news?"

Gutierrez gave him a grudging nod. The avian hadn't heard what passed between them. He was attempting to explain himself to an angry crowd. "... sincere belief Semlohcolresh may have been the victim of foul play."

A dozen voices dropped to a sneer, an eerie effect Reille y Sanchez thought. Empleado left his underlings and approached Gutierrez. "General, must we waste time listening to this? Does this thing actually expect us to accept excuses for not handing a murderer over?"

"Art," replied the general, "I want you to—"

"Twenny ferns," Broward Hake interrupted in a redneck accent which, with the rise of the ASSR, had fallen out of fashion in his native Texas, "says this Semlohcolresh slimed his way back t'someplace real people never evolved!"

The avian's hands fluttered like independent organisms. "General, help me! No matter how I explain the situation, your people won't understand!"

"Understand—just a minute." Hake had opened his mouth again, but Gutierrez spoke before he got a word out. "Arthur, front and center!"

Empleado's head snapped toward Gutierrez. "General?"

"Tell your Neanderthals if I'm interrupted once more, it isn't going to help that they belong to KGB. Do I make myself clear, Art?"

Empleado gulped and looked resentful. "Yes, General."

"Now, Aelbraugh Pritsch, you wanted us to understand something?"

"Yes, sir, I do. Regrettably, I can't explain a pivotal scientific fact when those I wish to explain it to lack the background to comprehend it."

"This," Gutierrez asked, "is leading somewhere?"

"General, it isn't our custom to keep secrets we can't profit by. Your technical education, that of your people, was to begin with the major's visit to our power plant. Mr. Thoggosh even intended to show you the dimensional translation machinery which brought us to 5023 Eris."

"Intentions," Gutierrez shook his head, "are the only thing cheaper than talk."

"Is that original, sir, or . . ." replied the bird being. "Never mind, to the point: in the absence of sufficient technical education, how can you appreciate the extreme difficulty, the overwhelming danger—''

"Not to mention the expense?"

"—the hideous expense interdimensional travel represents? I can't get your people to understand. Perhaps they won't understand. No one crosses world lines casually or secretly."

"Why not?" Roger Betal had an accent, too, similar to Hake's, although he and the major had a nation of ancestral origin in common. She'd learned to keep track of what the man did, rather than what he said. He could be agreeable, say anything to win a friend or avoid a fight, but when she'd made the mistake of accepting his invitation to a movie near the base where they'd been training, she'd seen him beat a vagrant half to death because the poor man had touched his uniform with dirty hands. Afterward, he'd relied on his credentials to avoid formal charges. Gutierrez gave him a glare, but left it at that, probably because he was curious about the answer.

"Because too much energy is expended. There are manifestations. It would be like taking off from Cape Canaveral without being seen or heard."

"To the extent that any of us believes you, Aelbraugh Pritsch," Empleado sneered, "you've just managed to make things worse!"

The avian turned to focus his amber eyes on the KGB man. "I'm afraid I fail to understand your meaning, this time, sir."

"Yes, Arthur," echoed the general, "meaning what?"

"That these *beasts*"—Empleado's face was red and his fists were clenched—"are conspiring! If Semlohcolresh didn't escape to avoid the consequences of his crime, his fellow creatures are helping him remain in hiding!"

"He's holed up," Hake seconded the motion, "and the rest are covering up!" Muttering, especially from Empleado's other three hirelings, agreed.

The major watched as the exasperated avian changed tactics. "General, I appeal to you." He spread his hands. "Whatever the truth, whoever killed Dr. Kamanov, don't you see that these events will plunge your entire Solar System, and all of us along with it, into war? I'm sure everybody, on every side, realizes one and only one thing can prevent such a catastrophe."

"Getting hold," Gutierrez agreed, "of Pete Kamanov's murderer."

"Guilty or not," a cynic among Sebastiano's group hissed under his breath, "as long as it's soon." Assenting noises were heard from others.

"Precisely," the avian replied, the major hoped, to the general rather than the joker. "Justice must be arrived at in a manner satisfactory to all."

"No small matter in itself," Gutierrez observed.

"The more reason both sides"—the avian turned to plead with all the humans—"must cooperate in trying to achieve it."

"This is bullshit!" Demene Wise complained. "Parrot shit!" amended Delbert Roo. "Chicken shit!" Wise tossed back. Nasty laughter from the other thugs wasn't shared this time by most of the humans.

"*Look at him!*" Reille y Sanchez startled herself by shouting. She strode forward, pointing a finger at Aelbraugh Pritsch. "Don't you morons understand that what you're hearing in his voice isn't fear for himself?"

"Estrellita," Gutierrez tried to interrupt, "what are you—"

"Sir, I've been thinking over what you said, about their not wanting our blood on their hands?" Gutierrez gestured for her to go on. She turned to the stirring of voices around them. "*The same principle that powers quasars!* Have you thought about that? Semlohcolresh stopped two bullets before they reached their target, bullets traveling over the speed of sound! If they wanted, they could wipe us off this rock any second! Instead, the idea seems to upset them more than if their own lives were on the line!"

In the silence following her outburst, Gutierrez seized the initiative. "Okay," he told the avian, "I may regret it, but I'm assuming you're on the up and up." Breaking precedent himself, the usually loquacious being nodded and Gutierrez went on. "If you're handling this mess for your—the nautiloids, somebody'll have to take charge of it for us. I'm an obvious candidate, or Art, but it'll have to be confirmed by higher authority before we start." He turned. "Juan, I want Washington on the line five minutes ago."

"Aye, aye, Commodore!" Grinning, Sebastiano jogged toward the flagship. "One long distance call, coming up!"

"General?" It was Rosalind Nguyen, carrying a small beaker of dark brown liquid. "May I speak with you a moment?"

Twenty minutes later, having seen Aelbraugh Pritsch off and attended a few matters around camp, Gutierrez followed Sebastiano aboard the *Moynihan*, squeezing through the hatch, and climbed up to the rear of the command deck. He settled the phones over his ears, bending the slender microphone pipette until it was in place before his lips. "Ampersand, this is Asterisk on Scramble Six. We've got a situation here, over."

Nearby, Reille y Sanchez was reminded of the lonely distance separating them from home. It would take over twenty-two minutes for his words to reach Earth—where the duty tech at Canaveral would have to summon a responsible officer, probably in Washington, adding to the delay—and another twenty-two to receive a reply. Gutierrez would like to spell their "situation" out this first time, she thought, but ASSR security measures forbade it. Unable to think of anything that could be done in the intervening hour, they waited, Empleado fidgeting beside her. Forty-seven minutes later, by her watch, a voice like crackling cellophane filtered into the general's phones and, at the same time, through a speaker on the panel.

"*Asterisk, this is Ampersand. Scramble Six negatively secure. Go to Scramble Nine or end transmission, over.*"

Surprised murmurs swept the deck. Gutierrez shook his head, a gesture of frustration lost over an audio link of half-a-billion kilometers. "Ampersand, Asterisk. Scramble Nine is no good, either, repeat, negatively good. Our, er, hosts can unscramble anything we can scramble, over." The general turned to those around him, giving them an ironic grin. "Three ways to do anything." He didn't need to finish the old army joke; they knew he meant the right way, the wrong way, and the government way. Experience indicated that there wasn't much difference between the latter two. "Would somebody like to make some real coffee while we wait?"

The suggestion was greeted with enthusiasm. Sometime during the long walk the general and the major had taken, Mr. Thoggosh had sent a generous supply of roasted whole beans—

his people had the habit, too—to the camp. Corporal Owen had cobbled up a drip device using laboratory filters and discarded food containers, but, wary of foreign substances, not to mention a murder already committed, Sebastiano had made everyone wait for Dr. Dr. Nguyen's analysis and Gutierrez's subsequent permission before brewing any.

This time the voice of Earth was impatient and peremptory. *"Asterisk, this is Ampersand. It isn't your 'hosts' we're concerned with. Leaders of the United World Soviet, here in the ASSR and in the USSR, have kept up to date on your mission and are conferring around the clock. Go to Scramble Nine immediately. Give us a telemetry update on the sideband while you're at it, over."*

On the command deck, the aggregate eyebrow level was raised a meter by the brief message. Beside the general, Sebastiano, a set of phones pressed to one ear, made adjustments and examined readouts. He glanced for confirmation at a tech standing in an identical posture on the side away from his boss, then back at the general, lifting a circled thumb and forefinger.

"Ampersand," Gutierrez told his mike, "this is Asterisk. Roger telemetry coming up on sideband at . . ." Sebastiano scribbled a figure on a pad velcroed to the panel. ". . . a hundred twenty-eight to one. Going to Scramble Nine as ordered in four seconds on my mark. Mark, one, two, three. Ampersand, this is Asterisk on Scramble Nine, do you still copy, over?"

"Around the clock?" Empleado's eyebrows were highest of all, making up in an odd way for his baldness. It would be forty-four minutes before they heard from Earth again. Two hours wasted, the major thought, on conversation which had so far been worth about two minutes. "Presumably our leaders differ on what Marxist conduct demands in this instance."

Gutierrez turned from the console. "You bet your ass they differ! Can't you see it, Congress and Politburo, President and Premier, dithering themselves to death, while the real negotiation—"

Empleado interrupted. "General, I—"

"Stow it, Art." He shot a glance at Reille y Sanchez. She

was reminded of their bargain: the truth, no matter what. "Everyone knows the Banker. Why pretend it's a deep, dark secret? It's what Pete said, we Americans, in the Russian view, haven't lived with Marxism long enough. Moscow—the Banker, his people—are bound to be more realistic and flexible than Washington, especially when matters of ideology conflict with common sense. Moscow wants peace with the Elders, to get their technology, no matter what."

"General, I—"

"Art, you're repeating yourself. Can I have another cup of coffee? Thanks, Major. You know, Pete once told me that to his people, Marxism's like the old man who lived with a family for years in an overcrowded apartment in Leningrad. He was filthy, smelled bad, his personal habits would've disgusted Rasputin. No one in the family liked him much, but no one had the courage to tell him to get out. Finally, the wife confronted her husband, saying that he must tell his uncle to leave.

" 'My uncle?' the husband replied, 'I thought he was your uncle!' "

"Sir, I was going to say . . ." Empleado paused as if expecting another interruption, seeming almost disappointed when it didn't happen. ". . . in the interest of survival, that our leaders, whose expedition this is supposed to be, may decide they can do without the advice of the world capital."

Gutierrez nodded. It was a surprising analysis, thought the major, considering the source. Like many Americans, she was aware that, for some time, Washington had only been paying lip service to Moscow.

"And now it's time"—Sebastiano reminded her of Kamanov's remark about Texas Marxism—"to show the world who's the biggest and best Marxist power?"

Half an hour went by. "*Asterisk, this is Ampersand.*" A different voice, someone with more authority, or the shifts had changed at the Cape. "*We copy you five by five on Scramble Nine, voice and telemetry. Now why the hell are you breaking radio silence? It better be good, over.*"

"Hasn't it been good for you?" Gutierrez fought annoyance the one way he knew, then apparently thought better of it. "Strike that, Ampersand. We've had a series of, ah, events, here. We've lost Colonel Richardson." He cleared his throat. "She isn't dead, repeat, negatively dead, just misplaced. She collapsed on landing and had to be sedated. Under therapy, she went berserk and escaped with a gun after trying unsuccessfully, repeat, unsuccessfully, to kill one of the Elders. We have search parties out, being relieved every couple of hours. Negative results so far." He gave his next words careful thought. "That's the short subject. Our feature presentation is that Dr. Kamanov, our geologist, appears to have been strangled to death by one of the nautiloids, an individual named Semlohcolresh, now negatively present, over."

Finding a spot on one of the jump seats behind the control seats, Reille y Sanchez dozed off thinking that this kind of communication always gave her a feeling of not knowing what to do with herself once the last few words had been said. She could see by his expression that the general felt that way. Somewhere among such thoughts she lost track of time and was awakened, with a sore back and stiffened muscles, by the radio.

"*Asterisk, this is Ampersand,*" came the voice of yet another faceless individual. "*For this you broke radio silence? What the fuck do you mean, negatively present? We don't understand why you broke fucking radio silence! Kamanov was nonessential personnel. Demand that the killer be turned over to you and execute it, SOP, over.*"

"Ampersand, it isn't that easy—I mean, this is Asterisk." Struggling with anger again, Gutierrez took deep breaths to prevent the words he wanted to say from escaping. "You idiots invented this lingo. Semlohcolresh, the apparent killer, repeat, apparent, subsequently disappeared and is negatively available. His people swear they don't know where he is. They suggest that he, too, may be a victim of some kind of violence, over."

This time, rather than fall asleep and wake up with a useless body, the major decided to spend the lag time walking around the camp.

"Cancer stick?" Danny Gutierrez grinned, a slim cylinder between his lips. The trailing wisp had an unmistakable, welcome aroma. Somewhere, somehow, someone had scrounged some cigarettes, maybe the same way as the coffee. Yet she remembered what the general had said: as far as Mr. Thoggosh knew, humans from her Earth were the only sapients anywhere, anywhen, dumb enough to have invented smoking. She took one—for her part, she didn't know any Marine, anywhere, anywhen, who wouldn't—it was South African, as it turned out, a Kendall—when it was offered with the wrist flick she'd never seen any non-American imitate successfully. Something sparked in the boy's hand, an emergency fire-lighter from one of the shuttle kits: a knurled carbide thumb-wheel in a brass fixture which held what was called flint, and a short length of fluffy cotton cord. It had been screwed onto an aluminum reservoir from an arctic-survival lip-gloss. Corporal Owen's handiwork. Reille y Sanchez bent over the tiny flame and drew smoke into her lungs.

"Thanks, Lieutenant." She exhaled. "Coffee and cigarettes. My life is complete. Feels like rain. How can that be?"

The air was as warm, damp, and close as if they were indoors. In a way, they were. The yellow sky, of course, was artificial, and never seemed to change. She found it getting on her nerves. Where she came from, sky that color meant tornadoes. The lieutenant blinked, puppy-bashful in a more normal manner than Pulaski's habitual shyness, the supply of small talk which protected him from good-looking female officers who outranked him used up. "Dr. Kamanov said it's a matter of volume. There are buildings on Earth where it rains. Before he . . . he expected it to happen before this."

In that instant they heard a noise they might have described as a "ping," if it hadn't been loud enough to deafen. Their attention, focused on the sky, was seized by the appearance, not quite overhead, more in the direction of the power plant, of a violet pinpoint bright enough to throw faint shadows on the grayish flank of the shuttle beside them.

"What the fu—sorry, Major!" Reille y Sanchez grinned despite a brief, dizzy feeling, as if her heart had missed a beat or a small tremor had lifted the ground under her feet. The violet spot began pulsing, throwing off a ring of brilliant blue. At the fifth pulse, another ring swelled outward, emerald green, and at the tenth, another, yellow-gold, contrasting with the indifferent mustard of the sky it was projected on. Each ring was broader than the one preceding, with no space visible between them.

Fascinated by the display, Reille y Sanchez lost count of the pulses, each accompanied by the fluttery sensation which made it difficult to breathe. An orange ring took its place outside the others. It was hard judging its size. She estimated it was nine or ten times the diameter of the Moon, as seen from Earth. It was joined by a larger orange ring, then a ring of ruby-red, its far edge hidden by the serried jungle horizon.

In the beginning, the rings pulsed together. Now they began to slip out of phase until, like a multicylindered engine, the sense of vibration spread evenly from moment to moment in a disturbing, low-throated growl. Reille y Sanchez felt her ears ringing. She was forced to concentrate to get her breath. The look on Danny's face, a softened version of the general's, was a mixture of fear and curiosity, probably identical to her own.

Without warning, another "ping" reverberated through the air. In a rush from the center, the rings suddenly reversed colors, violet outermost, shrank inward, and vanished. Before the major could decide what color of residual dazzle had imprinted itself on her retina, a blinding flash of lightning eradicated it. An ordinary peal of thunder followed. Rain began to fall as if directed downward at them through a fire hose. They ducked beneath the wing of the *Moynihan* to watch their fellow travelers, as enthralled as they themselves had been at the aerial display, scrambling for cover. "So *that's* what weather-making machinery's like." Danny, his earlier shyness forgotten, thrust thumb and forefinger into his breast pocket, extracting the pack of Kendalls. "Very impressive. Another cigarette, Major?"

She let him light it for her, and stood beside him, breathing smoke and watching the rain. When she returned to the flagship's command deck, it was in time to see the elder Gutierrez shaken out of sleep the same way she'd been. He'd slept through the spectacular beginning of the storm, but was alert the moment a voice issued from the radio.

"*Asterisk, this is Ampersand. This is a fucking stall and you ought to know it, Gutierrez, I mean Asterisk! Why haven't you ordered those vermin off the asteroid? Why haven't you ordered them to produce the killer? What's wrong with you, anyway, Asterisk? Over.*"

Rubbing an arm, the general lumbered to the mike, not bothering with the headphones. "Ampersand, this is Asterisk. I tried explaining last time. You didn't listen. These beings are five hundred million years ahead of us. They stop bullets and generate power with something so far beyond fusion I don't know how to ask what it is, let alone how it works. I'm in no position to order anybody to do anything. We're outgunned and living on favors. I'm looking into the murder, cooperating with what passes for authority here. I called, SOP as you say, to see who you want to head the investigation. We have an official of the American KGB—no, I can't remember his damned code name—also any unofficial representative you have aboard. Major Estrellita Reille y Sanchez, in charge of military security, might be a logical choice, considering the circumstances, over."

Surprised and pleased to have been mentioned, the major watched Gutierrez during the next endless lag, preparing himself for a counterblast. Instead, what they heard was: "*Stand by, Asterisk, over.*"

The general keyed his mike. "Ampersand, this is Asterisk, over." The hiss of empty airwaves filled headphones and speakers. "Ampersand," he insisted, "this is Asterisk, do you copy, over?"

"*Asterisk, this is Ampersand.*" Gutierrez jumped as the reply coincided with his futile attempt to elicit it. "*Negative your recommen—Jorge, what the fuck did you say the code name was? I dunno, how the fuck can I remember what you never told me, I'm just the fucking messenger boy! Well, fuck you and your pet iguana! Strike that, Asterisk. Orders from Washington, highest priority: the political officer's passed over without prejudice.*"

This, thought Reille y Sanchez, despite the fact that Empleado, at least until this afternoon, wholeheartedly supported ASSR policy. She wondered if it meant Washington knew something about him she didn't. She also wondered how it might have gone if the number two KGB officer hadn't lost her mind. Maybe Washington itself wasn't sure, judging by what came next.

"*For purposes of investigation, you'll place in charge Major*

Estrellita Reille y Sanchez, field appointment to full colonel, effective immediately, Russian KGB. Do you copy, Asterisk? Never mind, don't answer that, maintain radio silence. This is Ampersand, over and out."

XIII
Agent of Exultation

Rain roared on the overhead windows aft of the flagship's flight deck, reminding Reille y Sanchez of the semitropical monsoons which had often interrupted training in north Florida. There, it had been possible to stand in the sunshine and see a wall of falling water coming toward you. Here, amplified by the drum-like aluminum structure of the shuttle, it was more like being in a war zone during a firefight.

She tried to keep her mind on the ramifications of her latest assignment. Although it wasn't her responsibility—doubly so, now that she'd been publicly conscripted into the KGB—her first thought was for the hardware and electronics in the cargo bay. Designed for vacuum, incredible temperatures, and a lot of Gs, it had never been intended to get wet.

The doors were lined with superconducting solar collectors, the only new technology aboard. They lay open as they did in space, epoxy graphite clamshells in two sections which had once given this vehicle type the nickname "Polish Bomber." The largest such structures ever fabricated for flight, they were controlled from a panel near the aft windows. Closed, they were secured with thirty-two latches which had proven no more reliable on the outward journey than anything else the shuttles were equipped with.

Others were thinking, as well. She joined what turned into a rush, clambering down the "primary interdeck access" to the middeck with Betal, Empleado, and the general, shouldering out through the crew hatch. The crews of the other shuttles had the same idea. Those within the passenger containers jostled through the tiny airlocks into the bays. Shivering almost immediately, her ship-suit soaked, her thick auburn hair limp and streaming into her eyes, she emerged to climb another, cruder ladder of lashed branches onto the rain-slick starboard wing of the *Moynihan*. Her clothing already seemed impossibly heavy with the weight of absorbed water. Danny Gutierrez and Broward Hake were behind her, looking bedraggled.

Meters away, small figures struggled over the equally slippery airline-sized hulls of the *Metzenbaum* and *Wright*, heedless, in the light gravity, of the danger of falling or that they stood on "no step" areas. Reille y Sanchez made out the drenched forms of Marna and Nguyen: thumb-sized drops struck, thousands to the meter, atomizing themselves into a knee-deep coarse mist through which the lieutenant and the physician seemed to be wading.

The idea was to help the eighty-year-old motors close the doors, and fasten the recalcitrant latches. Reille y Sanchez brushed a hand across her eyes, noticing how the ends of her fingers were wrinkled and pale. She tried to catch a breath from an atmosphere that seemed solid with rain. Laboring beside Owen, Pulaski (less fragile than she appeared), and her other comrades, her holster slapping on her thigh through wet trousers, her thoughts abruptly flashed back to her *Spetznaz* training. Told it carried with it reserve status as a KGB officer, at the time, she'd regarded it as purely ceremonial and hadn't taken it seriously. She knew better now.

From this perspective, it was suddenly absurd that she'd wondered whether Richardson served Washington or the Banker (why did they call him that?) and his Moscow cutthroats. Like most people, Reille y Sanchez detested all KGB, American or Russian. Now she feared that, having worked for them even in an emergency like this, she might not be allowed to quit. What was perhaps worse, certain ugly inferences—and uglier nicknames than Polish Bomber—always seemed appropriate when a woman carried KGB credentials. She'd always been proud that her Marine rank and responsibilities had never had anything to do, as far as she knew, with her gender.

With Owen and Pulaski, she'd climbed to the flight-deck roof, and was standing over the windows she'd been standing under earlier. A dozen people, Gutierrez and his son, Delbert Roo, Demene Wise, had taken up positions along the wing root, working with a few brave souls perched atop the passenger insert. Across the camp, she saw Sebastiano bossing the same job from the roof of the *Wright*. Aboard the *Moynihan*, those along the wing lifted. She felt, rather than heard the whining of the elderly motors. The door rose with a series of jerks, a torrent sluicing down the curved photovoltaics, into the bay.

Those on the container seized the door, careful where they placed their hands, supporting it as it descended. Unsure whether she was helping, Reille y Sanchez held the front edge, as others at the tail fin, Empleado and Betal among them, held the rear. Someone shouted something, but she couldn't hear. Deafened by rain on the door, she tried to ignore the goose bumps covering her everywhere, tried not to ask herself what had caused them, dirty weather or dirtier politics. Her breath was visible when she exhaled.

The starboard door was down at last. Grinning at Pulaski and the machinist, she imitated them as she slid her feet carefully to the port side of the roof and prepared to be of what assistance she could. Thinking back to the EVA which had gotten her here, she realized the one good thing you could say about space was that it was dry.

Gutierrez had never really asked where she stood on the issues. He'd assumed she'd do her duty, possibly be one of the most vocal in favor of Washington's war. Scattered among the land mines in that assumption were reasons to feel complimented, she supposed. But she recognized other, dangerous possibilities inherent in perceived bias and conflict of—

Someone shouted again—Sebastiano, pointing at the sky—and at the same time she realized they'd managed to shut the second door. From inside the bay, she could hear somebody hammering at the stubborn latches. Reille y Sanchez stepped back, nearly losing her footing as she stumbled into Pulaski, who staggered against Corporal Owen, who fell from the roof, almost floating in the asteroidal gravity to land with a disgusting splash in the mud. He stood, wiping himself off with the edge of a broad hand—the rain was doing a better job of it—laughing.

Meanwhile, Reille y Sanchez looked in the direction Sebastiano had pointed, straining to hear, above the bumble and splatter of the rain, the keening of one of the electric aircraft which had brought many of them here. The encampment was about to have a visitor, and she was curious to see how a species five hundred million years old avoided getting wet in weather like this. As it materialized from the mist and began settling toward the streaming, muddy ground, she could see some object projecting from the blue metallic doughnut shape which hadn't been in evidence when she'd ridden a machine exactly like it from the cradle of plasticized mesh down to the infirmary. Aelbraugh Pritsch appeared to be holding a bright yellow, exceedingly large, and otherwise ordinary umbrella, attempting to keep not only his own feathers dry, but the forms of two other occupants, one of whom might not have appreciated the gesture.

It was a nautiloid, not just a tentacular extension. From the avian's bearing, Reille y Sanchez guessed it was Mr. Thoggosh in the flesh—and massive spiral shell—glistening within a covering of silvery-transparent plastic. The general's description, vivid as it had been, failed to convey how big the giant mollusc was. The grooved dome of his shell bulged shoulder-high from the open compartment of the vehicle, and several tentacles, draped casually over the side, perhaps to allow more room for his fellow passengers, touched ground before the undersurface of the machine.

The third rider was human, unfamiliar at this distance in the rain. She hadn't been aware someone was missing from the camp. As the machine squelched into the circle formed by the shuttles, a section of one side tucked itself away. Protected and concealed by the umbrella, the bipeds clambered from the vehicle, leaving the nautiloid. To her astonishment, Reille y Sanchez watched a large, white, shaggy dog jump from the machine to follow those beneath the umbrella, although it made no effort to stay out of the rain.

Creeping along the sealed door, she slid off onto the starboard wing, found the makeshift ladder at the same moment as the general and the political officer, and soon stood with them beneath the fuselage, up to her ankles in mud, waiting for those beneath the umbrella. Aelbraugh Pritsch folded the contrivance. Standing beside the bird-being was a man she'd never seen before, certainly not on the journey to 5023 Eris.

"General Gutierrez, Mr. Empleado," Aelbraugh Pritsch intoned, "Colonel Reille y Sanchez, late of the ASSR Marines. I congratulate you on your promotion, Colonel, and present my friend and associate, Eichra Oren."

Somehow, by a miracle of transportation or simple determination, Mr. Thoggosh had extricated himself from the aircraft without help and joined them under the wing of the shuttle. Behind him, between the two vehicles, his shell had left a deep groove in the mud, rapidly being eradicated by the rain. Introductions started again to include the Proprietor, with whom Reille y Sanchez managed to shake appendages without flinching. The strange man smiled and put out a hand. When it got to her, she unconsciously counted the fingers—the usual five—before taking it.

"Colonel, I'm pleased to meet you." For some reason he wore nylon running shoes, an obnoxious red and green Hawaiian shirt, and a pair of faded Levi's. He was of average height, well-muscled though a little thin, blond, tanned, and blue-eyed, but his voice, deep and mellow, wasn't that of the kid surfer from a long-gone era he resembled. He had the inward look of a combat veteran on temporary leave. In one hand he carried a leather case a meter long, half again as wide as her hand, five centimeters thick. "This"— he indicated the dog—"is Sam. Sam, Colonel Reille y Sanchez."

The dog barked, its own voice deeper and more powerful than she'd expected. For a moment she was afraid the animal would try to shake itself dry in the shelter beneath the wing, not that it would have made much difference to her uniform, or would jump up and put its paws on her. Instead it sat, mud and all, and raised its right paw toward her.

She took the paw, delighted. "I'm pleased to meet, you, Sam."

"Glad to hear it, Colonel," Sam replied. "You're very beautiful, if a bit wet. May I call you Estrellita?"

In the stunned silence that followed, the Proprietor's assistant, unaware of the shock the humans were coping with, went on. "As a *p'Nan* debt assessor of great reputation, exercising his talents on behalf of the Proprietor, Eichra Oren will be your opposite number, Colonel Reille y Sanchez."

"I see," she lied.

The avian paused, listening to something. Sam and Eichra Oren turned their heads to look at Mr. Thoggosh. "The Proprietor, unable to communicate owing to a lack of requisite equipment, asks me to explain that this means Eichra Oren will act as our investigator into the mystery of Dr. Kamanov's unfortunate demise."

"Lieutenant," Gutierrez picked his son out of the crowd gathering around them, "go inboard and patch one of the ATUs into the middeck intercom for Mr. Thoggosh. That's a portable transceiver," he explained, "over which he can broadcast to the audio system. You might inform him that Eichra Oren's sudden appearance on 5023 Eris represents something of a mystery in itself."

"As well it might," the avian replied, "if you're still unaware of the significance of this storm and the display preceding it. I believe I told you earlier that interdimensional travel, by means of which Eichra Oren's just arrived, occurs with rather spectacular side effects. And by the way, the Proprietor can hear you perfectly well."

"That's right," the general nodded, addressing Mr. Thoggosh, "you did say your hearing was good, didn't you?"

"*Indeed.*" The Proprietor's voice came from several sources, relayed through the unit plugged in by the younger Gutierrez. "*I'm surprised you remember, General, considering all you've been through. Aelbraugh Pritsch, having formally presented Eichra Oren, we'll retire and leave our old friends to become acquainted with our new friends. Eichra Oren, Sam, confer with me at your later convenience, if you will.*"

The nautiloid began to turn his ponderous shell and point

himself back toward the aircraft, with Aelbraugh Pritsch behind him.

"Just a minute!" Empleado squeezed between Reille y Sanchez and the general. "You've only managed to make things worse—again!"

The mollusc paused, causing his assistant to stumble into him. "*You're speaking to me, sir? I'm afraid I don't know what you're talking about. Perhaps by well-meaning inadvertence—*"

"I'm not speaking to Tweetybird." Empleado's tone was nasty. "Or to this ventriloquist and his trained mutt! If this Oren's as human as he looks, he won't be doing any investigating for anybody. It's my duty to claim him by virtue of the fact he's a civilian. Otherwise, he belongs to the general and Maj—Colonel Reille y Sanchez. I don't know where he came from, but he's a citizen of the United World Soviet whether he knows it—or wants to be—or not, and must therefore contribute to the general *human* welfare and obey the lawful orders of all duly constituted *human* authority."

Mr. Thoggosh waved a tentacle, preliminary to speaking. "Excuse me," Eichra Oren interrupted. He faced the KGB officer. "Mr. Empleado—Art—isn't this doctrine the basis for several violent disputes now taking place between the remaining nations of Earth?" Without waiting for an answer, he turned to the general. "Including the one, sir, that squandered the life of your eldest son not long ago?" In the embarrassed silence, someone hidden in the crowd laughed at the frustrated Empleado.

"*I might have anticipated this,*" sighed the Proprietor. "*I suppose it's best to initiate Eichra Oren's tenure with a declaration of his independence. As a p'Nan debt assessor, certified by the market he serves and the sword he carries, he's immune to the laws, customs, and authority of the American Soviet Socialist Republic, the Union of Soviet Socialist Republics, the United World Soviet, and both versions of the KGB. I assure you he comes well-equipped to enforce any status he wishes to claim in that regard.*"

"We'll see about that!" Empleado seized Eichra Oren's arm as his four enforcers elbowed their way through the crowd. It was a mistake. Empleado, a perplexed look on his face, discovered he was holding his own arm instead of Eichra

Oren's. The latter had tossed his case to Reille y Sanchez, who caught it automatically. Something heavy rattled inside.

Noncombatants, including Empleado, evaporated from beneath the wing. Broward Hake aimed broad, hardened knuckles at the side of the stranger's head, only to find his best punch captured in the man's left hand, where it landed without a sound. At the same time, Delbert Roo launched a back-kick at Eichra Oren's kidney. It arrived in the man's other cupped palm. Eichra Oren spread his arms wide, as if to fling the unwanted energy away, tossing Roo and Hake a full dozen meters in different directions, where they landed, with a spectacular double splash, in the mud.

Eichra Oren was the most beautiful being Reille y Sanchez had ever seen. Despite his unnatural speed and power, the strange warrior wasn't exerting himself. He showed no sign of sweating, no shortness of breath, his hair hardly stirred from its well-combed place.

She wished Gutierrez would do something, but the general seemed to be watching the fight with personal interest. From the way he bobbed and grimaced, raising his own fists and muttering, it was plain he wasn't siding with Empleado's men. His son, Danny, was shouting openly, taking the same side as his father, as did Lieutenant Marna.

Mr. Thoggosh had allowed his separable tentacle to wander to the other side of the camp, where it climbed onto the wing of the *Wright,* perhaps affording him a better view. Aelbraugh Pritsch might have been expected to be fluttering nervously, exclaiming how dreadful it all was. Instead, the avian stood calm, his furled umbrella tucked beneath one winglike arm, as if the outcome were already certain. Anybody else's dog would be leaping, barking, joining the fight. Sam sat where he was, as calmly as Aelbraugh Pritsch, apparently watching the fight with intelligent interest.

Sebastiano grinned each time one of Empleado's four absorbed punishment. Empleado's face became grimmer with each setback his men suffered. Undismayed or unobservant, Roger Betal and Demene Wise closed in. There was a lot of yelling from the fighters who fancied themselves martial artists, mixed with grunts of exertion and occasional screams of pain. It was difficult to hear them above the yelling from the crowd.

"Go Meany!" she presumed was for Demene Wise. Someone chanted Hake's name over and over again. It didn't make a bad cheer, at that, even if it did sound a bit Orwellian. "Punch him, Roger, put his lights out!" "Sic him, Del!" seemed a bit more to the point, given what she knew of Delbert Roo. It was foolhardy to be standing anywhere near Corporal Owen. Eyes glued on the fighting men, he swung his massive fists in unconscious sympathy, jabbing and punching the air, endangering everyone within two meters of his reach.

A flurry of movement was hidden in a confusion of shoulders and elbows. Eichra Oren stepped back, having *braided* the fingers of one assailant. The victim stared at the bizarre result, an inescapable, anatomically impossible pattern, in dumb astonishment. Reille y Sanchez suspected it would require a surgeon's help to rearrange Betal's fingers.

Rosalind Nguyen had disappeared when the first blow was struck. Now she was back again, ducking through the crew hatch of the *Moynihan*, carrying the squarish zippered nylon container which served her as the black bag of medical tradition.

Almost as an afterthought, Eichra Oren disabled Wise with a feathery toe-brush to the knee, the crack of the broken joint echoing sickeningly through the camp. As earlier, at the sight of Kamanov's body, Pulaski ran behind one of the landing-gear assemblies to throw up.

That didn't end the matter. Hake and Roo were back in the fray, advancing on the investigator, short knives with blackened blades appearing like magic in their fists. Eichra Oren's response resembled dancing more than fighting. Each movement of their feet threw sprays of mud into the crowd. Each of them, except for Eichra Oren, was plastered with mud, soaked to the bone. Reille y Sanchez was fascinated, watching his undisturbed face and fathomless eyes, believing she saw the same frightening exultation she'd seen before, in the line of duty, among the outlawed and legendary *Penitentes* of her native Southwest. It was as if the lovely, lethal dance he performed were a religious exercise, putting him in touch with another reality. The lower half of Hake's face looked like a bloody ruin, but it was only his nose bleeding.

Or maybe it was something sickening, she thought with a shudder which surprised her. Maybe what moved him to ecstasy was the idea of hurting, of killing or being killed. This, too, she was familiar with, from the classrooms, training fields, and barracks where she'd obtained her own training. Then he laughed, shattering the illusion as he bobbed and whirled through stylized motions, keeping up a conversation with his opponents, too quiet for her to hear, as if instructing them. She shivered, clutching the leather case to her breasts, terrified and fascinated all at once. Perhaps that was exactly what he was doing.

Water streamed off the shuttles in a tangle of rivulets, creating treacherous miniature gulleys through which the men splashed and stumbled as they fought. Eichra Oren elbowed his first opponent, Hake, into semiconsciousness. Roo was faster and came closest to scoring a blow, almost landing a heel in Eichra Oren's solar plexus. It was hard to follow the movements of either man, so fast were they. Compared to the others, it was like watching the same tape at a different speed. The newcomer took a step back, leaned in, and gave Roo's forehead a tap of his finger. Roo dropped to the mud and lay still, although no more so than three-dozen horrified observers. As Eichra Oren turned his back, Hake, lying on his back in the mud, fumbled in his pocket and produced a gun, another of the little SD9s, minus silencer, like Richardson had carried. He raised it toward the investigator.

Reille y Sanchez almost tossed the case to Eichra Oren. "Don't!" he shouted, at Hake not her, a gleaming weapon of his own materializing in his hand. He hadn't even turned around to see Hake. Now he did.

"Watch!" He raised whatever he carried, no bigger than a .25 automatic, and pointed it between the *Moynihan* and the *Metzenbaum* at a hillock just outside the camp. With an odd, muffled explosion, brief-lived smoke blossomed at the muzzle. The hillock vanished with a louder noise and a more impressive explosion. Where it had been, there now lay a deep, elliptical trench, the size of a human grave, into which water from the camp was already beginning to drain. Hake's mouth hung open. Climbing painfully to his feet, he dropped his pistol into the mud beside him, where it was quickly retrieved by Sebastiano.

"The little one hurried me," Eichra Oren told the people around him, his eyes going to those of Reille y Sanchez. "I didn't have time to measure the stroke. I apologize for having been compelled to kill him."

From somewhere outside the camp, a shot rang like a thunderclap. Hake's arms stiffened and he collapsed again, face-first, legs crossed at the ankles, a ragged exit wound between his shoulder blades mingling carmine with the wet soil. The bullet had passed within a centimeter of Eichra Oren.

"A forty-one!" Sebastiano cried. Judging by the sound, Reille y Sanchez agreed with him.

"Richardson's still out there somewhere!" the general added. "Juan, pick three people and go after her—and don't forget to duck!"

XIV
Horn of Unicorn

Empleado refused to let them bury Hake and Roo in the hole Eichra Oren had blasted from the ground. Instead, a handful of unlucky noncoms was given the task of digging a double grave out of crumbling carbonaceous chondrite and sticky mud. In a way, they were lucky—the rain had stopped. However the sky was beginning to dim; nightfall had come to 5023 Eris.

Reille y Sanchez had just returned from a long, fruitless couple of hours searching for Richardson. The first shift, just before hers, had discovered a spent cartridge case, .41x22m/m, in the trees close to the camp, but no trace of the missing woman. By the time the newly fledged KGB colonel was back from what she increasingly regarded as a futile expenditure of manpower, Dr. Nguyen had repaired Demene Wise's shattered knee as best she could.

It had been a bloody mess in the most literal sense. The physician had spent the same two hours picking bone splinters from the wound before calling for sutures and bandages. How Pulaski was able to assist her without getting sick was a mystery. The joint would never be the same, that being the way of knees, but in his own way, Wise was lucky, too. In this gravity he'd be ambulatory long before a similar recovery would have been possible on Earth. Eichra Oren would soon have to begin watching his back.

At least the so-called *p'Nan* debt assessor had saved Dr. Nguyen the time and energy involved in healing Roger Betal's "injury," which energy, given present technology and the minimal resources available, might otherwise have been as badly wasted as in the search for Richardson. Reille y Sanchez had watched Eichra Oren before returning what she presumed was his cased sword and leaving on her hopeless quest. He'd squatted beside the man, still conscious but far gone in shock and pain. Eichra Oren's ecstatic concentration had returned for a moment. Placing his hands over Betal's, he'd moved them in a complex pattern impossible for the eye to follow, as if casting a spell. When he lifted them, Betal's fingers had unlaced from one another. The KGB bully had sighed, a look of beatific gratitude on his face, and passed out.

Now Eichra Oren had a friend for life—and a couple of problems. Wise, despite his name, was too stupid to learn from experience, however painful. He'd pursue the man who'd crippled him, not giving up this side of the grave, probably his own. Betal, however, was a classic authoritarian: once beaten properly, he'd be loyal forever. On second thought, she grinned to herself, maybe Eichra Oren's problems were self-cancelling.

After changing to fresh clothes aboard the *Moynihan*—Richardson's, even the rank tabs were right—for the second time that day, she found him sitting among empty crates under the starboard wing of the *Metzenbaum*, drinking coffee with the doctor, who rose and left them, making noises about checking on her patients. The mysterious case lay across his legs. Sam, at his knee, grinned up at her, but his expression, like a dolphin's, seemed a permanent feature. The man lifted a thermos bottle. "Home is the hunter, and my fellow—or is it competitive?—investigator. Would you like some coffee?"

She smiled, taking a small crate on the opposite side of a large crate from his own. "Nothing I'd like better. This is comfortable, like a sidewalk cafe, complete with a billion-dollar aluminum-graphite awning. Let's leave it 'fellow investigator' as long as we can, shall we? Is your combat technique something special, or can anybody do it where you're from?"

"Wherever that is," he poured coffee for her into a paper cup, voicing her unspoken thought, "because God, or someone more acceptably Marxist, forbid that there may be more at home like me?"

She took a sip. "Look, Eichra Oren, I don't care if you agree with your boss's condescendingly negative opinion of Marxism or not. I'm just trying to have a nice, polite, diplomatic conversation—"

"At the same time obtaining whatever data you can persuade me to part with?" He leaned against the tire of the shuttle, shifted the leather case, and crossed his legs at the ankles (it was like watching a cat stretch, she thought), grinning as he looked her over from beneath annoyingly raised eyebrows. "Fair enough, fair Colonel, if you return the favor. What would you like to know? The gun I carry is fusion-powered—you'd call it a 'steam pistol'—with coaxial laser sights. Its power plant's about the size of a thimble, far beyond any current Soviet or American capability, and would serve the energy needs of all three of your spacecraft for a—"

She shook her head. Being a trained and experienced warrior herself, she was fascinated, astonished, by virtually every aspect of the man's appearance on 5023 Eris, but, at least for now, she'd leave the engineering questions to somebody else. "I know something about martial arts. Did you kill Roo by projecting your *ki* into him?"

"Nothing so romantic," he laughed, "just plain old hydrostatic shock."

More engineering. She knew this was a phenomenon associated with high-velocity bullets. "What I really wondered, is it something specially devised with the help of the Elders? They're so advanced—''

Eichra Oren laughed again, not in an unkindly way. He did that a lot, she realized, the same open, unguarded laughter as during the fight. For some reason she found it more terrifying than the even greater mysteries he represented. "Art's pathetic leg-breakers," he explained, "were doomed the moment they initiated force against me, Estrellita. Once committed, the poor devils never stood a chance."

"But they—''

"I know how they're carried on your expedition roster. Wise is supposedly a mining technician, Betal a structural engineer. Hake and Roo were agricultural equipment operators."

From the beginning, like everyone else, Reille y Sanchez had known the four worked for Empleado. In fact they were—had been—exactly what they seemed to be, even to someone as naive as Pulaski: tough, highly trained KGB enforcement agents.

"Their failure was by no means their fault," Eichra Oren went on, "this I swear to you." By now, the strange exultation she'd twice seen in his eyes seemed to have faded altogether. In her judgment, he seemed apologetic, ashamed of himself, of the amazing things he'd done—four to one, two armed with knives—afraid the survivors might be punished on his account. "Nor the fault of those—the Union of Soviet Socialist Republics, isn't it, or is it still sometimes called Russia?—who trained them."

She managed to summon up an official KGB frown far sterner than she actually felt. "What do you mean?"

"Their school of martial arts is simply more primitive than mine."

"How much''—she thought of the five hundred thousand millennia the nautiloid culture had existed—"more primitive?"

"Give or take a century or two, maybe fifteen thousand years. Like the Aztecs fighting your *Spetznaz*—did I say that right?—instead of Hernán Cortés. Only much worse."

They sat for a long moment in silence.

"Just who are you, anyway, Eichra Oren?" she demanded, reflecting on his weird talent and what kept striking her as the impossibility of his existence. "A whole lot more important from a strategic and tactical viewpoint, where the hell did you come from, all of a sudden?"

He spread his hands in a half-shrug, opening his mouth to speak.

"While I'm indulging myself," she interrupted, "asking questions that'll never be answered, what are the Elders searching for on Eris?" With a chill running up her spine, she realized she'd been saving the most frightening question for last. "What sort of terrible thing is it that an advanced people like the Elders need so desperately?"

"On our first date?" He took case in hand and arose from the crate he was sitting on. "My dear Colonel, I'm shocked. But I'll tell you what: I'm overdue to check in with the entity you call my boss. Until I do, believe it or not, I won't know a great deal more about all of this than you do. I'll leave Sam with you. Maybe he can answer some of your questions. All except that last one, that's—what's the expression?—'classified.' You're right, you'll probably never know the answer. Sam, remember you're with a lady and on your best behavior." With that, Eichra Oren turned and strode away from the shuttle, out into the jungle, and was gone.

"My first act as a KGB agent." She put her elbows on the makeshift table, chin in hands, glaring at the animal as it sat with its tongue hanging out through an idiot grin. "Interrogating a furry ventriloquist's dummy!"

The dog turned his head toward her. "Estrellita, I'll be nice if you will. That's what he meant, 'best behavior.' He always accuses me of being a wise guy, if that's the idiom. Me, I think my sense of humor's fifteen thousand years more advanced than his, give or take a century or two."

"So you *can* talk!" She glanced around, remembering the relay carried by Semlohcolresh's separable tentacle and suspecting some kind of practical joke. On the other hand, how reasonable was the idea of a giant squid running this entire show? By comparison, a talking dog seemed downright mundane.

"No," Sam replied, "it's your imagination. The strain you're under. You're cracking up."

"That I can believe." Coming to a decision, she stood. "But

cracking up or not, he said you'd answer my questions. Only let's take a walk, so I can enjoy my schizophrenia in privacy." They followed the route Eichra Oren had, slipping between two shuttles—she checked the contents of the chamber and magazine of her CZ99A1, mindful of another colonel whose uniform she wore—far enough into the trees so that she could still see by the half dozen lights Sebastiano had strung around the camp. "Wise guy's the correct idiom," she told the dog when they were out of human earshot, "although it's a bit dated. Your English is actually very good. So is Eichra Oren's. He also knows a lot about Earth's current and not-so-current history."

"Why shouldn't he?" Sam asked. "That's where he comes from. So do I."

Reille y Sanchez found a spot at the base of one of the giant growths where the ground was relatively dry despite the recent rain. She kept her pistol in her lap. "Yes, but what I've learned here, so far—almost the only thing I've learned—is that there's Earth and then again there's Earth. Which version are you and Eichra Oren from?"

Sam stretched and lay down on the ground. "That's an assumption, isn't it, that he and I are from the same Earth? You don't know, Estrellita, maybe I'm from the Planet of the Dogs."

She chuckled. "Like Aelbraugh Pritsch is from the Planet of the Birds?"

"Bird*brains*," he corrected, "and you're from the Planet of the Apes. But no, in this case your assumption's correct. It's an Earth where, for uncounted millennia, no sapient (including Eichra Oren, although I seem to be the cynical and worldly member of the firm) has ever known domination by, or of, another sapient. That's what scares you about him, Estrellita."

"What?"

"Didn't think I'd noticed, did you? I'm a dog, remember? I can smell fear. It smells like shit. You're frightened whenever he laughs. But, speaking of shit, with your political education, you've no way of realizing that it's merely the uncalculated laughter of a free individual, something you've never had a chance to see. Or be."

"There's a much simpler explanation than that, Sam." She took a deep breath. "Shit's all I seem to be wading through on my way to the truth. 'Uncounted millennia,' you say. Eichra Oren says 'fifteen thousand years.' On my Earth, fifteen thousand years ago, people were pretty much limited to stone knives and bear skins. What makes your Earth so different?"

Sam took several moments to answer. Deeper among the trees, Reille y Sanchez thought she saw fireflies winking. "Look," he told her, "suppose one of your space shuttles accidentally landed on some primitive island where people are *still* limited to stone knives and bear skins. There are places like that on your Earth, aren't there?"

She nodded. "I suppose so. Jungles in New Guinea, maybe."

"All right, now suppose for some reason you had to explain fully and accurately where you'd come from and how you'd gotten there. The natives' view of the universe revolves around magic and mythology. It doesn't include things like science or spaceflight. They don't even know the world is round. You'd have to do a lot of preliminary educating before you got around to things like airfoils and rocket engines, wouldn't you?"

"Yes, you would." She frowned. "What're you driving at, Sam?"

"New Guinea primitives mightn't like what you tell them. They might get scared and burn you at the stake or shrink your head or something. I'm trying to warn you, Estrellita, that a full and accurate understanding of, well, of Eichra Oren's origin, or mine, requires that you unlearn a lot that's taken for granted—mistakenly—by your own civilization."

This time it was her turn for a long, thoughtful pause. *I'm having this conversation,* she told herself again, *with a big white shaggy animal.* "Sam, I've been trying to cut down on burning people—and dogs—at the stake. It causes cancer. And I've given up shrinking heads for Lent. Will you please tell me what this is leading up to?"

"Simply that Eichra Oren's the descendent of an ancient civilization."

"That much I've managed to gather on my own, thank you."

Sam sat up. "Yes? Well, it's a civilization which existed on your very own alternate version of Earth, Estrellita. By a long, indirect route, he and I come from exactly the same place you do. Unfortunately, it happens to be a civilization none of your historians have ever heard of, one your archaeologists would maintain never existed.'' Observing her confused expression, he added, ''Any questions, so far?''

''Sure. Lots. At the moment, I find the most important is this one: is it at all intelligent to believe any of this nonsense you're telling me? Let me rephrase that: how can a person distinguish intellectual flexibility from foolish gullibility?''

''Between having an open mind and holes in your head?'' he asked. ''In my off moments, I've often pondered that never-ending conflict myself.''

She grinned at the dog and started, from reflex, to reach down and pat him on the head, stopping herself only at the last moment. ''Most of all,'' she told him, ''I wonder about myself, my own potential for both of those attributes. Would I have believed Galileo, for instance, when he told me what he'd just seen through his telescope? Or how about William Harvey, claiming that the heart's merely a mechanical pump?''

''Or whoever it was in your culture,'' Sam suggested, ''who discovered that most human evils are caused by invisible plant life?''

''Louis Pasteur,'' she nodded. ''On the other hand, would I have been able to spot Piltdown man or the Giant of Cardiff as hoaxes, or would I have been taken in, along with the rest of the crowd? Would I have dismissed truly revolutionary and valuable information as . . . as—''

''Having been decanted from a cracked pot?''

''Pretty good, Sam. You know, I remember reading somewhere that Sir Isaac Newton believed in astrology and numerology. He once conducted 'scientific' experiments with what he thought was the powder of ground unicorn horn. What was it you said? An Earth where, for uncounted millennia, no sapient being has dominated, or been dominated by, another sapient being? And you're right, it does scare me. It also sounds a lot like powdered horn of unicorn.''

''There's your answer, Estrellita, don't believe me. See for yourself." He reached up with a hind foot, scratched behind one ear, and Reille y Sanchez was reminded all over again what sort of creature she was discussing politics with. "Excuse me, you came to the right place for it."

"Well," she answered, giving it visible consideration. She'd meant her remark about unicorn horn, but maybe this was a way to draw him out. "I haven't seen any evidence of military discipline among the Proprietor's people—so many different weird and wonderful creatures. They don't seem to display anything resembling the legendary capitalist corporate loyalty. As far as I can tell, there isn't any clear-cut hierarchy of authority, no official table of organization, not even much of the minimal social pecking order I'd expect to see among intelligent and competitive beings."

"No distemper, worms, or rabies, either."

"Have it your way. Obviously you and Eichra Oren share the Elders' peculiar philosophy. Or is that an assumption, too? But it also means you're sitting ducks—you know that idiom?—for anybody better organized. You have no sense of internal security, no solidarity which would tend to protect you or your company secrets."

"Right again, Estrellita, try it for yourself. Within the bounds of whatever they regard as personal integrity, none of the Elders, nor any of their many associated species, will demonstrate even the slightest reluctance to tell you anything and everything you want to know."

She shifted the CZ99A1 in her lap, then discovered that some ground dampness was beginning to creep through her clothing after all, but decided to stick it out for a few more minutes. "The single exception being the precise reason or reason for their presence on the asteroid to begin with, apparently at the order or suggestion or request, I can't tell which, of the one identifiable authority figure, the so-called Proprietor."

"The big fat bum."

She leaned forward, concentrating. "And even that secret, I'm inclined to agree with General Gutierrez, seems to have religious undertones about it which make me doubt the value of ferreting it out."

"Didn't one of your own greatest philosophers once observe that one man's theology is another man's belly laugh?"

"Wait a minute"—she held up a hand—"let me think. I'll make a bet with you, Sam. If the people here turn out to be anything, it'll be *too* goddamned cooperative, won't it? As the expedition's—and my Earth's—official investigator, I'll find myself in the worst imaginable position, inundated with more information than I can possibly evaluate. That kind of generosity might be a pretty clever tactic in itself, mightn't it?"

Sam grinned and wagged his tail. "You say that with what sounds like a certain amount of grudging admiration."

"It's true," she replied distractedly, still thinking, then shifted her focus back to the here and now. "But it's also true that I pride myself on being a practical, efficient type at heart, afflicted with very little unbridled imagination or useless curiosity." She leaned back against the tree.

"Anyway," he suggested, "that's what you've always wanted to believe about yourself."

"Sam! I thought you were going to be nice if I was."

"A point, Estrellita, but I can smell other things besides fear, you know. Intelligence. Curiosity. Imagination. They smell nice. You reek of them, if you don't mind my saying so."

She crossed her arms. "That's a hell of a compliment. I'll just have to take immediate and stern measures to control them."

"Do that, Estrellita, it'll be interesting to watch. I'll—" He lifted his head, ears perked rigid. "But you'll have to excuse me, I'm being paged. 'His master's voice' and all that. Can you find your way back?"

"Thanks, I'm a sapient, too, you know." A bit stiff from dampness, she climbed to her feet. He grinned, turned, and ran off into the jungle.

But not very sapient, she thought. *I hardly found out anything I wanted to know, especially about where Eichra Oren came from.* Shrugging to herself, always the practical, efficient type, she simply added the task of discovering more about the mystery man to a long list of other chores she saw, in her incurious, unimaginative way, looming ahead of her.

XV
Empty Millennia

To sleep, perchance not to dream—if she was lucky.

Now, in Vivian Richardson's continuing absence, Reille y Sanchez, the expedition's newest second-highest-ranking officer, remembered that she rated a better place to toss and turn, a folding cot and sleeping bag—one of three available—in the relative privacy and luxury of the crew deck, aboard either the *Moynihan* or the *Metzenbaum*.

After being outdoors so much the last couple of days, her skin crawled at thought of the alternative. For most of the past year, eight hours a "day," she'd occupied twenty-five vertical centimeters between folding bunks arranged in two stacks of six in the cargo bay insert inboard the former vessel. Even as she strode alone through the trees on her way back to the camp, the idea of wedging herself once again into such confinement, of breathing air exhaled by others, of smelling their smells, gave her a feeling of suffocation.

Entering the lighted area around the shuttles, she brightened in more than a literal sense at a third possibility. She could follow the example of many of the crew who'd scrounged blankets and bags and were sleeping under the wings and hulls of the spacecraft. The idea appealed to her. She'd gotten almost nothing in the way of rest during the previous period of darkness, with Semlohcolresh's unexpected visit to the camp and the subsequent flap over the disappearance of the expedition's second in command. A few minutes, here and there, was all she'd had, sitting propped against the tanden-tired nose gear of the *Wright*, CZ99A1 in hand.

Glancing down now at the same kilo of Czechoslovakian steel and plastic hanging in her numb and aching fingers, she smiled sheepishly to herself. She was exhausted and becoming careless, forgetful. She slid the weapon into its holster, fastening the flap. At that, she thought, it hadn't been bad last night, all things considered, particularly the three-hundred-odd worse nights which had preceded it. It was warm enough outside that she shouldn't need much in the way of bedding. Maybe she could still find something fresh in the *Moynihan*'s emergency stores.

After a brief search, equipped with a lightweight silver and red plastic "space blanket" and a cup of tea courtesy of Corporal Owen's welding torch, Reille y Sanchez settled in under what was being called the "girl's wing" of the flagship, between Marna and Pulaski. She was too worn out for any more conversation and grateful that both young women were already sound asleep (the latter, she observed, with her thumb in her mouth again, as had been her unconscious habit throughout most of the journey to the asteroid). As tired as Reille y Sanchez was, disturbing thoughts and vivid images kept circling inside her head. Her mind wouldn't shut itself off.

Among other things, until now, she hadn't really had time to feel the full loss of Piotr Kamanov. For most of her life, all of the people around her had been just like she was: sober, literal-minded, duty-oriented. She'd never met a man quite like the geologist, who seemed to live life simply for the fun of it. She knew now that she'd miss him very badly, his silly joking, his habit of collecting and redistributing strange stories and ideas, his astonishing lack of respect for authority and established wisdom.

Most of all, she couldn't get the Russian's stupid, senseless murder out of her troubled mind, the horrifying sight of him, silent and slack-faced for the first time since she'd met him. She could think of a hundred individuals for whom the world would have been better off, had they died in his place. Now more than ever she understood that the general was right. The solution to their bizarre situation—to her own in particular—lay in somehow learning to think the way Kamanov had.

But Reille y Sanchez was a soldier. This sort of morbid preoccupation was unusual for the no-nonsense, action-oriented Marine officer, and she knew it. Finishing her tea, Reille y

Sanchez set the cup aside, along with what she realized (with a small start of surprise) was her grieving. Likewise, she temporarily abandoned the speculation over the reliability of Sam and Eichra Oren which had filled her mind before these thoughts of Kamanov had intruded, and simply promised herself that she'd try her best to evaluate the amazing information they'd given her as objectively as she could—tomorrow.

"Colonel?"

In a shorter time than seemed possible, the butterscotch-colored light of day had returned to the human encampment and sought out Reille y Sanchez where she lay, sweating under her plastic blanket, twitching occasionally in her sleep and mumbling to herself.

"Pulaski?" Blinking, Reille y Sanchez sat up, stiff and sore in every muscle, her mouth tasting like her idea of some nameless, ancient evil. Her right hip seemed particularly painful, as if she'd slept on a big rock. Pushing the blanket aside, she discovered that she'd fallen asleep still wearing her knife-and-pistol belt.

"Yes, ma'am. It's 0600, as near as anybody can figure, and I wondered if you'd like some coffee." The sergeant held a steaming cup under her nose, constructed neither of paper nor plastic, but of something somewhere between metal and ceramic, another gift from the strangely generous creatures Washington wanted them to fight a war with. The colonel's initial nausea at the aroma was immediately smothered by a wave of irresistible craving. She took a sip and swallowed.

"Thanks, Toya, stick around. You're just the person I wanted to see."

"Me, Colonel?"

Reille y Sanchez struggled to her feet, brushing at her uniform with one hand while she held onto her cup with the other. "No, Pulaski, me colonel, you sergeant." She grinned self-consciously. It wasn't as bad as one of Kamanov's, but at least she was trying. "Get yourself some coffee, if you want, while I go inside for PTA drill." She watched the girl blush, as she always did, at the figure of speech, peculiar to the female Marine Corps, which stood for those parts of her anatomy she intended giving a cursory rinse. The A stood for armpits. "We're going to talk over all these ancient matters you're supposed to know so much about."

Pulaski actually threw her a salute. "Yes, ma'am."

Minutes later, they were sitting back outdoors in sunshine which came, surprisingly strong, through the asteroid canopy. For a bench, Pulaski had commandeered a fair-sized log, fated for this evening's fire. They were somewhat startled to be watching their commander, stripped to the waist and sweating, laboriously cutting kindling with the almost useless saw-toothed back of a big hollow-handled knife exactly like the one Reille y Sanchez carried.

Adversity must be good for some people, Reille y Sanchez thought. The man seemed a lot less flabby than she recalled from their prevoyage physical training. Brigadier General Gutierrez was being assisted by Second Lieutenant Gutierrez—if the younger man had been a Marine, he'd still be in the brig for losing his pistol to Richardson, but the AeroSpace Force was infamous for gentle discipline—the first time she'd ever seen them like this, father and son. It was a pleasant picture. For some reason, it made her want to cry.

"Let me see," declared the expedition's amateur paleontologist, answering the first question Reille y Sanchez had asked her, "I think the oldest known fully human remains are about a quarter of a million years old. They were discovered a long time ago, somewhere in the British Isles. I don't remember exactly where or when."

"Okay," the colonel nodded, "how about the oldest known civilization?"

"In what sense," Pulaski frowned, "do you mean 'civilization?' "

"I don't know, Toya, what do I mean?" *No 'ma'am' when answering questions in her field,* observed Reille y Sanchez, who hated the word, let alone being called by it. *I'll have to remember that.* "Houses, buildings, cities? Doesn't 'civilization' mean cities?"

Pulaski blinked. "The most ancient known cluster of habitations which might—generously—be called a city, are about eight thousand years old. They were located somewhere in the

Middle East, the so-called cradle of civilization, before that whole area got slagged.''

Reille y Sanchez reflected without self-pity that these were items she might have been required to learn about, if she'd led anything resembling a normal life, growing up. Instead, on the basis of aptitudes she'd unknowingly demonstrated in written and athletic tests at the age of eight or nine, she'd been selected for special attention, taken from her family—tearfully proud to let their daughter go—and enrolled in a strictly supervised Soviet-American training academy.

She and her school had been interested in preparing her for a career as an officer. At the time, she'd have regarded any other kind of knowledge as useless mental clutter, possibly of mild interest but essentially irrelevant. This had certainly included subjects like paleontology, archaeology, and all but military history. If she'd ever heard anything about it, she'd promptly forgotten it, having no way of knowing that such information might someday prove critical to survival, not to mention her career.

Later, of course, she'd done some casual reading, a paperback purchased at a train station or base exchange, shoved as an afterthought into a rucksack or overnight bag. The hurry-up-and-wait existence led by any professional soldier affords plenty of time for casual reading. A surprising number of thick-necked, dog-faced grunts of her own acquaintance might easily have qualified for doctorates, based on this sort of casually acquired information, if they'd given a damn, which they didn't. Now, thanks to Pulaski, who more or less fit into the same category, Reille y Sanchez had been furnished with new data and a few refreshed memories.

"Thanks, Toya, that's about what I thought. And now I wonder why it's never occurred to anyone to ask one simple, highly disturbing question."

"Colonel?"

Better than 'ma'am'. Come to think of it, a lot better. "Well, if the oldest known fully human remains are two hundred fifty thousand years old, and the oldest known civilization only about eight thousand, what, in the semisacred name of the martyred Geraldo Rivera was *Homo sapiens* doing with himself during the intervening two hundred forty-two thousand years?''

Pulaski had an odd, frightened expression on her face. ''I don't believe I follow you, ma'am.''

The colonel was too deep in concentration to be annoyed at this relapse. ''Sure you do, Toya, look: it required only eighty centuries for mankind to step from your sunbaked adobe villages somewhere in the Middle East to the crater-marked surface of the Moon, right?''

''Right—'' A dismayed look on the girl's face indicated the suspicion that, perhaps by some tricky, characteristically military twisting of logic, her answer might somehow get her into trouble. Reille y Sanchez knew from her own military experience that such a suspicion, although groundless on this occasion, was as soundly rooted in reality as the great trees surrounding the encampment. ''I mean, yes, Colonel.''

''Relax, Toya, and answer this: could it actually have taken poor old Homo sap all of the preceding two hundred forty-two millennia to claw his way up from animal subsistence on the blood-soaked veldt of Africa to the same damned adobe villages?''

''That's colorful, Colonel.'' The sergeant swallowed, still uncomfortable. ''But not very, um, scientific—I mean I don't believe I ever thought much about it before.''

Reille y Sanchez laughed. ''That's exactly what I was warned you'd say, as a representative of established science. Well, it occurred to me to ask that question, or rather, it was asked for me last night. And now, either I can't leave it alone, or it won't leave me alone. Could our species, the supposedly human race, possibly be as slow-witted as that empty, accusing quarter of a million years seems to imply?''

''I, er—'' Pulaski closed her mouth, thinking.

''If that were truly so, how could they have survived all of those long, danger-filled tens of thousands of years in tooth-and-nail competition with what would, by logical comparison, have been vastly more intelligent species, for instance, turtles, parakeets, garden snails—''

Pulaski giggled. ''And giant ground sloths?''

''I think, Toya''—Reille y Sanchez laughed again—''that you've got the idea. No matter how hard I try—no matter how much the contrary proposition flies in the face of accepted scientific evidence—I can't bring myself to believe we're that dumb. You know, I never thought of myself as an optimist regarding human nature, but there it is."

"There what is, Estrellita?" A shadow fell across the women. Gutierrez stood before them bare-chested, toweling himself off, his shirt still tucked in and hanging from the waist. Across the campsite, Danny was stacking kindling under a shuttle wingtip.

The colonel eyed the general's hands, covered with painful-looking blisters, broken and weeping. "I could be wrong," she mused. "Still, two hundred forty-two thousand years. What if people were doing anything more ambitious, anything nobler, with all that spare time?"

"Like what?" Pulaski asked.

"What are you two talking about?" demanded the general.

Pulaski looked up, visibly embarrassed by his naked, hairy torso, and even more, the colonel thought, by his not-unpleasant male-animal odor. "Anthropology, sir, and prehistory." Together, the women explained what they'd been discussing.

He nodded, folding his legs beneath him and sitting on the ground. "So the question before us is: what if people were accomplishing something all that time—besides bashing cave bears, saber-toothed tigers, and each other over the heads and subsisting as the fur-clad stone-tooled Alley Oops you see in museum dioramas? Well, what about it?"

Reille y Sanchez took up where she'd left off. "Okay, why is it archaeologists and paleontologists, even when they're violating all accepted academic precedent looking for it—"

"Which, for the most part," Pulaski interrupted, surprising even herself, "they're decidedly not—"

"Why can't they find any physical trace of it?" the colonel finished.

"For the excellent reason . . ." The general thrust his arms into the sleeves of his shirt, pulled it around his shoulders, and closed the zipper halfway. From the way his uniform hung, she guessed he was still carrying the weapons left behind by Kamanov and Richardson. ". . . that the poor, ignorant, tenured schmucks've been looking in all the wrong places!"

Reille y Sanchez opened her mouth. She closed it.

"Don't look surprised," he told her. "I've been doing some snooping on my own, as I said I would, among the asteroid's better-informed inhabitants. For instance, I had a long, interesting talk with Eichra Oren yesterday, while some of you were out looking for Vivian. Funny kind of investigator. He answers a lot more questions than he asks. He suggested they'd be better off—your archaeologists and paleontologists—if they'd drill for evidence of archaic civilizations beneath the South Polar ice cap. They might even find something rewarding by randomly dragging the bottom of the Indian Ocean."

"For what?" both women demanded of the man.

"For what, sir?" Pulaski added, after a moment, in a small voice.

Gutierrez grinned. "For physical evidence of prehistoric civilization which it appears Mother Nature—or maybe it was Auntie Evolution—once shoved off the edge of a continental shelf."

Pulaski began nodding, understanding something Reille y Sanchez hadn't caught yet. "Tens of thousands of years ago," the girl declared, staring off at the treetops as if she were talking to herself, "what we regard as our hospitable home continent of North America was every bit as uninhabitable as the surface of the Moon."

"The whole thing was covered," agreed Gutierrez, "from the Arctic Sea almost to the Gulf of Mexico, by an ice sheet—as hard as it may be to imagine it—three kilometers thick in places."

They're both right, the colonel realized, remembering colored maps and artists' renderings from science and geographic magazines which, long after she'd left the academy and its narrow concerns, had never failed to fascinate her. "The North and South Poles," she volunteered, "were in different places only a few thousand years ago."

The general clapped his palms together. "As usual—Son of a bitch, look at those blisters, will you? I didn't realize I'd done that! So much for healthy physical labor! I was about to say, you've hit the nail on the head, Estrellita. And at the same time—well, you tell it, Sergeant. About Antarctica during the same period. It's your hobby, after all." He stared down at his hands and shook his head.

Pulaski smiled a shy smile; the general, too, had made a friend. "Well, sir—ma'am—the fossil record demonstrates that today's ice-bound Antarctica was, by contrast, a dry, warm, heavily forested environment, even though, on all Earth, it's now the bleakest and most barren."

"Right." In his enthusiasm, the general couldn't resist interrupting. "At least according to Eichra Oren, it wasn't in the so-called Fertile Crescent of the Middle East that the human race built its first real civilizations. In a sense, if you believe him, that's where they were forced, later on, to begin climbing to the stars all over again."

"I don't know, sir, if it's smart to believe everything we're told." Again Reille y Sanchez faced the dilemma of open-mindedness and gullibility. "What you're saying, what Eichra Oren maintains, is that civilization began in Antarctica, the least hospitable—"

He nodded. "Back when it was fab. I don't know whether we can believe him either, Estrellita, but it's fascinating to think about. Everything about Mr. Thoggosh's new deputy seems mysterious and unbelievable. But Eichra Oren says his immediate ancestors once lived there."

"On that little frozen-over continent?"

"Not that little, really. And only recently frozen over. Soviet science states—correctly, according to Eichra Oren—that human beings first arose as a sapient species in nearby southern Africa. Somehow, some of them managed to cross the water and made history for thousands of years—history which would have been lost to us forever if we hadn't met Eichra Oren—and learned and grew as a people. Which accounts for at least a part of your missing two hundred forty-two thousand years, Estrellita. I gather these people spent a lot of it building themselves a fairly impressive civilization, in every way comparable to the civilization achieved, oh, say by our European ancestors during the early Industrial Revolution."

Pulaski looked concerned. "But what became of them, sir?"

"Well, Toya, in a sense, nothing. Here we are, aren't we?"

Reille y Sanchez shook her head. "You mean to say, sir, that these ancient people we're just hearing about for the first time happen to be our ancestors, too?"

He stood up, grunting just a little. "By a more indirect route than they're Eichra Oren's, yes. Our remote ancestors. Now, if you ladies will excuse me, I'm going to find a Band-Aid or twelve."

"Our remote ancestors," Toya sighed.

"From the Lost Continent," the colonel answered, "of Antarctica."

XVI
Method, Motive, Opportunity

"I'm sorry," the rubber flower told her, "Tl*m*nch*l is out of the office. "I'm Llessure Knarrfic, his, er—excuse me, please."

Reille y Sanchez wondered what this being had evolved from. Impossibly thin greenish fingers, six or seven to a hand (of which there were four), clattered over a circular keyboard set in the top of the desklike piece of furniture behind which the lower half of the peculiar sapient was hidden.

The "office" was a roofless cubicle she'd found after wandering a maze of similar corridors for what seemed hours. Overhead, a Fresnel lens two meters square focused the canopy's diffuse sunlight on the desk's occupant. Nearby, a humidifier hissed, adding to the tropical heat and moisture of what already seemed a greenhouse.

From the general's description, Reille y Sanchez had imagined something like a big talking sunflower with petals around a "have-a-nice-day" face. This thing looked more like a pale green chrysanthemum with a blossom larger than a soccer ball. No eyes or other features could be seen, nor could she tell where the being's clear, androgynous voice was coming from.

Beneath the blossom, a stalk or torso of the same color branched at intervals to produce the arms before it disappeared behind the desk. Now, symbols appeared on a screen no thicker than cardboard, standing at one end of that desk.

"There it is, according to this glossary of the human language, I'm Tl*m*nch*l's 'secretary' or 'receptionist.' Can I help you, Colonel Sanchez?"

This Tl*m*nch*l (at least it sounded like that to Reille y Sanchez) was one of the sea scorpions, sapient crustaceans brought here by the Elders. Decorative frames on every wall except the one which had dilated to admit her made the colonel suspect this creature or its boss, head of the 'giant bugs with guns,' perceived light in different frequencies than human beings. Significant areas of the pictures seemed an empty, dull gray.

"Reille y Sanchez," the colonel corrected, "mine works differently than most human names. There's really more than one human language. Ask Aelbraugh Pritsch, he speaks lovely Spanish. You can tell me where Tlumunchul is, or when he's likely to be back."

The chrysanthemum made a noise, clearing whatever it used for a throat. "That's Tl*m*nch*l, Colonel Reille y Sanchez. Most sapients find his name, along with the rest of his language—his species has only one—difficult to pronounce and won't even try. He's busy somewhere, doing something I'm not supposed to talk about with you newcomers—"

Reille y Sanchez nodded. "The Elders' mysterious search for whatever?"

"I'm afraid," Llessure Knarrfic replied, ignoring the remark, "I don't know when he'll be back. Would you care to leave a message?"

"Sure. I'd like to speak with Tlemenchel about Piotr Kamanov's death. He's the Proprietor's chief of security, therefore my 'opposite number.' He's also the first nonhuman I happened to see here. I've never investigated a murder before, and I'm trying to be methodical."

"That's Tl*m*nch*l, Colonel Reille y Sanchez. I'll give him the message. Will there be anything else?"

"I'll—hold on a minute, one more thing, if you don't

mind.'' Excusing herself, Reille y Sanchez walked around the desk. Tucked beneath it were two pairs of fairly ordinary legs and feet, fairly ordinary considering that she'd expected to see a pot full of dirt. ''That'll be all, thanks. I'm going to look up Aelbraugh Pritsch, and can be reached there, wherever 'there' is.''

''Oh, fudge,'' answered the flower. ''I'm afraid you'll be disappointed again. Aelbraugh Pritsch happens to be with Tl*m*nch*l, as we speak.''

Reille y Sanchez suppressed the first response that came to mind. ''I'm afraid 'oh fudge' doesn't say it. Surprise the next human you talk to: check your glossary under sexual intercourse and bodily elimination.''

''I will.'' The petals constituting Llessure Knarrfic's face seemed to spread. ''And thank you, Colonel Reille y Sanchez!''

''Don't mention it.'' She grinned, walked out through the wall, and stopped the next sapient she ran into.

By chance—or perhaps not—Tl*m*nch*l's office was near the infirmary (at least on the more-or-less random course Reille y Sanchez was following) where, it felt like such a long time ago, Kamanov had been taken for his shoulder injury. ''Ran into'' was more than a figure of speech. The ''walking quilt'' Gutierrez had told them of, who dispensed refreshments, came close to running the colonel over with its pushcart.

''Oops! Excuse me,'' were the colonel's first, reflexive words, ''I'm Estrellita Reille y Sanchez. Have you seen Aelbraugh Pritsch or Tliminchil around anywhere? I need to speak with one of them.''

''Greetings, Estrellita Reille y Sanchez, Colonel in Fullity of Kaygeebee, I have pleasure to be Remaulthiek and regret to inform you that both worthy sapients after whom you inquire— and it is pronounced Tl*m*nch*l—are at this time occupied in righteous and sacred undertakings which are not to be discussed with homosapienses. May I do something to recompense the debt of civilty which this may otherwise create between us? You would, perhaps, delight to ingest caffeine infusion and a doughnut?''

Reille y Sanchez smiled. It was difficult to dislike these beings, even when they looked like GI-issue mummy bags sealed in Saran Wrap. "Thanks—let me get this one straight . . . Remaulthiek?—the coffee smells wonderful, and I will have a doughnut. You haven't created any debt. If these were ordinary circumstances, I'd just mind my own business. But I need to talk to somebody among your people, the nonhomosapienses, who knows something."

Beside the cart, she watched Remaulthiek treat itself—herself, the general had decided—using a flexible corner of her blanket shape to dissolve a doughnut in a cup of coffee, sipping the mess through a large-caliber straw thrust through her protective wrapper. As with Llessure Knarrfic, there was no expressive face to go by, no familiar body language, but Remaulthiek seemed to be pondering the request.

"Something, if I may ask, about what, Estrellita Reille y Sanchez?"

"I had definite ideas about that, earlier," the colonel replied. "Detective-type questions about Semlohcolresh, Mr. Thoggosh, the Elders' culture in general. Now, I'd settle for practically anything. What have you got in mind?"

"Please, if you wish it, to follow me."

Disposing of the cup and leaving the cart, the entity waddled toward a corridor wall and through, the colonel following. As the wall closed behind them, they encountered an insectile being, perhaps one of the surgeons who'd worked on Kamanov. It stood as tall as Reille y Sanchez, and was different from the sea scorpions. For one thing, it wasn't wearing the transparent plastic affected by them and Remaulthiek. Instead, it wore a garment made of hundreds of centimeter-wide strips of fluorescent orange and green fabric. It seemed to be examining a sheaf of papers on a clipboard.

"Remaulthiek," it rasped, apparently making sound by rubbing vestigial wing cases together under its clothing, "you never sicken, nor are you easily injured. What service may I do you?"

"Dlee Raftan Saon," intoned the quilt-being, "though denied in kindness, I pay a debt of civilty. Estrellita Reille y Sanchez, in Kaygeebee Full Colonelness, wishes to ask, of somebody who knows something, detective-type questions about Semlohcolresh, Mr. Thoggosh, the Elders' culture, practically anything in general. Estrellita Reille y Sanchez, Dlee Raftan Saon, Restorer-of-Health, who knows much about many things.''

Reille y Sanchez put out a hand. "Thank you, Remaulthiek, and for the, er, caffeine infusion and doughnut.''

Remaulthiek bent a corner, touching her hand. "Welcome, Estrellita Reille y Sanchez. I have savored the sweet scent of your naming and return to my occupation." With that, she walked through the wall.

Through its tattered, dazzling attire, the insect extended a bristly limb which the colonel accepted without examining closely. "Sit, my dear, while I finish these confounded records. May I call you Estrellita? Then we'll sneak out of this sweetshop—correct?—for a bit and a bite of talk, or is it the other way round? No matter, tell me, this is your wish, to ask questions? It's difficult with Remaulthiek, her species communicates with pheromones and I've never quite trusted their translating software."

She sat, although she wasn't sure whether she'd chosen a tall bench or a low table. "You're actually speaking English, whereas Remaulthiek . . . how about Llessure Knarrfic, Tlomonchol's secretary, does it—''

"It's Tl*m*nch*l, Estrellita, and *she*. Llessure Knarrfic's quite as irresistibly feminine, in her specific way—that's a pun—as your charming self. There are many differing theories on the evolution of sapience. One I agree with claims it's impossible in life-forms not divided into genders. I might add, it wouldn't be much fun." The physician flipped papers back over the clipboard and set it on another piece of furniture. "I happen to be male, and of so remarkably advanced an age that my enthusiastic interest in the opposite sex is seldom taken seriously by females of my species until it's too late for the little darlings. Shall we go to lunch?"

With the colonel hanging dubiously on one of his four available arms, they strolled down the corridor, entering what she guessed was a cafeteria. Around the walls of an area large enough for basketball, she saw waist-high counters heaped with steaming dishes, dishes at room temperature, dishes on ice. Much of what was offered looked and smelled appealing after shipboard rations. Other selections, those still squirming in their stainless warmers, made her want to run to the nearest bathroom (God alone knew what *that* was like) with both hands over her mouth.

"I didn't realize," exclaimed the doctor, noting her reaction, "this would be an ordeal. A moment's thought—here, find us an isolated table. Having treated one of your species, I've an idea of your requirements and can guess your preferences." He gave her arm a pat. "Perhaps by the window?"

Gulping her revulsion, she set a course for the indicated spot, closed her eyes, navigated by memory through a gauntlet of occupied tables laden with stuff which set her stomach churning. Like any place where hundreds gathered to eat together, the room was filled with chatter. Like any place where those hundreds were all foreigners, it consisted of incomprehensible gabble. Here, where Reille y Sanchez was the only human, the whooping, screeching, and buzzing of the dozens of life-forms around her made it sound like a weird combination of cabinet factory and sheet-metal shop, set in the middle of a jungle (which it was) populated by noisy insects and tropical birds. The table she chose had potted ferns on either side, sparing her further visual unpleasantness. She thanked whoever had designed the ventilation system that she couldn't smell most of what the others here seemed to be enjoying.

"You haven't found a seat." Dlee Raftan Saon arrived at her heels with a tray. "Don't you know how?" He set tray on table, eliciting a pinging noise. "Dlee Saon," he told it. "Reille y Sanchez." Chairs sprouted, one obviously for human use, the other an uncomfortable-looking rack resembling an upside-down director's chair. The table chimed until he fed it copper-colored coins.

Hitching her weapons belt, she sat. "Dlee—Doctor, I can't let you pay for lunch! Especially since I probably won't be able to eat it."

"Come, Estrellita, I know you haven't any money. You repay me with your delectable presence." Arranging himself on his rack, he slid the tray toward her. "See what I've chosen: uncooked greens in sweet, savory sauce. Muscle protein from an herbivorous animal, minced, boiled in its own lipids until uniform in color and texture. Ground graminid kernels, leavened, heated until brown. Sliced tubers, also boiled in lipids, lightly salted. Coffee, seldom a wrong guess for any sapient. A bit short on certain essentials, but no one meal accomplishes everything. How have I done?''

She laughed, suddenly hungry. ''Salad, hamburger complete with bun, and fries? Doc, pass the ketchup. What're you having, ants? I haven't had any ants since survival school. I wonder what Tlamanchal's secretary over there is eating. And don't bother, I know I can't pronounce it.''

''That's twice you've said that, Estrellita.'' His blue-green faceted eyes glittered in his heart-shaped, toast-colored face. She thought he looked like a mantis, although the swell of the skull (did insects have skulls?) behind his eyes was enormous. Hands at the ends of two-elbowed arms were like the armored gloves of a knight. The vestigial wings she'd guessed at lay under strips of colored cloth at the back of his neck, no bigger than the silver dollars her mother had once hidden under the basement floor. His antennae, jointed like a goosenecked lamp, made him look like a cartoon bug. ''Must be something amiss with Knarrfic's software, too. She isn't Tl*m*nch*l's secretary, but his employer, under contract to Mr. Thoggosh.''

''That makes me feel better.'' She tried a bit of the burger. It tasted more like lamb than beef, and was delicious. More than that, she didn't want to know. ''The only two nonhuman females I've met here, so far, and both of them menials? That doesn't speak well—''

Dlee Raftan Saon looked up from his food, live insects in a bowl with slick, in-tilted sides so they couldn't get out onto the table. A utensil in one hand was a spoon with a lid like a beer stein. Another was a miniature whisk broom. ''My dear, you're mistaken. Remaulthiek's a wealthy being. Long ago, she did a great wrong by our standards, I don't know what. It was the decision of the debt assessor she engaged that she succor, not those who become ill or injured, but those who love them and wait in anguish to hear their fate. She comes to this asteroid for the same reason we all have, as Mr. Thoggosh's employees, investors, or both. Unlike most of us, she brings with her the necessity to pay the moral debt she incurred.'' He took a sip of coffee. "There are others you may consult about such matters. I'm best qualified to advise you on biology. How may I help?"

"Just being here with you"—she blinked at the change of subjects—"adds to my knowledge. There's a basic logic to investigation, the discovery of 'method, motive, and opportunity,' but here that isn't enough. I don't know what motivates nonhumans. I need to know more about the Elders, physical facts, as you say. And maybe I can pick up pointers from this—debt assessor?—Eichra Oren, if you tell me about the way he works. He's no doubt adding to his knowledge of my culture as we speak."

"I see." He sat a while, thinking. Reille y Sanchez paid attention to her lunch. "To begin with your first question, our esteemed benefactors are water-breathing creatures."

She nodded. "Although they're capable, in certain circumstances, of existing in the same environment as land sapients."

"For limited periods of time," Dlee Raftan Saon agreed, "and primarily by virtue of the almost nonexistent gravity on this asteroid, which makes up for a lack of bouyancy. In the water, you know, they can fill those awkward shells of theirs with air, rising and falling like . . . like—"

"Like submarines?" She raised her eyebrows.

"They propel themselves at great velocities, like submarines, employing respiratory siphons like the nonsapient octopi you know. By contrast, on land, in full gravity, their shells weigh hundreds, sometimes even thousands of—I don't recall the name of your unit of measure."

Reille y Sanchez swallowed coffee. "Kilograms. Or pounds."

"Depending on their age," he finished, "for they continue growing all their lives. That may be one reason they live so long."

She wanted to ask how long, but stuck to immediate business. "I've noticed that, exposed to air, like other aquatic species here, they wear a kind of space suit, practically invisible, which, I suppose, in addition to supplying breathable liquid, keeps their gills and other tissues moist. But I also know that, on some occasions, simply sitting in shallow water, out of direct sunlight, and splashing their gills seems to be sufficient."

Dlee Raftan Saon pushed his bowl aside, pouring coffee for

both of them from a carafe. "In his personal quarters, Mr. Thoggosh compromises all these possibilities, steeping himself in an oxygenated chemical which air-breathers like ourselves are able to survive in, although they may not like it much."

"General Gutierrez took a swim with Mr. Thoggosh the first day we were here." She grinned. "It sounded like quite an experience."

"It's an expensive, somewhat experimental medium. Mr. Thoggosh's use of the substance identifies him as progressive and forward-thinking. The fact is, he's one of the most radical individuals among the Elders."

"None of us," the colonel replied, "had enough data to appreciate that."

He leaned toward her. "We've been studying your species—are you going to finish your tubers?—a popular form of entertainment. As our computers sort your broadcasts, we've been catching up on thousands of years of history, one thrilling episode after another. I can tell you Mr. Thoggosh is like your early aviation pioneers, radio tinkerers, women's suffragists. If it's new, he's interested. Semlohcolresh is more representative of Elders in general, which is why this asteroid venture is Mr. Thoggosh's enterprise, not theirs. His enthusiasms invariably prove profitable."

"He's"—she searched for the hated epithet—"an entrepreneur?"

"Yes. For example, that chemical stuff makes it possible for members of more than one species to meet face-to-face, something he finds essential. It accounts, in part, for many of his past competitive—"

"*Aha, Dlee Raftan Saon, I might have known! Colonel, here you are!*" She turned toward a voice she recognized. What she saw was a tentacle wheeling toward them on a metal contrivance, like a snake on a bicycle. "*I heard you seek my friend, Tulominchel—confound it, I'll never be able to pronounce his name—and my assistant. They're occupied, as indeed I am, but perhaps this surrogate will do. May it join you?*"

XVII
The Lost Continent

"Just in time," Dlee Raftan Saon exclaimed. "Estrellita asks after the biology of your species, with an eye toward learning what constitutes a motive for murder among the Elders."

The limb wheeled to the table, taking a position between them. *"Aside from wealth,"* it asked, *"the universal motive? I'll be of what assistance I can, Raftan. What would you like to know, Colonel?"*

She shook her head. "I'm poking around at random, satisfying personal curiosity. Biology seemed the best place to start. You might tell me more about the nautiloid separable tentacle."

"As you wish, Colonel." The extension of Mr. Thoggosh made up and down motions at its small end, nodding, as it explained unabashedly, *"In primitive species of cephalopods, it was a sexual organ, which swam away from the male, carrying sperm to the female."*

"This, too," added Dlee Raftan Saon, "is true of species familiar to humans. The 'Stone Age' precursors of Mr. Thoggosh's people, for some reason, altered their sexual practices rather late in evolutionary history—"

"Doctor, I—"

"Precisely," Mr. Thoggosh pointed out, *"as happened with the ancestors of human beings. Shortly after being driven out of increasingly scarce trees by bigger and stronger monkeys, in an Africa going through a prolonged drought cycle, they, too, switched, from rear to frontal—"*

"Mr. Thoggosh, I—"

"You're discomfited, Colonel, yet you did ask. But then

your species is rather easily embarrassed. Your own Mark Twain observed that you're the only organisms who blush—or need to. Or was it H. L. Mencken? Do I fail to employ the language with sufficient clinical detachment?''

"You're both doing fine." She rubbed her hands over her face. "It's just me, too many surprises, too close together. Please go on."

"Very well," replied the physician, pouring himself more coffee. "With both prehumans and their molluscan equivalent, this small change caused greater changes, behavioral and physical, either accelerating development of speech in both species or being greatly influenced by it."

"Students of evolution," the tentacle offered, *"have never been entirely certain which. Raftan, I wish I'd attended this lecture in person. That coffee smells good."*

The doctor nodded. "Next time, you'll know better." He turned to Reille y Sanchez. "It's one of those lizard-and-egg things, Estrellita, impossible to say which came first. The result was the same in both instances. Intimate personal relations became, well, more intimate and personal, because they became more verbal. Thus, with the ancestors of the Elders, the sperm-bearing tentacle became an evolutionary redundancy."

"As you see"—the tentacle gave a ripple, showing itself off, a display that struck her as somewhat obscene, considering the topic—*"it didn't atrophy away. Evolution's conservative. Instead, it underwent metamorphosis, changing relatively quickly— in the geological scheme of things."*

"By stages," explained Dlee Raftan Saon, "it became a remote-controlled general-purpose manipulator. Needing something to be controlled by, its existence encouraged the evolution of greater intelligence, as speech or the possession of thumbs may have done with your species."

Mr. Thoggosh, or his general-purpose manipulator, went on. *"Its first new function, paleobiologists believe, was as a decoy, expendably sent into harm's way to appease predators, as a lizard's tail, since you brought lizards up, Raftan, is sacrificed. The theory derives from the fact that, among the primitive species, it grows back in time for the next mating season. In later species found in the fossil record, that process was accelerated."*

If I stop for a second, thought Reille y Sanchez, her attention momentarily wandering, *to consider what a weird conversation this really is, I'll end up running through the woods like Richardson.*

". . . confers survival advantages," the doctor was saying, "and would never have evolved had the species from which the Elders sprang not been unique in another—"

"*Raftan.*" The tentacle waved an admonitory tip. "*I believe we stray from the immediate interests of the colonel.*"

Dlee Raftan Saon saw her expression. "I'm afraid we have. What else should we discuss, my dear?"

She cleared her throat. "Tell me about Eichra Oren. It was a surprise, meeting another human here. Where does he come from?"

Something, not the table, began beeping. "If you'll both excuse me," the doctor declared, rising, "it's back to indentured servitude. Estrellita." He bent over her hand and brushed it with complex mouth parts. It gave her a chill, not because he was an insect, but because the gesture, although she'd never seen the late geologist do it, somehow reminded her of Kamanov. "I've savored, to put it Remaulthiek's poetic way, the sweet scent of your naming. Come see me any time you wish, as long as you make it soon."

She felt herself blush like Toya. "Thank you, Dlee Raftan Saon, I will." Making his way among the crowded tables, he departed. She turned to the tentacle, which left the wheeled contraption to twine itself around the seat abandoned by the doctor. "You were telling me about Eichra Oren."

"*So I—*" Part of the noise must have been recorded music, for now she heard, all about her, Paul McCartney's "Yesterday," presumably sorted from a welter of signals received from Earth. It was good to hear, but must have been a South African or Swiss broadcast, possibly Israeli or Chinese, because such music had been illegal—which didn't mean she hadn't enjoyed it all her life—since before she was born. "*Someone's noticed your presence, Colonel, and altered the entertainment program in your honor. I suppose we'll have to sit and listen politely to that outlandish racket. Then I suggest we find a place to converse without quite so much interference. You're aware that*

Eichra Oren's descended from ancient Antarcticans in your own continuum?''

"Yes." Outside, morning had been acquiring tints of jungle afternoon. Exotic birds fluttered from branch to branch amid giant orchids. Mosses and ferns filled the area between the great trees. She fought back tears evoked by the "outlandish racket." Was it possible that she, of all people, was homesick? "That's what he told the general, something about a great seafaring people wiped out by a sudden change of climate."

"Indeed," the Proprietor replied, apparently unaware of her struggle. *"In their time, thousands of years ago, the Antarcticans built complex, efficient ocean-going ships, constructed, if you'll believe it, entirely of wood. Some boasted hundreds of sails, supported by masts of sixty or seventy meters. Often they had crews consisting of several hundred men and women—there, it's over with at last. Shall we leave, Colonel, before they honor you once more with something even more unbearable?"*

Reille y Sanchez raised her eyebrows. "Women?"

The tentacle somehow conveyed a shrug. *'A wise arrangement for those planning voyages lasting years. They knew the compass and sextant, although they were still at something of a loss regarding the calculation of longitude at sea. In this they were like the navies of your own civilization, well into the nineteenth century. I suggest we go to my office for further discussion. I'll have the rest of me meet us there."*

Reille y Sanchez wasn't looking forward to her first dip in fluorocarbon. They followed Dlee Raftan Saon's footsteps out, the sound system blaring Sousa's "Stars and Stripes Forever." *"That's more to my liking,"* exclaimed the tentacle wheeling beside her. *"The subtleties! The intricacy! You people can produce real music, after all!"*

"What was that," she had to shout, "about Earth's nineteenth-century navies?"

"Without offense," the voice suggested, *"it occurs to me that you're unschooled in your own history. Mind you, I shouldn't want to give you the impression the Antarcticans were supernaturally skilled mariners. They did attain estimable heights of navigational proficiency, exploring and mapping most of what was then the Earth's surface. It's in this respect,*

although you may not be aware of it, that they were like the navy of your own British Empire at about the time of the Napoleonic—excuse me."

One of the lobster people stopped them just outside, apparently to talk business. Wondering if it was Tl*m*nch*l, Reille y Sanchez tried not to be conspicuous as she also tried to hear what was being said.

"Yes, Subbotsirrh, what is it?"

"English? Very well—and it's pronounced S*bb*ts*rrh. About these drilling-equipment invoices . . ." Whatever S*bb*ts*rrh needed, it didn't take long. Mr. Thoggosh and Reille y Sanchez were soon strolling down the corridor again, in the direction, she assumed, of his office.

"Now, what was it we were discussing? Navigation?"

"My British Empire," she replied. "Mr. Thoggosh, I'm just a soldier. An American soldier. You know more about my world than I do. You even speak the language better. Everybody here does."

"My dear Colonel, unlike stupidity, ignorance is a curable condition. And unlike British mercantilists, the Antarcticans were basically free traders. As with many other such throughout sapient history, they welcomed innovation, and were in the initial stages of inventing mass production and the steam engine. Yet for all that, they were helpless when an incredible worldwide disaster—yes, what is it, Nellus?"

Again he was interrupted, this time by a furry animal which would have been taller than Reille y Sanchez had it not walked with a stoop. Its long, whiskered muzzle ended in a restless nose. Behind it lashed a hairless tail. It spoke a language consisting of squeaks and whistles.

"Colonel, this is Nellus Glaser, proprietor of the restaurant we just left. He wishes to know if you found your meal satisfactory."

Preoccupied with other matters, she had to think to remember what she'd just eaten. "I had no idea it was a private establishment. I assumed—I didn't see any signs. But yes," she grinned, "absolutely the best burger and fries I've ever had on another planet."

The tentacle emitted whistles and squeaks. So did Nellus

Glaser, passing a handful of something metallic to it. It extended and dropped coins in her palm. *"The restaurant's signs are posted in radio frequencies you aren't equipped to perceive. Your fellow mammal wishes you to accept lunch as his guest. He asks whether he may quote you regarding the food."*

"I guess it won't do any harm." She looked at the money in her hand, the amount Dlee Raftan Saon had fed into the table. "This is the doctor's. But ask him not to mention it to the general or Mr. Empleado."

"I wondered," replied the tentacle, *"whether KGB officers made a habit of commercial endorsements. Keep the coins as souvenirs. Raftan would be pleased."* More shrill communication took place, the cafeteria owner shook hands with Reille y Sanchez, and they were on their way down the corridor again. *"I'm not certain what you assumed, but I refuse to attempt explaining the complex division-of-investment economy we've brought to 5023 Eris, until you understand more basic facts about us. What were we talking about?"*

"Worldwide disaster. Shifting poles and the change in climate."

"Someone's been curing your ignorance already. Yes, the Earth processed—wobbled in orbit—and the treacherous poles began wandering again."

"Again?"

"They've done so on many previous occasions. As long as continents drift, they'll do so again. Timing—whether or not a people has achieved sufficient sophistication to withstand such an event—has made all the difference in the survival or extinction of many sapient species. The poles' inconstancy is written in alternating magnetic patterns laid down, like your ferromagnetic musical recordings, in the great stone pillows of extruded lava in the bottommost abysses of Earth's deepest—what is it this time?"

In that moment, she came closest to imitating Richardson, paralyzed by primordial fear, even her saw-backed knife and CZ99A1 forgotten on her hips. Before them, on eight legs, not six, was a hairy presence the size of the proverbial Buick. Its overall color was straw gold, mottled with black which ran in stripes down its flying-buttress legs. The leglets—she couldn't remember what they were called—guarding the mandibles looked like a pair of brooms. The face—four visible eyes set in a horizontal line, two large between two smaller—was a painted-looking red. The giant spider hissed and bubbled at the Proprietor's surrogate.

"Moltchirtber," Mr. Thoggosh told her, *"my friend and first assistant chief engineer. Moltchirtber, forgive my snapping at you, dear. My talk with this lady's been much interrupted. May I present Colonel Estrellita Reille y Sanchez?"*

Please, God, she thought, *or whoever has the duty, don't let it want to shake hands.*

"Kindly accept apologies," the spider replied in an impatient but human-sounding voice, "for not beginning this in English. You vertebrates all look alike to me—a bit frightening, actually—and I wasn't aware you were one of our recent guests. Mr. Thoggosh, your integrated presence is urgently required at Shaft Thirteen, where we've experienced an equipment breakage. No casualties, this time, thanks be to Aelbraugh Pritsch's Cosmic Egg, but when we return home, a manufacturer I know will be consulting his debt assessor, or my name's not Moltchirtber!"

"Tell them I'll be there, at once," he answered, as the spider turned and sped away. *"Colonel, we must alter our plans. We can continue to converse, if you care to accompany me."* Reversing directions, they hurried along the corridor until they came to a spot on the wall which let them outside to where an aircraft was waiting. As they climbed in—no pilot, no visible controls—Reille y Sanchez was out of breath. The machine lifted them a hundred meters and zoomed forward. Mr. Thoggosh went on as before.

'As far as the Antarctican disaster's concerned, on a planetary scale, the degree of shift was small, probably not noticeable to an observer on some neighboring world. For Earth's inhabitants, it was a cataclysm. One day it began snowing in what had been the semitropics. It didn't stop again, winter or summer, for hundreds of years. The first snowfall compressed under a load of new precipitation into steely ice which crushed the Antarcticans' greatest artifacts to powder, destroying every trace of their once great civilization. Dying of the cold or fleeing from it, they were decimated, scattered. The little remaining evidence of their existence was scraped, by the

slowly flowing glaciers, off the edges of the continent, into the surrounding oceans."

The craft tilted, giving them a view of the human encampment. She waved at Toya, at the center, but the machine was almost silent, the girl didn't look up. With its stale woodsmoke and latrine smells, the place was hardly a model of rustic charm. Surprised when he didn't land to let her off, she thought Mr. Thoggosh was polite not to mention it. She asked a question which had puzzled her. "Surely archaeologists would find something left."

"Outside their cities, Colonel, now lost forever beneath miles—pardon—kilometers of ice, they worked primarily in wood, again much like nineteenth-century Britain. After all these millennia, very little remains. From time to time, an inexplicable bit of stone or glasswork may show up, like an orphan, among the remnants of later civilizations, no more than a token of its creators' former greatness. There, if you look closely, you may see our destination, that deforested rise and a cluster of low buildings. The question naturally arises, could such a disaster repeat itself? If so, how much of today's human civilization will be left after fifteen thousand years? Certainly nothing identifiable of nineteenth-century Britain will survive. What would, neglected for a period of a hundred fifty centuries? Brace yourself for landing, Colonel. Out in the countryside, this thing believes it's a jeep."

"But something survived. What about Eichra Oren?"

"People being sturdier than artifacts, some Antarcticans escaped. For a variety of reasons, their choice of avenues appeared more limited than it was. They falsely believed Australia was an uninhabitable wasteland. It's said they'd enemies in Africa, on whom a superstitious few among them blamed the catastrophe. If it ever truly existed, which I myself doubt, that culture also perished, for no trace of it remains. Thus it was to the southern tip of India the refugees came, with little more than the clothing they wore."

Mr. Thoggosh had been correct about the landing. They bumped down in a trampled field sloping upward to become the ridge he'd mentioned. Aelbraugh Pritsch met them, comically attired in a workman's hard hat, a fireman's heavy coat, and a pair of odd boots, all of it, including what parts of him were visible, covered with dirt as if he'd been doing demolition work. Before the voluble avian could get a word out, another aircraft landed virtually on top of them. Mr. Thoggosh climbed out. His tentacle slithered over the side of the machine Reille y Sanchez sat in, and integrated with its owner.

"There's a regrettable lack of data," he continued, as if he'd been with her all along, "for the next fifteen thousand years. Our ethnographers base their surmises on legends and linguistics. The Antarcticans may have been ancestral to certain wanderers who, migrating north and westward—perhaps out of fear of something they no longer remembered clearly—came to dominate Europe, North America, and your modern world. Now, Colonel, I must hand you off, in a manner of speaking, to my assistant, and attend a smaller disaster of my own."

"But you haven't explained Eichra Oren!"

"So I haven't. One thing we know with certainty: by coincidence, during this period, interdimensional translation was being invented by those among us who called themselves natural philosophers. Conducting a monumental cross-probability survey of your Earth and several others, they 'collected' and saved a single shipload of glacial refugees. Eichra Oren's a descendent of these so-called Appropriated Persons."

XVIII
The Cage of Freedom

"Do please come in, Colonel Reille y Sanchez."

Aelbraugh Pritsch led the human female to the construction office, a self-fabricating structure which the Proprietor had ordered planted when this location was selected. A light but thoroughly depressing drizzle was falling, no doubt due to

Eichra Oren's recent arrival and its effects on the closed environment of the asteroid. Perhaps the atmosphere required readjusting. They climbed an uncovered flight of stairs to a deck where he manipulated the knob of a crude mechanical entrance.

"I'm afraid I must begin by anticipating your first question and refusing to say precisely what we're attempting to accomplish on this site. We can speak of anything else you wish. I spend an increasing amount of time here, so I've arranged things to my own taste and comfort. One item still sorely lacking is a humor door, although I'm not certain the place merits it."

The bits of fur over her eyes climbed her forehead. "A humidor?"

"Humor door, customary in the dwellings of my people, Colonel, which entertains a visitor with a riddle or joke as he waits for the occupant to answer. No house is properly a home without one. Perhaps before the next consignment—but no, I'm not sure we'll be here long enough to justify the expense. Nevertheless, I'm quite proud of what I've accomplished in these rustic conditions. May I offer you something to drink?"

Inside, it was all one large, high-ceilinged room, although it was difficult to find a level expanse larger than a desk. The building consisted of little besides stairs, landings, and lofts. He found broad, flat expanses as boring as his guest might have found a room painted a uniform gray.

"Not at the moment, thanks. As I explained to Dlee Raftan Saon and Mr. Thoggosh, I'm trying to learn what I can of nautiloid biology. The doctor said something about the evolution of the Elders that intrigued me, but he got interrupted and didn't finish. Something about some other attribute, besides the separable tentacle, that made the Elders what they are?"

Stripping off coat, hat, and boots near the entrance—his symbiote poked its blue-green head from his feathers for its first breath of fresh air in hours—he extracted a hot, wet cloth from the greeting bowl, refraining from offering one to the human. He led her to the room's center where, under a screen which kept him from singeing himself and protected his symbiote from even greater tragedy, a brazier of heated stones glowed.

"Colonel, I believe you'll find that padded swing comfortable. I'll perch here and get a little of this mud off my face. Grooming in the company of others is the custom of my people, so, if you don't mind that I do it, I won't mind that you don't do it. You're sure I can't offer you something? That, I do believe, is the custom of your people."

She sat and let her legs dangle, settling against the backrest. "Maybe a little later, if you don't mind. I just ate."

"I've been thinking it over." He took a place on a nearby perching rack and began toweling his face. "I can't imagine what Raftan referred to unless—of course. One takes it so much for granted. The Elders' ancestors were powerful 'electric fish.' They're still capable of generating a respectable current. You're familiar with eels, skates, rays, other aquatic nonsapients which do this with special cells in their nervous systems?"

She nodded. "Yes, I am. I hadn't noticed anything like that with the nautiloids, maybe because of the transparent—unless—that isn't how Semlohcolresh stopped Colonel Richardson's bullets, is it?"

He lowered the towel and looked at her. "Dear me, no. I don't know what you saw, but it was no doubt part of the technology built into his protective covering. The Elders' capabilities are orders of magnitude less powerful than that, Colonel. Such an ability sometimes serves more than simple purposes of defense. As with many modern species, it helped primitive molluscs with navigation, to remain in formation within schools, and in, er, finding and courting mates. The Elders' species generates a sort of biological radio energy little different in principle."

"I see." The human bobbed her head up and down, completely out of timing with the swing, which he discovered got on his nerves. "The famous nautiloid telepathy General Gutierrez told us about?"

Knowing that her disturbing lack of rhythm wasn't her fault, he tried to keep irritability out of his voice. These creatures were so sensitive. "The species is telepathic only in the sense that its fields are undetectable by other species unaided by technology. Nautiloids employ them to control their remote tentacles and to communicate among one another. This latter use is limited to relatively short distances, analogous to those covered by our voices. Species employing sound communications seem 'telepathic' to the Elders.''

She exposed her fangs, something he struggled, against the racing of his heart—his symbiote buried its jewel-scaled head deep in his feathers—to remember had evolved into an expression of cordiality among these creatures. His species lacked them altogether, although they were as predatory in their heritage as humans. ''Radio. Unless they can turn it off, doesn't that make it hard to think or get a night's sleep without distractions?''

''How perceptive, Colonel.'' He chuckled. ''Knowing no more than you do, you've put a foreclaw on a pivotal fact of history. Unlike a human being, the nautiloid encounters unique difficulties whenever he seeks solitude or quiet. He must confine himself within the sanctuary of a well-grounded shelter of metallic mesh, a basic amenity the species lacked for millions of years.''

''One would think,'' she suggested, again nodding out of rhythm, ''that the evolutionary result would be some sort of ultimate collectivism. Organisms like that might even develop a species-wide group mind.''

''True.'' He gave his symbiote's face a swipe, put the soiled towel aside on a dish for that purpose, and rose from his perch, hungry after the morning's work and wondering what he could do about it politely. ''That's where the Elders might have found themselves, in a state of nature. However, it's equally true that the first imperative of evolution is diversity.''

She stopped swinging. ''I thought it was survival of the fittest.''

''Survival of the *fit*, Colonel. The implications are worlds apart. Bereft of a vital aspect of diversity, the Elders might have died out. In their barbaric past, privacy deprivation was a dreaded punishment, much like imprisonment in your culture, which I believe practices solitary confinement, yet its precise opposite. The Proprietor says one has only to experience collectivism of the mind to hate all forms of collectivism thoroughly. Artificial privacy was his culture's most historically important invention, fully equivalent to your invention of the wheel.''

Again the female bared her fangs, his heart began to flutter, and his symbiote dived for cover. ''Did they ever get around to inventing the wheel?''

''That, of course, an aquatic species had small use for until, like your astronauts exploring space, they began exploring the land. Its early remnants are seen at paleontological, rather than archaeological sites, but the invention of privacy is older. In a sense, it allowed them to invent individualism itself. Over two hundred million years, they've refined it to an amazing degree.''

''Oh?'' The fangs disappeared, which he knew wasn't a good sign, although he felt relieved. Ignoring a growling stomach, he sat again.

''Indeed. They've no authority you'd recognize, having discovered—having been compelled to discover, over and over, through a long, bloody history—that, of the many things which may be said of it, foremost is that authority's always established for the opposite reasons its advocates claim.''

''But that's anarchy!'' He was momentarily gratified, not without a pang of guilt, to see so fearsome a creature terrified at something he'd said. ''What protects them from chaos? What holds their society together?''

He raised a hand. ''Calm yourself, Colonel. The Elders, and those like my people who've learned from them, practice the philosophy of *p'Na*, an ethical conceit far older than mankind which has proven stable and workable. Although adept at self-defense and ruthless in its application, they believe it the most heinous violation of *p'Na* to interfere without justification in the lives of innocent sapients.''

She opened her mouth, but he didn't give her a chance. ''I've studied you enough to know that the word 'interference' takes on what may seem strange connotations, employed by someone such as myself, taught by the Elders. Their customary measure of unethical interference is the use of force in the absence of force initiated by another.''

She nodded, mollified. ''There are other ways to interfere with people.''

''There are. The least aesthetic, in their view, is the most insidiously attractive, consisting of an attempt, invariably well-meaning, to save others, willing or otherwise, from the effects of 'the Forge of Adversity.' By this they mean everyday vicissitudes which educate the individual, or what you mean by the process of natural selection which educates entire species.'' He cast an eye toward the stasis-preserver at another level of the room and rose again. His symbiote slithered out and raced upstairs in anticipation. ''If you'll excuse me, Colonel, it's been a long morning. I'm going to get something to eat. Do you still wish nothing?''

''I'll take something to drink.'' She put feet on the floor, arose with him, followed him upstairs to watch him place spiced, frozen grubs into an oiled pan. Sitting at the edge of the counter, his symbiote watched, too. When the grubs were sizzling nicely on the element, he began making a pot of coffee. ''You know,'' declared the female, ''we have a name for what you call the Forge of Adversity: Social Darwinism. It was used to justify inhumane treatment of workers by antisocial industrial criminals and robber barons.''

He gave the pan a shake before replying. ''And like your word 'anarchy,' Colonel, its function in your language is to prevent further consideration of whatever you don't want to consider further. The opposite of the way words ought to be used. Could you give the matter further consideration, you'd see at once that such a philosophy informs us, in a manner verifiable by science, that our suffering may mean something after all, in a universe which otherwise doesn't seem to make sense very often.''

She took a step backward, raising her voice. ''But it's so cruel!''

''Far from being cruel . . .'' He turned, missing his symbiote—it had fled to a cupboard, where its slender, projecting tail gave it away—feeling himself tremble as he answered and striving to keep it from his voice. ''. . . It's a deal more than religion or the state was ever able to deliver.''

This, of course, evoked a flood of expostulation. Her passion rattled him, but she was ill-prepared to evaluate, let alone accept, any answers he offered, neither facts established by science nor validated by the experience (vicarious on his part, he admitted) of two million centuries. Gratified that she had no way of knowing how nervous she made him, he poured two large cups of coffee and a tiny one, offering her a variety of condiments, shuffled food from the pan, and gathered utensils. Still arguing, they returned to swing and perch. He placed a small plate on an end table for his symbiote, which glanced at them, picked up a feather-fine fork, and began to eat.

"What you refer to as 'Scientific Socialism,'" Aelbraugh Pritsch told her between bites, "has nothing to do with science. It consists, instead, of unexamined emotions and a desperate political need to justify the wholesale abuse and slaughter of billions of sapients for some imaginary—and, at its roots, purely mystical—'greater good.' The Proprietor warned me of this. Even after this much discussion, Colonel, I can see that the concept of the Forge remains unclear because you don't wish to understand it."

Holding the cup to warm her hands, she sipped her coffee. "Wait," she demanded, "didn't you say any well-meaning attempt to protect another sapient, willing or otherwise, from everyday natural selection deprives the individual and his species of education and constitutes the least aesthetic form of unethical interference?"

"That isn't precisely what I said"—he set his empty plate aside, taking up his own cup—"but it will do for purposes of this discussion."

"Okay, then," she went on, "wouldn't it be more consistent to let them run around naked and hungry, killing each other, being eaten by predators, dying of diseases we found cures for centuries ago?"

He blinked. "More consistent with what? Who do you mean by 'them'?"

"More consistent than protecting people from the Forge of Adversity, as we obviously do in both our societies, by means of education, an industrial economy, and humane—or whatever you call it—medicine?"

He put his cup down. "I see. It would help if you limited yourself to one question at a time. Regrettably, your upbringing's left you ignorant of logic, let alone a profit-and-loss system of distribution and allocation and the voluntary division of labor. Such systems require an exchange of values. Life becomes easier, but none of the benefits arrive without thought and effort which are themselves part of the workings of the Forge.''

''And as usual,'' she sneered, ''the rich get richer while we dismiss the poor as unfit. There isn't much difference between your views and those of so-called intellectuals we were warned about in school, Nietzsche, Stirner, Rand, others nobody reads any more, except a few South Africans or Israelis.''

He chuckled. ''Or a billion Chinese. The ideas you speak of aren't frequently broadcast, and my acquaintance with them is slight. But to the extent I'm familiar with them, I believe I detect within them an element of gratuitous contempt for others—life is difficult enough already—as if their originators weren't entirely certain of themselves or their ideas.''

She raised her eyebrows. ''Contempt? I call it class hatred.''

''I imagine you would, but even I overstate the case, in particular where Rand's concerned. One is certain of that which he earns for himself. One with certainty possesses self-esteem. One possessed of self-esteem relates to others in a mutually satisfactory manner. Our culture, harsh as it may seem, makes more tolerance, respect, and love possible than any collective striving to protect those huddled within it. What yours protects them from is a benevolent regard for others with foundations in reality, the opportunity to grow beyond difficulty. Whatever else the concept of the Forge is, it precludes such stultifying interference. Do you care for more coffee?''

''I'm about coffeed out, thanks. Aelbraugh Pritsch, such an opportunity exists,'' she objected, ''in our society, as long as its only object is to do things for others, rather than yourself.''

''The limitation,'' he countered, spreading his hands, ''imposed at bayonet-point or through guilt-feelings, denies sapients any genuine motivation for growth. It steals from them a chance to transcend themselves, for their own sake, in both an individual and evolutionary sense. It denies them self-esteem, the cornerstone of any sane being's existence.''

She stood, jamming her hands in her pockets. ''But what about the needs of the community, of society or the nation?

Aren't they larger than any single individual and worthy of self-sacrifice?"

Looking up, he shook his head. "Colonel, if your interest lies with the group, consider that it consists of nothing but individuals. What else exists for it to consist of? And it's from individuals that its survival, all its growth and progress, derive. Where else could they come from? Suppress the individual, you suppress the group, defeating your original purpose."

The human began to answer before what he'd said began to register. When it did, she closed her mouth, a puzzled expression distorting her features. At that, it was better than when she smiled. When she did speak, she wondered aloud whether his ideas mightn't represent a viewpoint biologically peculiar to the Elders, and therefore not applicable to humans or any other species.

"Colonel, you're an officer of Marines and the KGB. You've been indoctrinated all your life in a centuries-old tradition of collectivism, imposed, against your natural inclination, with gun, whip, and fist. But understand this: centuries are an eye-blink. Already your values devour you, or you wouldn't be here. They run counter to more billions of years of evolution than any single species has seen. Any species which practiced them consistently would soon render itself extinct—as I gather your species is doing. Fortunately for us all, collectivism and self-sacrifice are impossible to practice consistently."

Turning her back, she gazed into the glowing stones. "I admit none of us is perfect. Nobody ever said it would be easy to measure up to what's right all the time." She turned to face him. "I was simply trying to understand your Elders, wondering whether this selfishness they've made a virtue of might not be, well, an instinct with them."

"So they aren't culpable for what you see as moral failure? No, *p'Na*'s by no means an instinct. Few beings evolve to sapience without having lost all such inbuilt guides. But it consists of something almost as—"

"Hey, birdbrain," a third voice demanded, "ask her when the last time was she screwed her father!"

"What?" Aelbraugh Pritsch leaped up, filled with alarm and unsure, in the interest of continued survival, which direction he should watch. Behind him, half a level up from perch, swing, and brazier, the front door swung open, pushed by a damp, black nose.

"Mammalshit," muttered his symbiote, setting its little cup down and diving back into his feathers, "it's that dog again!"

XIX
Crystalline Music

The nose was only the beginning. Following behind it, its owner, then the Proprietor, entered the office, halting on the landing above the lounging area where Aelbraugh Pritsch and Reille y Sanchez had been talking for the past half hour. A damp, cold draft and a wisp of fog sneaked in with them before they shut the door.

"I expect," the Elder told the colonel, "lest you give up on us as hopelessly barbaric, Oasam's remark may require as radical a readjustment as we've just performed on our atmosphere. With your assistance, gentle beings?"

The Proprietor dragged himself perilously close to the edge of the steps, rising on the ends of his tentacles as on tiptoe. Aelbraugh Pritsch thought he resembled a grotesque spider, but his employer was never conscious of his dignity when he wanted something concrete accomplished, preferring to leave such aesthetic considerations to others. Reille y Sanchez hurried to help, while his assistant assisted from behind, straining under the rough-surfaced, massive shell. It would have been an impossible task on Earth, given the mollusc's enormous weight. Here on the asteroid, half-floating the bulky Elder down a narrow flight of stairs was much like handling a fiber carton greater than one's own height and width, but empty.

Acting as host, the avian started another pot of coffee

brewing and resumed the perch he'd occupied. Reille y Sanchez went back to the padded swing, Sam lying on the floor at her knee.

The Proprietor trundled into place between them. "Given the broad individual variation inevitably—and happily—found among all sapients," he continued for the human female's benefit, "I suspect some few among your number, Colonel, would perceive nothing untoward in seeking reproductive converse with a parent—"

"*Mr. Thoggosh!*"

"Aha! Enlighten me: does the shock and disgust with which you audibly and visibly apprehend such a proposition represent an instinctive reaction on your part, indelibly imprinted on your genetic material?"

She didn't answer. Aelbraugh Pritsch gave puzzled thought to what his own answer might have been, grateful he hadn't been asked. Had he been capable, he might have blushed as furiously as she was doing now.

The Proprietor supplied his own reply. "I suspect the contrary. As my assistant indicated, it's something else, is it not? Something very powerful which must be reckoned with, if—as all reflective beings must—we aspire to know ourselves and act in accordance with our natures?"

"Alternatively," offered Aelbraugh Pritsch, "whenever one believes it necessary or advantageous to act against his nature, it's prudent, to say the least, to do so advisedly."

"If I follow you," Reille y Sanchez frowned, "you're saying this *p'Na* business isn't instinctive, as I suggested, but, like the human distaste for incest, merely a longstanding social prohibition?"

The nautiloid waved a tentacle in a negative gesture. "The word 'merely' doesn't come into it. All sapient species, even your own, have a distaste for incest, grounded not in instinct, but in experience at a level of reality so fundamental it can't be denied without terrible consequences."

"And *p'Na*?"

"Your species hasn't had the equivalent experience, yet, in those areas of reality which bear on it. It took mine millions of yours to reach our present level of understanding. But given time—provided you live through the terrible consequences you now suffer out of ignorance—you, too, will create a concept so like *p'Na* as to be indistinguishable from it. It's a necessity for survival, both for individuals and whole species."

"Then maybe what I'm trying to do here isn't a total loss," she replied, "though it's a strange way to investigate a murder. The general maintains that the key to understanding you people— which he regards as a necessity for *our* survival—is through your most fundamental beliefs. That's why I started with basic biology."

At a signal from the heating element in the kitchen, Aelbraugh Pritsch got up to pour coffee for himself, his symbiote, Oasam, and the Proprietor—Reille y Sanchez having turned him down again—bringing it to the nautiloid in a wide-bottomed flask with a long, flexible sipping tube. Sam, as he recalled, preferred his coffee in a shallow bowl or saucer, with milk. He set it on the floor beside the dog. Mammals.

"Your general," Mr. Thoggosh told her, "is an astute individual, Colonel. It's exactly what Eichra Oren's doing with your party now, examining your most fundamental beliefs. Very well, let's discuss mine. Although customarily derived from first principles, for your purposes the first tenet's this: if, for whatever reason, one of us should injure another, the *p'Na* system requires that he make appropriate restitution to the victim of his act." He glanced at Aelbraugh Pritsch and Sam. "Would you say that sums it up?"

"Why, yes, sir." The avian nodded.

The dog yawned: "I hear enough of this stuff at home."

The human shrugged. "It seems straightforward and comprehensible. Human ethics say the same thing: 'An eye for an eye and a tooth for a tooth.' "

"But you only have so much jaw-room"—Sam sat up— "and did you ever ask yourself what you'd do with a spare eye?"

"Oasam, don't confuse her." The Elder smiled at her, although Aelbraugh Pritsch knew she might not have been aware of it. "Estrellita, I speak of a thing distinct from Biblical retribution. Its opposite, in fact. The next logical, customary step may not be quite so comprehensible. If restitution can't possibly be made, our sense of justice—and, in a manner you may find difficult to appreciate, our sense of humor—demands that, in its place, the responsible party offer up his one irreplaceable asset."

"His life, of course. It sounds pretty Biblical to me."

"I believe we'll eventually persuade you of the difference. Although, of course, it may come to his life, in the end. If, for example, he's caused a wrongful death, or otherwise created an unpayable moral debt. Rather than payment, think of it as a token of acknowledgment of that debt."

"Mr. Thoggosh, that isn't quite as incomprehensible as you may think it is," she replied. "Aside from what you said about your sense of humor—which I admit I didn't get at all, and which I won't ask you to explain just now—in some ways it resembles the Japanese custom of seppuku, with which I'm reasonably familiar."

"Ah, the picturesque intestine-cutting ceremony. The spectacular rending of viscera." He raised a tentacle. "I trust you won't be too disappointed to learn that our custom's to avoid gratuitous suffering, where possible. And there are significant differences on our part regarding motivation. The samurai strives to meet what he imagines are the expectations of his ancestors. Unlike him, or your advocates of capital punishment for that matter, we're all too well aware that our deadly ritual restores nothing owed the damaged party. We recognize that it doesn't—that it can't—ever put back what was lost or damaged."

"That's the point," added Aelbraugh Pritsch. "It's an unpayable debt, and only an unpayable debt, which can create this rare and peculiar situation. I spoke of the importance to the Elders, as well as those they've influenced, of self-esteem. We speak now of an attempt to regain or repair it, before the end, through an ultimate display, on the part of those who create unpayable moral debts, of a willingness to make up for such mistakes, were it logically possible—which, in these circumstances, it isn't."

"Well," Reille y Sanchez shook her head in confusion, "that certainly muddies things up nicely."

At her feet, Sam permitted himself an undoglike chuckle.

"I'll try again," the Proprietor told her, interrupting whatever reply Aelbraugh Pritsch intended making. "Although this dramatic phenomenon is often referred to as the ultimate restitution, it's never actually considered to be the restitution itself, which, in cases like this, is acknowledged by everyone as impossible by its very nature."

"So why," asked the colonel, "try?"

"Well, in a sense, the individual in question's concerned with payment of a debt which he also believes he owes himself. In that sense, his death represents a place-holder, a token, a customarily accepted substitute, however unsatisfactory, for the more desirable restitution which could be made in less restrictive circumstances. Moreover, most individuals, however culpable, recognize the importance of not creating yet another debt by imposing the burden of doing the right thing on another being."

"Please understand, Colonel"—Aelbraugh Pritsch leaned forward on his perch and spread his hands to her—"that this is much more than mere lofty theorizing. You wished to know about our culture, and such considerations have previously been known—"

"On more than one occasion," the Proprietor interposed.

"—to have interrupted the otherwise stately progress of the Elders' cultural history." The avian glanced at his employer, then back at Reille y Sanchez. "Given current events, a notorious example arises in the mind."

"Here it comes," warned Sam.

"Yes," Mr. Thoggosh agreed. "It seems that certain scientists among us—perhaps 'natural philosophers' might be a better translation—had devised a novel and intriguing application for the then newly invented and otherwise useless curiosity of dimensional translation."

The human female nodded. "So I've been told."

Aelbraugh Pritsch turned to the Proprietor. "I mentioned this to her already, sir, since it was during the period which happened to coincide with the Antarctican disaster. She knows they'd begun collecting life-forms from divergent branches of galactic history."

"I see," the mollusc answered with a hint of annoyance before continuing. "Now here's something you've not been told, for I don't believe my assistant's aware of this detail. It's well known that many nonsapient species, what you call pack rats, for example, and several bright species of squid, like collecting colorful shiny objects. Natural philosophers had long known that virtually all creatures advanced beyond the gobble-it-raw-before-it-can-gobble-you stage appeared to be partial to such objects as well, although they tended to carry the fascination further than nonsapients.''

Reille y Sanchez smiled. ''Diamonds are a girl's best friend.''

''You'll be gratified to know,'' the Proprietor replied, ''that the same is true of females of my species. Now, as luck would have it, the deliberate cutting or faceting of certain brilliantly colorful artificial gemstones creates a brief but unmistakable, very subtle and complex piezo-electric impulse in certain radio frequencies. It happens, as you know, that we're natural transmitters and receivers of such waves. Thus we were sensitive to these piezo-electric gem-cutting impulses.''

''Hold on,'' she asked, ''you mean you could actually 'hear' these things being cut? From a distance?''

''In fact,'' he answered with an affirmative gesture of a tentacle, ''their generation for pleasure was something of a musical art early in our history. The philosophers, remembering that, reasoned that such gemstones might be deliberately scattered to good effect throughout an area about to be studied. The effort, however, would aid scientific, rather than aesthetic values.''

The colonel grinned. ''I get it—it might safely be assumed that any resulting electronic impulses would signify the presence of sapient life-forms, since nonsapients which found the gemstones would merely collect them, not cut them. Pretty neat.''

The Proprietor chuckled. ''As you say, pretty neat, indeed. With relatively little effort, the philosophers could reliably detect the presence of tool-making species in virtually any of the many universes of alternative probability which they purposed exploring. And it was in this way that, not just human beings, but many other intelligent species were discovered and subsequently 'sampled' by our dimensional translators.''

Aelbraugh Pritsch nodded. ''Including my own.''

Sam lifted his head. "And that, lovely Estrellita, was only the beginning of the bad news."

"Oh?"

"Oasam's quite correct," Mr. Thoggosh told her, "all good things have finite limits. There immediately ensued a prolonged and general debate, lasting hundreds of years, concerning the nature of what had been done and the fate of those it had been done to. At times, it came close to splitting our ancient culture down the middle."

"Like one of the gems," she suggested.

"During this time, as you may imagine," added Aelbraugh Pritsch, "every effort was expended to extend the lives of the individuals under debate."

"Yes," finished the Proprietor, "and, in the end, after much searching, they arrived at an answer which, however unpleasant its implications, they all agreed was preferable to the ongoing argument. It was decided that the tenets and precepts of *p'Na* were supreme. It was agreed—for reasons I shan't elaborate—that, according to those tenets and precepts, all rights derive from sapience. Despite their unenviably primitive estate, the collected beings—Appropriated Persons—were nonetheless sapient. That was the reason they'd been collected in the first place."

She nodded. "I take it this was bad news for the scientists?"

"You take it correctly," the Proprietor confirmed. "*P'Na* had to be applied equally to 'savage' sapients as well as civilized molluscs. This being so, their involuntary collection had been a forbidden act, constituting the grossest possible violation of an intelligent life-form's rights. Given universal recognition of the Forge of Adversity concept, this was true even when it happened to save their lives, as it may have with the Antarctican humans my assistant told you about. The result was unintentional creation of an enormous and so far unpaid debt."

Mr. Thoggosh fell silent. As it became apparent he was through talking for the moment, Aelbraugh Pritsch took up the story. "This dismaying—and retroactively obvious—realization on their part resulted in unprecedented trauma, a fatal discontinuity in the lives of a normally placid and far-seeing people. At stake was their ancient civilization, everything it stood for, their leisurely view of things. To this day, that discontinuity and its astonishing aftermath are an embarrassment. To many, being the long-lived species they are, it's recent history, but history they feel uncomfortable remembering, despite its generally beneficial outcome.''

The human female set her feet on the floor and leaned forward, directing a gently toned question at the Proprietor, who still seemed lost in memory or contemplation. ''How was the debt paid?''

Mr. Thoggosh blinked and looked back at her. ''Owing to the amount of time which had passed, as well as the immense difficulty and danger of interdimensional travel, the philosophers were physically unable to replace their living 'samples.' That, of course, did nothing to remove the burden of obligation from their figurative shoulders. There could be no statute of limitations on seeing that right was done. And this time, given the circumstances, expense didn't come into the picture.''

''I see. And?''

''Nor were any other potentially negative effects on our society to be taken into account. At the time, it was generally predicted that the slow, inexorable progress of science might be measurably retarded. Nevertheless, such an irreplaceable loss of talent all at once was an unavoidable price that had to be paid.''

''I think you lost me somewhere. What loss of talent? What happened?''

''Why, what else? In the most ancient and honored tradition of *p'Na*, those individuals who considered themselves most responsible for the ethical travesty, the physicists, specimen collectors, and their various associates, suicided honorably.''

XX
The Great Restitution

"I've been higher than this," Reille y Sanchez told him, "on Earth, in the Rockies and the Sierra Nevada, and here on Eris. I don't remember being more intimidated by the height."

Eichra Oren nodded. They stood alone together on a balcony of the plastic-covered mesh the Elders seemed to use for everything here, half a kilometer from the surface. It was attached to the massive trunk of one of the giant trees which created and held up the canopy. Below, in the gathering twilight, they could see the site Mr. Thoggosh wouldn't tell the woman about, laid out like a miniature model. Whatever adjustment had been made to the atmosphere, following the disturbance of his own arrival, it had been correct. The air around them was warm for this late in the day, drier than it had been, she said, since the Soviet-American expedition had landed. At this altitude, there was a fair breeze which, he observed with interest, put color in her face and ruffled her thick auburn hair.

"I've heard it said heights aren't impressive unless something in your field of vision—like this tree—establishes an unbroken perspective, from bottom to top." He didn't relish standing close to the flimsy-looking rail himself, although he thought it unlikely a fall of that distance, in this gravity, would injure. "But you didn't climb up here to discuss the weather or the altitude. Sam mentioned you'd been talking to Mr. Thoggosh and Aelbraugh Pritsch about the Great Restitution."

"Sam told me how to find you. I thought you two were in constant touch. It's that radio thing the Elders do, isn't it?"

She turned from the dizzying view to face him. "I didn't climb up here to talk about that, either. I'm trying to figure out what makes them tick. One minute I think I understand, and the next, somebody throws something at me that confuses me all over again." She indicated the broad-bladed sword with its wire-wrapped handle and heavy brass-colored pommel and guard, leaning in is scabbard beside him. "You're human, but you also know the nautiloid culture. I decided to ask you why all those scientists killed themselves."

"I see." He turned, finding it hard to look into her eyes and think at the same time, to gaze out at the darkening landscape. "It might help to tell you about others, perhaps objectively less guilty, who didn't kill themselves. In a way it was harder for them. They'd supported the research, benefitted from the knowledge it produced, so they felt a measure of responsibility."

"What did they do?"

"To the Elders, the beings they called Appropriated Persons were alien, repugnant creatures. Nevertheless, and although they had no moral obligation in my opinion, supposedly that of an expert, thousands personally adopted nonnautiloid sapients with the objective of bringing them fully into the culture. Appropriated Persons would enjoy exactly the same status as the Elders themselves. It couldn't have been easy, not after two hundred million years of being the only people they knew about. As I say, it may have been harder than for those who took an easier way out. Even so, it happened faster than anyone, including the Elders, expected. The process was already well under way by the time the decision was arrived at formally."

She stepped closer. "I don't think I follow you."

He turned back, unable to keep his eyes off her. "Well, it may be significant to you that the complete nonexistence of anything resembling politics helped in a major way. There wasn't anything to interfere with what would have been a complicated process to plan—one that happened anyway, without anyone planning it. For example, they spoke of providing collectees with an education in any one of thousands of different fields. By the time anybody got around to it, they discovered the opportunity was already being provided by private parties through the market process."

"But why? I mean, aside from the restitution we've been talking about, why would anybody want to do something like that?"

He shrugged. "Why not? If you're an Elder, and you've a job that can be done better by a human or an avian or a sea scorpion than another Elder, that's who you hire. If they need education first, technical or academic, you provide it if you want the job done badly enough. One way or another, the Elders were making their former 'victims' a remarkable open-handed gift, giving away everything it had taken them millions of years to learn. But they didn't look at it that way. Once the decision was made, once it was discovered that the decision was irrelevant, many said special care should be exercised to avoid injuring the beneficiaries inadvertently."

Her eyes widened, and she spread her hands, palms up. "Now I'm really lost. Injuring them? By educating them, giving them work?"

"Your culture has an expression about killing with kindness. Some of the Elders worried that Appropriated Persons might become helpless, dependent welfare recipients. Remember, they had a long history, during which they'd made about every mistake a people can make and live to tell about it. So they concocted all sorts of complicated plans. An Appropriated Person's education, they decided, should be as self-directed as possible. Productive employment should be offered as soon as Appropriated Persons qualified for it. Under their voluntarist— what you call laissez-faire—economy, these measures, they felt, would prevent a welfare mentality."

She opened her mouth and closed it again. He was well aware that, from her Marxist viewpoint, there were so many things wrong with what he'd just said she didn't know where to begin replying to it. He laughed. "Before any of it was thought out, it was done, out of self-interest. Cortical implants, keyed to the Elders' frequencies, allowed others to share their 'telepathy.' Soon, other life-forms acquired the artificial equivalent of separable tentacles, a convenience as necessary as clothing in your culture. In my case, it's an energetic, long-haired dog with a lopsided grin. He's the remote I'd have if I'd been born a thinking mollusc, instead of a naked—and Sam says, *sometimes* thinking—ape. The integration of Appropriated Persons into the Elders' world was swifter and smoother than anybody expected and, in time, they simply became *persons*."

"Okay." Reille y Sanchez nodded. "That explains something Aelbraugh Pritsch said about the nautiloids benefitting as much as those they were trying to recompense. In the end, their economy wound up with more manpower—beingpower—and more consumers."

He shook his head. "There's more. In addition to whatever culture Appropriated Persons brought with them—plenty, even if they were less advanced than the Elders—the climate encouraged cross-fertilization. New ideas, inventions, businesses sprang up overnight. The stubbornest Elder came to see that civilization had become—stagnant isn't the word—sluggish, before the 'victims' arrived. In the end—if such processes ever truly end—the Elders never abandoned *p'Na*. They'd learned the hard way, over a span of two hundred million years, and it was *p'Na* which made everything else possible. But in other ways, they soon found themselves strangers in their own land, as much in need of reeducation as the adoptees, and surprised to be exploring a brand-new culture they'd all built together by accident."

She raised her eyebrows. "And none of this violated the *p'Nan* principle of the Forge of Adversity?"

"On the contrary," he explained, "to the Elders it represented payment of a vast and terrible debt, to people they saw as having been brutally kidnapped. Which, of course, is why the scientists killed themselves. Do you have any more questions, Colonel Reille y Sanchez?"

She ran a self-conscious thumb around the top of her pistol belt before resting her palm of the pommel of her knife. "You could call me Estrellita. And since you invite it, this may be a minor mystery on the grand scale, but it's irritating. I'd resolved to speak with you or Sam about it, anyway."

"And what might that be . . . Estrellita?" He wondered whether she knew how beautiful her name was. Or how beautiful she was, for that matter.

"Well," she began, "you call him 'Oasam' sometimes, or often just 'Sam.' "

He nodded. "And sometimes 'Otusam,' as well."

"Okay, that raises a couple of questions. It must be coincidence that he resembles the Samoyed breed you may not even be familiar with. After all, his name's a word in Antarctican or some other language unknown on Earth. I don't understand why or how everybody gives him three different names, and I don't know whether I'll ever have the chance to acquire sufficient vocabulary in your native language to..."

She stopped, apparently embarrassed. He smiled. "And it never occurred to you, in this connection, to make count of the various names and titles by which different people address you in different contexts, former Major and now Colonel Estrellita Reille y Sanchez?"

She smiled back at him. "I've noticed that, on principle, he's as disrespectful as he can be to the Elders. The Proprietor, however, appears to have a well-developed sense of humor, and, as a consequence—"

"Mr. Thoggosh enjoys Sam's sassiness. Sam's especially merciless with Aelbraugh Pritsch, often referring to him as the Proprietor's spare separable tentacle. The fellow can be pretty humorless, and more than a little pompous, even if he's harmless. Aelbraugh Pritsch enjoys it less than Mr. Thoggosh, who encourages it because he thinks it's healthy. Sam—"

"Aha! That's why my ears were burning!" They turned to the spiral stairs wrapped around the tree, now almost lost in the dimness, by way of which they'd each climbed here in the first place. "Despite the beautiful Estrellita's undisguised astonishment—as well as her initial scornful disbelief—regarding talking dogs, I can speak as well for myself as any beneficiary of cortical augmentation, thank you, ma'am."

Eichra Oren laughed. Reille y Sanchez frowned. "Cortical augmentation? You started to say something about that."

He nodded. "A sophisticated surgical process performed in utero, common in our society. I also meant to tell you, when you mentioned Samoyeds, that Sam's descended from animals aboard the Antarctican refugee ship you were told about, when it departed the Lost Continent. Your Samoyeds probably descend from the ones who weren't Appropriated. In his case, augmentation had the effect of enhancing a suitable brain with the aid of electronics, until it was raised to the qualitative level of human sapience."

"Quite a mouthful." Sam grinned up at her. "Looked at differently, I'm a powerful cybernetic system riding around in a doggy's body. Not too bad a deal, let me tell you, for computer or doggy. Do you know what a gentleman's gentleman is?"

She put her fingers to her temples. "You're making my head ache, both of you. Do you know how deep a person has to reach for vocabulary as dangerous as that and almost a century out of date? A gentleman's gentleman. That's like a butler or a valet, isn't it? So what?"

"So I'm a sapient's sapient. Look, Boss, she's still thinking, can she really be talking to, and getting answers from, a hound? If this poochie's as Elderblessedly brilliant as he sounds, why is he content to act as a lowly, if rather insubordinate, servant? And she's thinking, how can such a thing be possible in a civilization founded on self-interest?"

She dropped her hands and laughed. "Wrong. I'm thinking I now have you in a logical trap. What I ask is, if you're a sapient being yourself, where the hell's *your* separable tentacle?"

Eichra Oren folded his arms and leaned against the trunk, grinning in the shadows. Sam sat and panted. It had been a long climb. "You'll be surprised to learn I wonder about that myself, at what you might call a philosophical level. I'm considered an independent being by the Elders, who define that status, somewhat circularly, in terms of the possession of sapience itself. What troubles me more is whether my intelligence is real or artificial, and, in my more ironic moments, whether it makes any difference."

"I don't know what you mean," Reille y Sanchez admitted.

"If he means anything at all," suggested Eichra Oren. "This is his poor, confused little canine genius routine. He's fond of human females, and it nearly always gets to them."

"Boss, this is serious! And before she gets the wrong idea, you'd better explain that I like human females because, back home, they always have canine female companions. What I wonder is if I'd be a different individual if my cybernetic component had been implanted, say, in the nervous system of that little blue-green lizard Aelbraugh Pritsch carries with him."

Reille y Sanchez looked at Eichra Oren. "I suspect what he wonders about is why, regardless of his status as independent sapient, he feels most comfortable as your companion. I'll bet he often feels a little lost on those occasions when you're not together. Most of all, he wonders how much of his contentment with his lot is real, and how much was programmed into him."

"Watch out," warned Eichra Oren. "I think she's got you, Sam."

Sam sighed. "I've gone over all of my programming and every one of my circuit diagrams myself, many times. I've never found a satisfactory answer to any of those questions."

"In the meantime, Eichra Oren," she went on, "regardless of the reason, he remains fondly loyal to you, a noble individual he feels deserving of nothing but fond loyalty. He sees himself, possibly with justification, as squire to a famous and formidable knight, although, talking to him, it sometimes seems he thinks of you as his appendage, rather than the other way around. Maybe that's the secret of his peculiar contentment. What do you think, Mr. Famous *p'Nan* Debt Assessor—whatever that title actually means?"

"I think"—Eichra Oren pushed himself from the tree and stood erect—"I'm not the only one who's formidable, and that whoever killed your friend Kamanov is in a great deal of trouble."

"I think," Sam added, "that it's getting late and I'd better get back to the surface and finish my errands. If you two can get along without me." He started down the stairs. "Don't do anything I wouldn't!"

Eichra Oren ignored the dog's advice and took a step closer to her. It was nearly dark. "As for my title, as close as English gets to the concept, I'm simply a kind of ethical bill collector."

She took a step closer to him. "Meaning you collect bills ethically, or you collect ethical bills?"

"Emphasis on the latter." He closed all but the last centimeters of distance between them. "I'm a debt assessor, employed most of the time by the parties I end up collecting from. I deduce logical answers to their questions regarding what you might call the balance of their moral accounts. It usually comes down to a simple matter of being asked to settle honest disputes of fact or intention between individuals of good will. On occasion, clients will want to be certain of the proper course ahead of time, before they act; I'll admit I've a good deal fewer clients of this sort than I might wish. In any case, once the equation's calculated, I prescribe a course of action to restore the balance, and sometimes act directly to restore it myself."

"Pretty words . . ." Reille y Sanchez cast a significant glance toward the sword, gleaming in the day's last light where it leaned against the rail. The expression on her face wasn't revulsion. ". . . Which means you function as judge, jury, and executioner."

"Does spreading the responsibility," he countered, shrugging, "really lessen it?" Although there wasn't enough light to see her clearly by, he turned to face her directly, seized her by the upper arms, pulling her close against him. She, with more training in the martial arts than the art of love, raised her forearms reflexively, trying to break the hold.

Before her body knew she wasn't being attacked, he'd released her shoulders, taking her by the wrists instead, bending her arms, not roughly, behind her back where he held them crossed and pinned as he kissed her in the warm dark. Kissing wasn't commonly done among his people. He'd studied it for this assignment and was curious. After a startled instant of resistance, her mouth softened under his and opened. She closed her eyes—he could feel her lashes on his cheek—and relaxed against his arms.

Nighttime had come to Eris once again.

XXI
Pleasure Before Business

Eichra Oren felt a tautness in his body, a singing in his nerves and muscles, a pleasure that was almost pain. Within the circle of his arms, Estrellita trembled and a tear escaped from the long sweep of her lashes. He released her wrists, keeping his arms around her. "Is it possible," he whispered, "that this incurs a moral debt on my part?"

"I hope—" Her voice came in a rusty croak. She inhaled and began over. "If you're applogizing, Eichra Oren, I, er, deny the debt."

He kissed her again. When some time had passed he told her, "For the first time I regret the structure of my language. I haven't a shorter name for you to call me by. 'Eichra' and 'Oren' mean nothing, separate from one another. You've a beautiful name—I meant to tell you that before—and appropriate, since you're beautiful yourself."

She buried her face against him, her shoulders worked, he felt dampness through his clothing, although she made no sound. He laid the palm of a hand along her cheek and gently turned her head to see her eyes. "You're crying," he told her, and felt like an idiot for stating the obvious.

"You don't know," she answered bitterly. "I'm far from beautiful inside! I'm a Marine officer, a trained killer, and now I'm—"

"And what am I?" he demanded. "The blood of a thousand sapients is on my hands." In the darkness, she heard the whisper of an aircraft as it rose level with the balcony. He turned her so that she stood facing it. "Come," he told her, "we'll steal a few hours and see what you and I are like inside. My wager's that you're beautiful that way, as well."

Without waiting for an answer, he lifted her in his arms, carried her to the rail, and set her in the machine, where he climbed in beside her. Pilotless, the electrostat slipped sideways from the balcony, gaining altitude. Half reclining in the bottom of the craft, she brushed tears from her cheeks with a sleeve. "You've forgotten your sword."

He shook his head. "I can't forget it, Estrellita, but I can leave it behind a while. It'll be there when I come back. Unfortunately." One arm beneath her shoulders, he leaned over to place his mouth on hers again. His other hand operated the release of her weapons belt. Knife and pistol slid to the floor with a dull clunk. He took the toggle of her suit zipper, pulled it down between her breasts to the waist. She wrapped her arms around his neck and clung to him as the aircraft swooped toward the night-black canopy.

Later, she faced him cross-legged, holding his hands in hers, palms up. They rested on bare flesh; her uniform, which couldn't be said to be lying discarded in a corner only because there were no corners, had been discarded nonetheless. Soft light glowed beneath the compartment rim. She looked at his hands, which she said seemed perfectly ordinary to her, and, at the same time, perfectly extraordinary, then up into his eyes.

"A thousand sapients."

As naked to her as she was to him, he looked at his hands as if they were strange to him, then met her eyes by a more circuitous route than she'd taken, having decided she was very beautiful indeed. "It doesn't happen every day," he told her. "Most of the time, I'm an arbiter in small matters of rights or property, rather than life. Often my presence will be requested to witness a personal or business agreement, or a potentially disputed event."

"In your official capacity?" she asked.

He smiled, enjoying the feel of the night around them. "I've no official capacity, Estrellita, only a customary one. Occasionally, a client will ask the most awful and fascinating question ever put to me. It's always an uncomfortable moment, and it's long established in formula: 'Am I allowing my existence to continue in ignorance of some irreversible breach I've unknowingly committed, some irrevocable restitution I've neglected to make?'"

With a frown, she repeated the words, "'Am I allowing my existence to continue in ignorance of some irreversible breach I've unknowingly committed, some irrevocable restitution I've neglected to make?'"

"Have a care," he warned, reaching to brush a strand of hair from her eyes. She ducked her head, caressed his palm with her cheek and kissed it. "Once the words are spoken in earnest, they can't be taken back. I've no choice but to find an answer and recommend action to be taken as a consequence. Sometimes— it's never pleasant—I must take action myself. In your terms, my profession combines aspects of rabbi, policeman, psychiatrist, lawyer, accountant, referee, father-confessor, judge, family doctor, philosopher, and, in the ultimate resort, executioner.''

She released his hand, leaned back against the side of the vehicle, and straightened her legs across his thighs. "I get around, for a twenty-nine-year-old former virgin. A rabbi, cop, shrink, lawyer, accountant, referee, priest, judge, doctor, philosopher, and executioner, all in one day?"

"You've an excellent memory, Estrellita." He let his hands travel the length of her legs, enjoying her soft, flawless skin and the muscles lying beneath. "And not as good an opinion of yourself as you deserve. It's true that, because of that last aspect, my work brings me, on rare occasion, into violent contact with others—what individual would be willing to trust me in small matters if I hadn't proven myself reliable in large ones?—or at least it presents its more physically active moments."

She laughed, pulling herself forward into his lap and wrapping her legs around his waist. "And what do you call this?"

He let his mouth and hands wander before he answered. "A splendid spirit of cooperation between two investigators. In fact, I'm ready to cooperate all over again, if you are." He moved and she settled lower in his lap.

She sighed, closed her eyes, and enjoyed a pleasant shudder. "So you are! No, don't turn out the lights. This time I want to see your face."

For an hour they were oblivious to anything but one another. Afterward, he set the 'stat on a random course among the trees, where lights twinkled here and there and she saw things strange and wonderful to her. They skimmed, at a modest distance, past a party of Aelbraugh Pritsch's species, celebrating their first hatching on the asteroid with traditional percussion music which sounded to her unaccustomed ear like an industrial accident. In their midst, a great arachnid held the equivalent of bagpipes to spiracles along its abdomen, adding to the racket.

Another pass took them by an off-duty mining crew of sea scorpions and cartiloids, no doubt discussing their latest failure as they shared a titanic keg of beer. Aboard the aircraft, Reille y Sanchez and Eichra Oren's own talk returned to his profession. She expressed surprise that a species as wise and ancient as the Elders needed someone like him, in her words, to maintain order.

"Wise and ancient they may be," he replied, "the Elders are no angels. Their history embraces every good or evil which we, mere butterflies to them, ever conceived in our paltry million years. They've seen five *hundred* million, and they've long memories. They regard a certain amount of crime as thermodynamically inevitable. It may even measure a culture's health."

She raised her eyebrows. "Crime as a sign of health?"

He nodded. "There's no surer sign that a culture's sickly and on the edge of collapse than lack of gumption among its crime-prone members. No matter how much progress is made, it'll always be easier to steal something than to earn it. That's why theft will exist, as Mr. Thoggosh says, for as long as stars of the nth generation continue to fuse hydrogen. No matter what happens, it'll always be easier to destroy something—"

"And even easier," she added, "just to threaten its destruction."

"Statements of equal relevance to the phenomena of entropy and extortion. The Elders are optimistic, they feel both facts have more to do with the way the universe is constructed than with the behavior of sapients living in it. However, there'll always be people capable of reasoning only as far as those facts and no further—and of making criminal plans predicated on them."

"Which is why you still need police?"

"On the contrary, Estrellita, I'm not a policeman. The persistence of crime reveals too much about the origins of authority. In what way could it have begun, other than by some gang threatening a farmer's crops—and the farmer with them—unless he agreed to part with a portion in order to protect the rest? That's the relationship between death and taxes."

"Anarchist! Lenin warned us about you." She laughed and shook her head. "And none of the younger species ever gives the Elders an argument?"

"The Elders detest appealing to seniority for validation. Still, over the years they've seen this process many times among many different species, beginning with their own. It's also characteristic of them that they're inclined to blame the farmer for inventing agriculture which, by its nature, rendered him helpless in the first place."

"Maybe farmers invented authority to protect them from gangs."

"Authority's always supposed, by history revised after the fact, to have arisen to prevent or punish the acts which, in truth, sustain it. How long could authority continue if it were effectively forbidden to steal what others earn, to destroy—or threaten to destroy—what others create?"

"I won't answer"—this time her mouth and hands did the wandering—"until you tell me how long I have to wait until you make love to me again."

He laughed. "Keep doing that, and—damn!" His implant shrilled, and for the first time the 'stat faltered in its flight. They were in no danger; the warning was advisory, intended to protect the colony's only means, however imperfect, of returning to the home continuum. "Look," he told her, pointing over the rim of the craft, "it's the dimensional translator!"

It was the largest building on 5023 Eris. He tried to look at it as she must be seeing it. It could have been a particle accelerator, even a raceway or athletic field. His layman's knowledge of the Elders' ultimate triumph in physics rendered him little less ignorant of its operation than she was. Its foundation, surrounded by the jungle, was an enormous blue isolation field a hundred meters square, inset with a wheel-rim construction almost as large, split into rectangular sections—more correctly, truncated wedges—seven meters wide, marching around the rim. Half-a-dozen pathways, made of the same sections, met at a hexagon in the center, where he and Sam had materialized not long ago amidst artificial lightning and a howling storm.

"Pretty," was her only comment. "You're easily distracted, Eichra Oren." She pulled him down, back to the center of the compartment, as the craft steered past the installation and away. It was a matter of a minute before she had his full attention again. After a considerably longer interval, their conversation returned, as it always must with the kind of people they were, to their responsibilities.

"Sometimes I'm compelled—" He stroked her head, which lay against his thigh.

She grinned. "Employing the least of your many amazing abilities—"

"As you suggest, to assist some clients with that sword which constitutes my badge of . . . there isn't a word for it in your language. 'Office' or 'authority' won't do at all. I said earlier, this is only in the uncommon instance of those few who, for one reason or another, happen to be—perhaps less morally capable—of making ultimate restitution themselves."

She sat up and turned to face him. "So you force them?"

"On the contrary, Estrellita, no one's ever forced to make the ultimate restitution. It's not even remotely related to capital punishment. But it'll happen that, in the course of collecting lesser debts, or defending my life while trying to do so, I'm called on to collect a life. If they've time under such circumstances, even these unwilling clients are sometimes grateful for my assistance. If not, their families or associates seldom fail to express a measure of gratitude."

She shook her head. "Sounds crazy to me."

He put a hand on her shoulder, although it displayed a tendency to explore elsewhere. "In a trade society, unwillingness or inability to pay a debt is the worst disgrace imaginable, spoken of afterward, sometimes for millennia, to the detriment of the defaulter's interests. It doesn't happen often."

Despite his martial skills, advanced weaponry, and a sword of—'office' wasn't the word—Eichra Oren was much more, in his own mind and in those of others, than a bloody-handed executioner. Trouble came when he tried explaining it to someone with Estrellita's background. He pointed out that Earth's barbaric past—not to mention its barbaric present—had plenty of the executioner type. "They do nothing to maintain the moral elevation of cultures they infest. I gather some of these butchers even stoop to torture. That kind of savagery, like taxation or slavery, has been absent from our society for millions of years."

She laid a hand on his cheek. "I believe you're not a torturer. Every time you touch me you tell me what you are."

He shrugged. "I'm one of a handful of individuals . . ."

She interrupted. "Unusually capable individuals, Mr. Thoggosh told me, upon which all civilization depends. His exact words."

"He exaggerates the qualities of all who work with him. I'd say, due to my basic character, as well as later training, I'm simply able to take the process of moral reasoning to a conclusion, regardless of what may happen as a consequence."

"And no one," she confirmed, "ever benefits from your, er, services unless they contract and pay for them voluntarily?"

"That's absolutely—" He frowned. "Damn, it's more complicated than that. They may, indeed, come to require them as the inevitable result of a chain of events which they initiated by choice."

She nodded. "Like saying a burglar or mugger or rapist dying at the hands of his victim has chosen a complicated way of committing suicide?"

"What else? I'm grateful that, rather than being feared or hated or avoided because of the more sanguinary aspects of my profession, I'm honored out of proportion to my talents or accomplishments."

"You're like a celebrated surgeon," she told him, "one of those rare and valued individuals practicing a profession who are able to do it competently."

He shook his head. "It's seen as having little to do with me. As with your burglar, responsibility lies with the one who came to need my services. I'm seen by everyone, and see myself, as the instrument of his will. Also, despite its fascination, situations which end in bloodshed are extremely rare. In the ordinary course of my profession, I'm more concerned with those who aren't criminals. It's the fervently held wish of all ordinary individuals never, by accident, ignorance, even appearance, to become such. It's my function to help them any way I can, consistent with principle, to fulfill that wish."

"Don't do me any favors!" She laughed, but there was a nervous tone beneath it. "What about those who won't volunteer?"

"It's true," he mused, "there always exist those who, for one reason or another, are not so particular about maintaining their moral status."

"Sociopaths."

"I've heard the word," he told her. "I disbelieve it has a real referent. The Elders are concerned with the consequences of an individual's acts. Reasons he may present for them are considered secondary, if they're considered."

Her eyes widened. "No extenuating circumstances? No mercy?"

"I didn't say that, Estrellita. Putting accountability first, they feel, is responsible for the longevity of their culture and the level of peace, freedom, and prosperity within it."

She looked at her hands. "You didn't answer about nonvolunteers."

"As one of your own philosophers once put it, life becomes impossible for them. No one will trade with them—hire, house, clothe, feed them—no matter what they offer. They wander the land becoming more ragged each day until, from desperation, they turn back—to find me following them."

She shivered and wrapped her arms around herself.

"You're right," he told her, "that few moral cripples such as these are grateful to me. So, out of a prudent regard for survival, let alone my professional reputation, in addition to pursuing philosophy and deduction I've become proficient at the martial arts."

"Be good at it, Eichra Oren." She placed her hands on either side of his face. "Be as good as you are at making a girl feel decent about herself for a few minutes for the first time in her life!"

She wept again for a little while, and then they made love all through the remainder of the night.

XXII
Mass Insanity

Daylight brought them back to reality and the human encampment. They'd stopped, high among the trees, to dress and reaccoutre themselves aboard the aircraft, and wash and eat breakfast at a little balcony café run by one of the "rat-things" Estrellita said she'd seen earlier with Mr. Thoggosh. Now the electrostat hovered over the shuttles. It felt, beneath their weight, as reluctant as they were about landing. Lost in thought, Eichra Oren turned as she spoke his name. "Speaking as a cooperating investigator," she asked, "what are you planning to do now?"

He grinned. "After I've caught up on sleep? I've talked to almost all of your people. Now I'll check in with Sam and start with mine."

" 'Check in with Sam,' he says. Are you claiming that dog of yours wasn't eavesdropping electronically on us all night?"

"I hope you're not disappointed." The electrostat settled with a bump outside the triangular circle of spacecraft. He rose, tucking his sword under his arm. "I locked out everything except that alarm, never having cared much for an audience. Oops, here's your general. You're sure we shouldn't have landed in the trees and let you walk in by yourself?"

"I believe you're trying to be a gentleman, unless you're worried about your own reputation. I just realized I know nothing—well, practically nothing—of Antarctican customs." She smiled and touched his cheek. "I'm not ashamed of anything I do with you, Eichra Oren. If anybody gives me any grief about it, I'll resign my commission and join the nautiloid foreign legion, just to be with you."

As the side of the craft shrank into itself and they alighted, the only humans who seemed to notice their arrival were Arthur Empleado and one of his surviving henchmen, Roger Betal, who slipped from between two of the shuttles and approached them. "Well, Colonel," asked the KGB man, "did you enjoy your dirty little interlude with this race traitor?"

Estrellita stiffened. Beside her, Eichra Oren was mystified to find himself despised. To the extent he understood it, the man's expression spoke of an ugly concept the Antarctican found devoid of meaning, and, at the same time, infuriating. He stepped forward.

"Arthur," Estrellita demanded, before Eichra Oren could reply, "I've hardly pulled my new rank on anybody yet, but it's about time. You justify your insubordinate innuendo, or you're in real trouble.''

"There are limits to anyone's authority, Colonel,'' Empleado sneered, "and apparently more than one way to abuse it. What else but 'race traitor' is it reasonable to call a human who willingly works for these inhuman, regressive individualistic monsters? Ruthlessly exploitive capitalists, striving selfishly for personal profit? Isn't he committing a crime against the collective interests of his own, naturally altruistic species? And what do you call one of us who, er, collaborates with him—all night?''

"Stop!'' This time, Eichra Oren wouldn't be interrupted. His warning had an effect, since they'd all seen what had happened the last time he'd shouted that word. He stepped up to Empleado until he could see the pores on the man's nose, but didn't touch him. "Nothing would give me greater pleasure than to make you eat those insults and your teeth along with them. I may yet. But for the time being, I'm the closest thing to a detective the Elders have produced—or needed to—and they've asked me to investigate a murder, using my own judgment. That's exactly what I'm doing.''

"Roger!'' Sweating profusely, Empleado appealed to his underling for support. Betal grinned at his boss, then at Eichra Oren, shrugged, and made no other move. Empleado gulped. Eichra Oren turned to face the small crowd beginning to filter out of the camp and gather around.

"I haven't refused to discuss my background with anyone interested enough to ask. For my part, I mistrust translation software. I'd risk offending my cosapients''—he glared at Empleado—"that's you—by breaking off this delightful conversation and asking to borrow a dictionary to look up the words you just threw at the colonel, except I'm feeling good this morning, and I don't want to start being sick to my stomach!''

At last, he turned to Reille y Sanchez. "Sorry, Estrellita, I thought something like this might happen.''

She shook her head. "I told you what I thought already. Don't worry about it. Are you going back to—''

"I'm going for a walk, then to speak with some of Mr.

Thoggosh's people, as I said. The electrostat will find its own way home. I'll be back toward evening to see you."

Looking around self-consciously, she smiled, then stood on tiptoe and kissed him on the cheek. "I'll look forward to it."

He turned, heading for the jungle, where he'd been vaguely aware that a shaggy dog was waiting for him. "Good speech, Boss. Have a good time last night?"

"Not you, too, Sam!" They walked together into the leaves, Eichra Oren swatting absently at random stalks with his sheathed sword. "I never get any closer to understanding what motivates these people. It must be something other than mere loyalty or affection such as we feel toward one another or my mother or Mr. Thoggosh. They're strange beings. They look human enough if one goes by outward appearance. From time to time they even manifest what I'm forced to admit is evidence that they're capable of rational thought and behavior. Simply getting here in these primitive rockets of theirs represents a respectable feat, like sailing around the Earth in a canoe."

"Therefore," the dog answered, taking up the man's tone, "and despite evidence to the contrary, they presumably fit somewhere in that broad class of entities with which we personally identify, sapient organisms."

Eichra Oren ducked to avoid brushing a dew-damp fern frond. Or perhaps it was still wet from yesterday's rain. "Presumably. Yet their inexplicable everyday behavior, their unfathomable thoughts and feelings, their hostile attitude toward me, before they knew anything about me . . ."

"That's what you're good at, solving mysteries."

Eichra Oren pondered the elaborate metal handle of his sword. "Yes? Well, I've tried to take the long view of the Elders. I've considered the possibility that these people are bent on suicide, that they're some recent, nonviable mutation yet to be weeded out by natural selection."

They went on for a while, in silence. Finally, Eichra Oren spoke. "Sam, they're more alien than any of the nonhuman species we've grown up with, lived among, been ourselves a part of, all our lives. Even the best of them, Gutierrez, Pulaski, the doctor, are preoccupied with a bizarre, dangerous, difficult, and not even particularly interesting, game."

Sam looked up at his human. "And the lovely Estrellita— *your* lovely Estrellita?"

He shook his head. "I don't know, Sam. Her worst of all, maybe. Or maybe I'm more sensitive where she's concerned. At first, try as I might, even with the help of Mr. Thoggosh and the data you were gathering, I couldn't deduce the rules governing this pointless, painful competition. In the absence of contradictory evidence, its only purpose seems to be to determine which of them gets to tell all the others what to do."

"What connection does that have"—the dog stopped to scratch behind an ear—"with investigating a murder?"

The man shrugged, waiting for the dog to finish. "Well, it seems like a lot of trouble to go to, just to win a prize consisting of being stuck with an unnecessary and objectionable task. Running other people's lives must be very unpleasant. It must take up time and energy more purposefully and pleasurably spent thousands of other ways. It's like holding an arm-wrestling contest where the winner gets to clean out a septic tank—"

Sam grinned. "Or gets to pick everybody else's nose."

"You're disgusting." Eichra Oren frowned. "Furthermore, it's impossible to accomplish without damaging those lives. I asked about that, over and over again. Sam, this revolting pursuit represents the only joy and satisfaction these people ever derive from their lives. Otherwise, their one consistent emotion is anger at everything and everybody, especially at themselves."

"And they never wonder if that isn't connected with the game they play?"

"None of them came even close to understanding what I was getting at. Like you, they wanted to know what it had to do with my investigation. I tried, without success, to warn them that a *p'Nan* debt assessor isn't equivalent to any of the roles they're familiar with, that this was a necessary part of my work, that I had to weigh this strange behavior pattern, establish its dimensions and extent, integrate it into my other deductions."

"And?"

"Nothing. You want to know the most mysterious and

frustrating facet of this mindless, self-destructive, sacrificial obedience I've observed being practiced among the members of the expedition?''

Sam sniffed at the base of a tree. "No."

"Good, I'll tell you." He stopped walking and concentrated on what he was saying, despite the fact that the dog yawned conspicuously. "The game's rigged so you can never win the prize that'd be worth winning: control over your own life. A few individuals back on Earth seem to have won permanently, and the perpetual losers feel they owe everything to them. One thing's clear, at their current, laughable level of technology, Earth's authorities are far too distant for simple fear to account for the observed phenomenon. How could they offer a credible threat to the lives or safety of the members of this expedition they've all but abandoned?''

If a dog had been capable of shrugging, Sam would have shrugged. "The general and his friends have to go back sometime."

The man nodded. "They should. They've a lot of houseceaning to do. But they won't. I'm tempted to regard it as perversion. Three billion years evolving a brain to run your own affairs, then you meekly, eagerly, hand them over to somebody whose credentials aren't superior knowledge or wisdom—''

"Simply the brute power," Sam replied, sitting on his haunches, "to beat you up and kill you if you won't.''

"Any rational, feeling individual may be motivated readily enough to act against his interests or will by sufficiently dire threats," Eichra Oren protested. "He can be moved by personal fear of physical injury or death to himself or someone he cares for. It's an historically common phenomenon. Yet this primitive, if understandable, motivation doesn't seem to be the pivotal factor. Taken by itself, it can't be the primary driving force behind this sickening phenomenon of 'obedience to authority.' ''

"You'll find authority itself," a new voice interposed, *"an even more difficult phenomenon to grasp, nothing more than one incomprehensible act of obedience piled on another, into pyramids."*

They whirled to see a large, glistening snake. "Mr. Thoggosh?''

"In the tentacle, if not the flesh. Good morning, Eichra Oren, Sam. Having discussed it at length with several of them, after all's said and done, I'm still no closer to understanding it myself. It's often seemed to me that unthinking obedience ought be physically impossible. Had such a suicidal behavior pattern even begun to develop at any time in evolutionary history, it should have been immediately self-extinguishing."

"Go on," urged Eichra Oren, "I'm listening."

"Well, suppose an individual became deranged, perhaps through some near-fatal illness or injury, so that it seemed rational to him to demand that other people obey his every command. Wouldn't the majority rise up, immediately and spontaneously, and put the would-be dictator out of their misery? It would be easy: he's sick or injured. Yet, here we are, face-to-face with the nth generation of victims of power, confronted, as it were, with the tangible consequence of an impossible mass insanity, well-established on this version of Earth for thousands of years."

"What's even worse," Sam told the appendage, "is the embarrassing fact that it's this particular Earth."

"That's right, isn't it? Had your own forebears, both of you, not been Appropriated—"

"Rescued," the man insisted, "but you're right, these *aliens* could have been my descendants. Which means their culture, to dignify it in a way it doesn't deserve, somehow evolved from the remnants of my own."

"Perhaps it was the pole-reversal," the mollusc mused, *"a rearrangement of worldwide patterns of glaciation, the overwhelming cataclysm which resulted in the Loss of the Continent."*

Eichra Oren nodded, mentally inventorying recently acquired information about Earth's history since the Loss. "I wonder if the story wasn't passed down as the sinking of Atlantis. Perhaps it scarred the survivors so badly, those who weren't rescued by the Elders, that it became the source of this mass aberration. But blast it all, where does a hypothesis like that get us? Whatever else it's worth, it doesn't tell us a thing about what happened to Semlohcolresh, or who killed Kam—"

"I did it! I did it!" The wild-eyed, torn, disheveled appari-

tion springing from the bushes was hardly recognizable as human, let alone the human who'd been Vivian Richardson. Her suit, dirty and wet, was tattered. Through the rents, her skin was bruised and cut by days spent as an animal in hiding. Her hair was full of woods debris. Her hands, extended in front of her in a rigid triangle, were full of large-bore service automatic.

"I did it!" she screamed. "I sawed that fucking monster's slimy arm off and strangled the shit out of that revisionist bastard with it! Now I'm gonna do you! All of you!" Nervously, she shifted her weight from foot to foot, pointing the gun first at Eichra Oren, then at Mr. Thoggosh's tentacle, even at Sam, and back at Eichra Oren again.

"What became of Semlohcolresh?" the Antarctican stepped forward and asked in a firm, gentle voice.

"Down the dumpster, and who wants to know?" Still shifting side to side, she, too, came a few steps forward. Deep in her skull, her eyes were red with veining, ringed with blue-black circles. "Who the hell're you, white boy? I don't know you!" Keeping her right hand on the grip of the pistol, she rocked the hammer back with her left thumb.

"*Dumpster?*" Mr. Thoggosh demanded. "*What's she talking about?*"

"I think she's talking about the manual waste imports on your mass-energy converter," Sam told him.

"*How in blazes could she know how to work the mass-energy converter? I hadn't shown any of them the power plant yet.*"

"I don't think that matters." Sam watched as Eichra Oren, eyes locked on Richardson's, extended a hand for her gun as the other crept to his waist. "Easy enough, anyway. The input looks like one of their own waste-disposal systems—how many different ways can you build a trash bin?—and the rest is automated. Garbage in, gigawatts out."

"Give me the weapon," Eichra Oren told her. "There's food, and you'll be dry and warm. No one will hurt you."

"Damn straight nobody's gonna hurt me!" She lifted the CZ99A1 a bare centimeter, sighting it on his face. He could see the blunt end of the bullet gleaming dully in the chamber. "I did it! I did it! Let's—"

Behind him, a double explosion erupted. She was lifted off her feet and thrown against a tree, where she hit with an ugly noise and slid to the ground, a pair of close-spaced scarlet blossoms soaking her uniform. A second noise, a snapped twig, caught his attention and he whirled. Sebastiano came from the undergrowth, followed by young Gutierrez and two others. "I see you found her," the shuttle captain observed. "Did you have to shoot her?"

"I didn't." He discovered that, without being aware of it, he'd drawn his little weapon and pointed it at the motionless figure on the ground. He stepped to her and pried the .41x22m/m from her cold, dead fingers.

"I did." From another direction, Reille y Sanchez strode out onto the path, her own pistol smoking in her hand. "Another half second and she'd have fired."

Eichra Oren rose. "Thanks, Estrellita, but not with this." He held the CZ99A1 for her to examine. "Days in the rain and damp. It's rusted solid."

XXIII
The Fatal Question

"What now?"

"What?" Reille y Sanchez looked up from the path she and Eichra Oren followed, away from the encampment, through the jungle toward the Elders' establishment. They'd been going through the formalities associated with Richardson's confession and death for several hours. Now they had free time and had decided, without discussion, to spend it together.

"What's customary among your people?" he asked shuffling

beside her with his sword tucked beneath one arm and his hands in his pants pockets. "What'll you do now?"

She shrugged. "Oh, paperwork. I have to get a report ready for the general to send back to Earth."

He nodded without looking up. "To the KGB?"

"Yes, that's who I'm working for. Why?"

Taking his sword in one hand, with the other he held a leafy branch out of the way to let her through and followed. They crossed a little stream she said she recognized and began working their way along its low bank toward whatever source it flowed from. "Curiosity. I've no paperwork to do. The Elders are wary of it. If they weren't, after five hundred million years, their entire Earth would be buried under glaciers made of wood pulp or plastic instead of ice. Also, I've no one to report to. The surrogate of Mr. Thoggosh was present, and in general, my clients are either satisfied with my work or not."

She stopped to face him, laying a hand on his arm and looking into his eyes. "Will you and Sam be going home now, to that other Earth?"

"Will you, Estrellita?" He covered her fingers with his free hand, shaking his head. "Nothing's been resolved here, you know. Your authorities still dispute our claim. Your orders to drive us off, however futile and inconsiderate of your survival, are still in effect. And, as Aelbraugh Pritsch would be the first to tell you, dimensional translation's too expensive and spectacular in its side effects to be used casually, even to get us back. Remember what happened last time."

She smiled. "The rain."

"The rain." They resumed walking until they came to the little waterfall that broke the course of the stream not far from the sprawling roots of an enormous canopy tree, thirty or thirty-five meters in diameter. "So I guess we're stuck here for the duration," he concluded, "whatever that turns out to be. Or until sufficient reasons accumulate to use the translator." He turned to look at her. "It could be quite a long while."

Again she smiled, shyly this time. "Is that so terrible?"

"It's why we're here, you and I, in this spot. I wanted to show you something." He reached into a pocket and held an object out, knowing it would look to her like an undersized golf ball, complete to color and texture. "That's my office and personal quarters, Estrellita. At least it will be in a few days. You'd call it a seed, with engineered genes. Don't drop it, or it'll try to take root."

He took the object from her, stepped to the tree, reached as high as he could and touched it to the trunk. When he took his hand away, it stayed in place. "When it's mature, it'll be cantilevered out over the stream, and I can fall asleep listening to the waterfall. This location's exactly halfway between your camp and the Elders' settlement, which sort of describes my position, as well. While I'm here, I'll act as liaison between humans and nonhumans on the asteroid."

"Good," she replied, finding a mossy place near the base of the tree to sit down, "you can begin with me."

He smiled back self-consciously and joined her where she sat, propping sword and scabbard against the tree beside him and taking her hand. "Why, I believe I have. This report you'll make, part of its purpose will be to wrap up the loose ends?"

"Loose ends? There aren't any." Keeping his hand, she ticked off the fingers of her other hand. "Method: after she struck him down, Richardson strangled Piotr with one of Semlohcolresh's tentacles. She probably shot the nautiloid. Her gun wasn't rusty then, she'd just taken it from Danny Gutierrez. Semlohcolresh would have been an easy mark. He wasn't wearing a protective suit. Opportunity: it was pitch dark. According to Sebastiano and others searching for Richardson, Semlohcolresh and Piotr were alone at the pool. Motive: Richardson was crazy."

Eichra Oren took her hand in both of his. "Estrellita, life consists of little besides loose ends. Sometimes that's the only thing that gives survivors a reason for going on."

"All right, if you're so smart," she retorted, "give me an example of a loose end."

He nodded. "I'll give you a good one. Your people in their camp should have heard that shot you mentioned, if that's how Semlohcolresh died. Those pistols of yours are loud. I found that out this morning."

"Because the bullet went right by you, silly. Semlohcolresh's pool was almost a klick from the camp. The forest would have absorbed the sound. Next loose end, please.''

"Motive." He shook his head. "Crazy's too easy, Estrellita, and at the same time, it's too hard."

She rolled her eyes and answered with exasperation. "Is this going to be some more of your deep philosophical and psychological ponderings? What do you mean, too hard?"

"In the sense that it violates parsimony, the principle of the fewest variables. What you call least reactance or Occam's razor. A lone individual striking on her own? Why? You people are hard to understand, but you aren't that crazy, even the deranged Colonel Richardson. Nor, I regret to say, are you that individualistic. There's a perfect motive still lying around unused, Estrellita, a single reason for that particular double murder which makes sense in the light of everything else."

"And that is?" she asked, in mock resignation.

"What it always was, to provoke conflict between humans and the Elders. Therefore it must have been done on orders from your ASSR leaders. I've learned enough about affairs on Earth to know that Moscow had no wish to antagonize the Elders."

She turned where she sat and faced him, taking both of his hands. "Now that you mention it, I do have a few unanswered questions of my own, mostly making certain I understand what the nautiloids and their friends seem to imply about their way of looking at things."

He raised his eyebrows. "We're still talking about motive?"

She nodded. "In a way. Given the nautiloids' five-hundred-million-year advantage, everybody but the government assumes we'll be wiped out the instant hostilities begin. But from what I've seen for myself, and from what they've told me, I'm seeing what I think could be a fatal weakness on their part, if it came to conflict. I could hardly believe it myself, at first, it sounds so childish and naive. It appears your Elders can't use what they call weapons of indiscriminate mass destruction."

"You're entirely correct, Estrellita, they can't." He paused, then added, "We can't."

She laughed gently. "Do you mean to tell me that all these gun-toting monsters are effectively disarmed by what's supposed to be a purely selfish, individualistic philosophy? They're prohibited from using fission or fusion bombs, even high explosives or hand grenades, no matter how desperate the circumstances?''

"Antimatter bombs, too. It must seem strange and contradictory to you. For their part, I imagine they can hardly believe it necessary to explain such an elementary matter of ethics to a person who represents herself as a reasoning being. The use of such nondiscriminating weapons is monstrous, Estrellita. No value it could possibly achieve would outweigh the values it destroyed. The Elders aren't pacifists, as you know. But this would inevitably involve, in their view, inflicting injury or death on innocent individuals who are not party to whatever dispute's being settled. Will this, too, be in your report?''

She shrugged, and for the first time there was unhappiness on her face. "I don't see how I can avoid it. The Elders have already become aware of any number of politically dangerous facts. United or not, the World Soviet's very fragile, and that knowledge alone, in the hands of an enemy, could damage it beyond repair. Now I've learned a hidden vulnerability of the Elders, and you know I have. For the sake of your culture's survival, you'll try to keep it from the ASSR. With what the two of us know together, mutual, horrifying discoveries, we might even bring about the thermonuclear war which, until our arrival on this asteroid, everybody thought had been avoided.''

"Peace, through bloodless capitulation?''

"Almost bloodless. There are always a few who can't see the handwriting on the wall, and it took people like Horatio Gutierrez to deal with them. It cost so much of so many, and now we can destroy it all by ourselves, Eichra Oren. Wouldn't that be something to be proud of?''

He couldn't think of anything to say before she went on.

"As a result of those discoveries, I'd come to a decision. I'm a Marine, a veteran, proud to have earned my rank the hard way in a man's world. Now I'm KGB, whether I like it or not. My opinion of agents willing to use sex as a weapon has always been low. I was happy it hadn't ever been required of me. To be completely truthful, Eichra Oren, I'd managed to fall in love with a mysterious stranger—no, don't say anything—

and part of that happiness is that I slept with him for its own sake, outside the line of duty.''

He sat up. "Why is all of this in the past perfect tense?"

She wouldn't meet his eyes. "Because I'd hoped, without much basis, that after this mess was over with, something more might come of you and me. With all my heart, Eichra Oren, I loathed the idea of cheapening the first feelings like this I've ever had. But even though I made the decision despising myself, I could conceive of no option except to kill you!''

"Your duty to obey authority," he reflected, placing a hand on her shoulder. "And now?"

"Loathsome as it would have been, the task didn't appear difficult. We'd begin right now, making love. I'd pretend to be as relaxed and open toward you as I was last night." She reached to her belt and drew her fighting knife. "When your relaxation appeared complete"—she raised it to his chin—"when you seemed off your guard"—the point touched his skin, indented it—"I'd discover I can't take your life!" She hurled the knife into the ground, where the blade stuck, quivering, and turned her back.

They were both silent for a long time, then Eichra Oren sighed. "For my part, Estrellita, I couldn't have made love to you this afternoon, because I've something I must tell you. Although I don't want to. Like you, I've pondered hard over this turn of events, always coming to the same miserable conclusion. The problem's my inability to understand my fellow beings, including most of all a beautiful, intelligent, accomplished young woman whom I've come in only a short time to love deeply. And to condemn."

She snapped around to face him. "Condemn? Why—"

He turned his hands over in an expression of helplessness. "Why would anyone betray what they value? Why would they destroy something—someone—they admire? Can it be, as they tell me, that they're obligated to obey some other sapient? Despite whatever education and intelligence I have, I've been unable to discover an answer that satisfies me, or any alternative to what must be done. Loathing myself, as you say you did yourself, I'm forced to speak now, Estrellita—because you murdered Piotr Kamanov and Semlohcolresh!"

Her eyes widened, and she didn't quite stop the gasp this provoked.

"I became suspicious," he continued, "when Dlee Raftan Saon told me you'd mentioned a nautiloid habit of venturing unprotected into the air to converse with land beings. You mentioned it again, just now. *No such habit exists.* Semlohcolresh's dislike for liquid fluorocarbon and protective suits was a personal eccentricity, as was lying in shallow water, splashing his gills. You could only have seen it from some hiding place when he and Kamanov conversed, the night they were both killed. Semlohcolresh was well-defended, but probably mistook you for one of the party searching for Richardson. It was you who strangled Kamanov, acting on orders from the American KGB which I'd guess you were given in secret, before you received your official, public promotion."

She protested, "But how could you—"

"I lack direct evidence for this last surmise. The Elders listen to your transmissions and can understand any encrypted message, but they couldn't recognize orders couched in terms of one of your previous missions: 'Do what was done on such and such a date in such and such a place.' Washington's objective was to provoke trouble. You pursued that objective, despite the fact that you liked and respected Kamanov. He was chosen to die because that might help alter Moscow's attitude. Even the murder weapon appears chosen to maximize hostility between the species, although I'll never be certain whether the murder of Semlohcolresh was your own idea, and that makes me sick."

"Eichra Oren, I—"

"I'll never know all the details, and you needn't supply them. Kamanov started home through the jungle and you knocked him out. At the pool you shot Semlohcolresh with the silenced SD9 from the Russian's pocket, and replaced it when you cut off Semlohcolresh's limb and finished Kamanov. Afterward, in the late night or early morning before your visit, you dragged the Elder's body to the mass-energy converter, easy in this gravity, and disposed of it, so it would look like Semlohcolresh killed Kamanov and ran away. You didn't know Richardson watched every step of the process. She was crazy enough to claim your deeds for her own. My suspicion was confirmed when you shot her, knowing that Mr. Thoggosh was well-protected and that I'm quite able to take care of myself."

"I didn't know." She let her head fall to his shoulder and began to cry softly. "I only wanted to . . ."

He stroked her hair. "At that, you might have gotten away with it, but you didn't think of everything, my love. You'd seen Sam, who has a mind of his own. You'd seen Aelbraugh Pritsch's reptile companion. I don't know why it didn't occur to you that they're modeled on the nautiloid separable tentacle, a semi-independent being with complex nerve bundles, and therefore—like Sam—some independent intelligence. Semlohcolresh's tentacle survived the death of its owner, Estrellita. It crawled into the jungle and lived long enough to identify you, by your red hair."

Not denying it, she sat back and looked at him, her expression that of a trusting child. Tears streamed down her cheeks without a sound to accompany them. Her voice was formal, as he'd specified, and in earnest. "God help me, Eichra Oren, am I allowing my existence to continue in ignorance of some irreversible breach I've unknowingly committed, some irrevocable restitution I've neglected to make?"

His tone was equally disconsolate as he reached behind him for his sword. "I wish I had a god to help me, Estrellita, because I lied. Separable limbs only survive their owners by a few minutes. Semlohcolresh's was never found."

She smiled through her tears. "I love you, Eichra Oren. I've never said that to a man before. I more or less expected, maybe I even hoped, things would turn out this way." She touched his arm. "I hate the idea of that sword of yours. So, having seen you fight four men at once, I'm going to make another sort of restitution, in advance, to you. Someday you'll be grateful that I made this a matter of self-defense for you, that you didn't have a choice."

She drew her pistol and was pulling the long, hard double-action trigger as the weapon leveled on his body. Before his conscious mind could interfere, his unconscious mind responded. Seizing her gun hand by the wrist, he paralyzed it with a touch before the gun could fire, pressing her carotid arteries with the thumb and forefinger of his other hand. Whether her heart and mind were in the effort, her body struggled to survive. The effort was futile; his grip was steel. Estrellita relaxed and breathed her last breath.

Afterward, he held her pistol to his temple for a long while, but he never pulled the trigger.

Epilogue
P'na

They watched him from over half a kilometer away.

Eichra Oren was a tiny figure sitting on the tree balcony, where Sam had left him and a happy Estrellita only the previous evening, staring out over the landscape at his soul. Mr. Thoggosh had come to the encampment, "in the flesh," to help his p'Nan debt assessor explain to General Gutierrez what had happened, but he'd wound up helping Sam, while the dog's companion climbed those spiral stairs to be alone.

"No, sir," the mollusc told the human, "it doesn't make him feel a bit better that, thanks to her, it was an act of self-defense. Colonel Reille y Sanchez never had a chance to know that, in addition to the incredible reflexes she counted on, Eichra Oren had already responded consciously to principle. He understands that, in order to fulfill a function he long ago willingly accepted, he'd have had to help her make the ultimate restitution sooner or later. Whether he cared for her or not, as I gather he did rather deeply, wouldn't have made any difference."

The general shook his head. They sat outside the circled shuttles in the waning light of late afternoon, Gutierrez on an improvised log bench, the Proprietor beside him on the ground. Nearby, the Elder's electrostat seemed to be waiting patiently. "She was wrong," replied the human, "because it was her duty to kill someone she cared for. He's right because it was his duty to kill someone he cared for. What's the difference?''

Mr. Thoggosh raised a tentacle. ''The difference, General, is that he'll eventually get over the horror, where someone else, like Reille y Sanchez, without the benefit of his philosophy, might never have. There's all the difference in the world—in several worlds—between acting against your own judgment on someone else's orders and committing what perhaps amounts to the same physical act for the sake of principle. He'll live and go forward because he acted consistently with what he believes.''

Gutierrez folded his arms in front of his chest. ''What he believes? Killing someone over a philosophical point?''

''Perhaps I use a word carelessly. In his view, and in my own, *p'Na*'s a fundamental feature of the material universe, no different from the operation of gravity—although quite distinct from foolish artificial laws made up by primitive sapients—and subject to the same processes of verification. *P'Na* required, for the debt Colonel Reille y Sanchez owed the sapients she murdered, that she make restitution. As a law of nature, this would be true whether she accepted it or not, although the question he says she asked, her token attempt to kill Eichra Oren, demonstrated acceptance of her fate.''

The general shook his head. ''And there he is, without her.''

The Elder pulled himself around to look the human in the eye. ''Not by any act on Eichra Oren's part, but because of a chain of events which she began, of which he was but the final, inevitable link. From your expression, if I've learned to read it correctly, you fail to find that satisfying.''

Gutierrez nodded, anger, disgust, and resignation coloring his tone. ''You could say that, Mr. Thoggosh.''

''Then consider: it could also be said he acted according to another principle. We'll never know. Ultimately, despite the pain it cost him, Eichra Oren acted because an abomination like socialism—or any sort of collectivism—must be eradicated, if for no other reason than its power to corrupt love, such as he and Estrellita found too late.''

Gutierrez rubbed his chin in thought. ''The colonel was accused, tried, sentenced, and executed according to the laws—''

''Customs,'' the nautiloid insisted.

"Of the world she committed her crimes on." He stood. "Forgive me, Mr. Thoggosh, if I limit myself to that when I report to the KGB."

"I shall, General, I shall, indeed." With a tentacle, he indicated the electrostat he'd come in. "Now, I've brought some refreshment along, will you join me? I'm having beer."